The House
of the Prophets

A NOVEL

Translation by Julia Allen

DOUBLEDAY & COMPANY, INC.
GARDEN CITY, NEW YORK
1985

NICOLAS SAUDRAY

The House
of the Prophets

Library of Congress Cataloging in Publication Data

Saudray, Nicolas.
  The house of the prophets.

  Translation of: La maison des prophètes.
  I. Title.
PQ2679.A847M2913   1985   843'.914
ISBN 0-385-19840-X
Library of Congress Catalog Card Number: 85-1488
English translation © 1985 by Doubleday and Company, Inc.
Originally published in French as *La Maison des Prophètes* by Editions du Seuil,
1984.

Religion is one. The Prophets have differed only on details. But God in His wisdom has decreed that men would not be united in one faith. Only the return of the Messiah will put an end to their divergences.

Emir ABD-EL-KADER
Letter to the French people

A simple idea is ravaging the East. An idea we are only too familiar with: death to diversity.

We know what happened to the Armenians. The Greeks of Anatolia, who had survived all invasions entrenched in their underground settlements, were driven out by a modern government. A similar fate befell the Balkan Turks, whose religious observance was often all that was Turkish about them. From Mogador to Babylon, the Jews were hunted down and in turn became hunters. Iran is exterminating its Bahais. Cyprus has been cut in two. Lebanon is struggling under the knives of partitioners.

The West is not entirely innocent of such inhumanity. For the West goes in for clear-cut solutions. And, it must be admitted, civil wars liven up the television news!

Nevertheless, the old Levant must go on living. Ancient land of symbiosis, with its frictions, its injustices, but also its wealth. Mosaic of cultures and creeds, precious for its very diversity. The threat which hung over the Copts of the Nile seems to have become less acute. An orthodox patriarch has been allowed to address the assembled heads of the Islamic States. Might peaceful coexistence still be possible in the land of Abraham?

It is to this wounded civilization, to this cradle of pluralism, that I dedicate my story.

N.S.

The House
of the Prophets

Often, when I think of our city, I see it from the Chapel of the Transfiguration, that tiny white building that our fathers' fathers perched on top of the hostile mountain. People would go up there to give thanks for good tidings, or simply for the light of day. It was but yesterday.

The friendly old tram had hauled Mark and me up to its terminus, Aïn-el-Bey. We dipped our heads in the Bey's pool—a raised basin surrounded by cypresses and untouched by the sun's rays. We may have murmured a few words for the inhabitants of that cool water, the brown, blind fish, which the simple folk see as imprisoned souls.

We started up the steep path that winds past villas and orchards to the tomb of Saint El Tunsi, then follows a little gully and loses itself in scrubland. Sap from the rockroses stained our trouser legs. I'd left behind the new world blanketed in snow and here the midday sun was already beating down hard. For a moment I couldn't get my breath. Mark didn't notice; he kept running on ahead, disappearing, then calling to me from on top of some boulder.

Suddenly we came to a great opening and the city lay dazzling and shimmering at our feet. From here, the houses and palaces looked even more inextricably jumbled than when seen from below. Shading our eyes, we picked out the Andalusian Mosque, with its turquoise tiles and three balls skewered on a lightning rod; the more recent Mehmet Pasha Mosque, the only Hanafite mosque in our city; the Jewish quarter, so crushed against the seawall you expected it to fall into the harbor.

"I am the city," it said, "I am Marsana,* the fruit of the patience of generations. You too shall add your stone."

Mark leaned over the edge and watched the tram going down the slopes of Tijarine; we thought we could hear its unmistakable clanking. The magnolia-covered terrace. The Berthome Bey Hospital. After that just gardens, tenaciously clinging to the precipice.

Allah, says their Book, *purchased from the faithful their lives and worldly goods, and in return has promised the garden of delight.†*

Down in the harbor toy freighters were being unloaded. I dared not look beyond, knowing only too well what I'd see: the immense, incongruous tower that I'd been given the job of completing. Next to it, even taller still, was a crane on hire from Yokohama. These two giants stood side by side, barring the entrance to an ill-defined area of lagoons, spits of sand, drained swamps where the Ministry of Agriculture had taken it into its head to grow rice.

Our hilltop chapel contained a modest icon someone had brought from Saint Catherine of Sinai. The door was never locked, but no one would have dreamed of stealing the smoke-blackened image. Even the Muslims worshipped it; their women had tied propitiatory strips of cloth to the bushes round about.

I too felt I owed an offering. Mark looked on puzzled while I built a small cairn. Hell, I am an architect.

"What's that supposed to mean?"

"That our country's the most beautiful in all the world and that I'll never leave it."

The boy thrust his hands into his pockets and made a wry face.

"Well, I wouldn't mind seeing Paris. Or San Francisco."

* Marsana, capital of Marsania. (See glossary, page 252.)
† Koran, IX, 111

Then, with a sly gleam in his eye, he said, "It seems you're going to marry Eudoxia."

"Who says?"

"Just about everyone."

So while I'd been learning my trade in Cincinnati, my future had been settled for me. Marsania hadn't changed much. I burst out laughing. "There's a mistake, old fellow. Eudoxia's rich."

"But you're *going to be* rich, and that's a lot better."

Just rich in ideas at the moment. My studies abroad had been paid for by a sponsor, who happened to be Eudoxia's father. I'd worked like a dog to justify his faith in me. Now they'd see what I could do. For a moment I played along with Mark: "How do you like my fiancée?"

"It's stupid to get married," he burst out. And he flung his arms around my neck to beg forgiveness. Poor Mark, sensitive, possessive, longing for affection, we'd taken him in when my uncle died and he clung to us like ivy.

A light north wind had sprung up: the jiss. Out at sea lay the Taffarine Islands, looking like a school of whales with the currents swirling around them. Farther on, jagged shapes hovered over the horizon, standing out almost too sharply in the clear winter light. That was the broken coastline across the water.

"Let's light a fire," Mark suggested.

"Why?"

"For the ships at sea." He was always getting ideas like that. But there was no wood.

"Do you know what, Mark? On the night of your sixteenth birthday I promise we'll come up here together and light a great blaze in the dark."

When he passed through our city, El Bekri, the eminent geographer, author of The Book of Roads and Kingdoms, *called it the city of the seven secrets, but he did not explain what he meant.*

"Of course," *says Katrin-who-knows-everything,* "the first is syrr. The second is honey, the third is bitterness."

The children sit around her in a circle.

"The fourth is *the white demon flies at noon.* The fifth, ansur."

"Ansur?"

"Yes, ansur." *The old woman smiles her gap-toothed smile.*

"There are two more secrets," *cries young Gabriel.*

"I'll tell you them when you're grown up, my little lion."

But he already knows them. The sixth is from stairway to stairway. *And the seventh is* seven colors.

I couldn't put off calling on our archbishop. That was our order of precedence. Without our religion we wouldn't even have existed. When Sarun the magnificent had put up the scholarship, Monsignor Elias had arranged for me to get it. I loved him, but I was also afraid of him. He could be too demanding, too perceptive. For a long time he had cut a fine figure, but that couldn't last forever. At any rate he was a man of some importance. His predecessors had run our community: they had settled its quarrels, vouched for its loyalty, taken responsibility for its taxes. He had inherited their moral authority if not their prerogatives.

Elias VIII, archbishop of Pelusa, exarch of Marsania, Cyrenaica and of the land of the Garamentes. . . . Absurd old titles, preserved like relics.

There he sits in his little tiled courtyard full of overblown roses. While we talk, he holds my hand in his like a blind man.

"Well, Gabriel, is it true? Are you really back for good?"

His magnificent eyes are dim and his beard, as neat as ever, is now completely white. I've brought him a religious book, a gift from the metropolitan of Baltimore. He wants to know all about the States: universities, customs, drugs. He listens to my stories, now and again giving a little burst of incredulous laughter and repeating, as if to reassure himself, "Even so, it's a very great nation."

Small birds are hopping about on the tiny lawn, begging for crumbs. Mar Elias gives them his special protection.

"I can hear them better than I can see them," he admits. "This is the house of little wings." Some other birds—we call them bluecaps—are squabbling in a huge, ornate cage. "When I die," my host adds, "they'll be able to fly off wherever they please. It's the custom—every living thing in the house must be set free. They won't have long to wait now."

I protest politely. He brings the conversation around to my future and my family.

"You're now of an age to marry, Gabriel."

"So people keep telling me."

"You'll be spoilt for choice."

"But I'm only just beginning my career."

"Tss. Tss."

An American magazine, containing a glowing account of my contribution to the Pittsburgh Community Center, had been passed around. I'm also considered good-looking in a sturdy sort of way, which I cultivate to inspire confidence.

"And you be careful," the exarch goes on, "don't be like the Westerners, who think only about the girl. Here, remember, you marry the family too."

He's so solemn. Might he by any chance be pulling my leg?

"Gabriel, you must marry into an influential family. An architect needs contacts."

"In America, talent is thought to be enough."

"Hmm. Not here. There's no harm in hedging your bets. As far as I know, you haven't taken a vow of poverty."

Elias himself had sold the family pharmacy and given the proceeds to the poor in order to enter Saint Saba's monastery in Judaea. He had thought he was quits with the world, but he'd forgotten the tradition whereby our bishops are chosen from among the monks. When Exarch Romanos had died, Elias had been brought back from the wilderness, shy, furtive, amazed at finding the city had grown so big. But the moment the interests of his flock are at stake, he drops his scruples. He can be demanding, humiliating.

I tease him a little.

"And supposing the family is better than the girl? Then what?"

"I think you'll be spared that sort of dilemma, Gabriel."

He's obviously got someone in mind, but delicacy prevents him from naming her. He'll leave that to the voices of the town. No matter, I already know. Young Mark hadn't spoken her name by chance.

"Tell me about your work. Are you going to build us something fine?"

"I don't know about that. I've been given the job of finishing the Tower."

"If it's been started then it must be finished," observes Monsignor Elias philosophically.

We fall silent. I take a deep breath before getting to the hardest part of the interview.

"The Tower is simply a means of earning a living. What really interests me is the harbor mosque."

"Have they entrusted you with their mosque?"

"Not yet, but I'm entering the competition."

To tell the truth, that's why I'd come back. I'd been doing well in the States, with a wonderful boss and plenty of work. Then I got a letter from Ruwan, my Muslim friend, telling me that the warehouses of the old port were to be pulled down to make room for a big mosque right on the promontory that separates the harbor basins. The best location in the city. "And," Ruwan added, "they're looking for an architect who's worth his salt." I'd packed my bags then and there. My illustrious boss thought I was crazy. My illustrious boss wept. But my illustrious boss doesn't know what it is to be born a Christian in a Muslim country.

"A salutary shock is needed," I explain. "A son of the Cross must build for the Crescent."

My host shakes his head. "You could just as well have built a church."

"I'll be ready when you are."

Our community has built too much and it's now ruining itself with upkeep. But the Muslims have just woken up. They're building all over the place. An atrocious vermicelli style is running rampant here and in neighboring countries. I swear I can do better than that, or they can put a yellow cap on my head and parade me through the streets sitting backward on an ass.

"Even if I had the choice, with all due respect, Mar Elias, I'd opt for the mosque. To build a church is laudable, to build a mosque is a historic event. Don't you agree?"

"I wish you luck," says the old man. Usually he gives his blessing.

Then he murmurs, "Stay a moment longer, there's something I want to ask you."

Ask a greenhorn like me? You flatter me, Monsignor. He grips the arms of his chair. His breath reeks of medication.

"Tell me, suppose something were to happen in Marsania?"

I don't see what he's driving at.

"Trouble, unrest. Do you think the Americans would step in?"

Certainly not. The Americans have taken enough knocks in the world. What they want is peace.

7

"Even if there's a massacre of the innocents? If the port is taken over by a foreign fleet?"

He keeps at me, almost imploringly. I enlighten him gently. We can't count on the United States, or France, or anyone. But why worry? We've got no oil and we're happy.

He raises his gentle, tired eyes under their beetling brows and stares into space; he's forgotten me. I still wonder what he saw that evening through the whitewashed wall.

"We'll need young men like you," he says after a long pause.

Nearby, the cathedral bell tinkles. Mar Elias's predecessors had wanted the sound to be soft, so as not to give offence in this city where we are so much in the minority. Then comes the call to prayer from the Firdussiya Mosque, a motionless praise of God, no doubt sung with closed eyes and repeated from crier to crier right to the end of the city.

"Their prayers are recorded nowadays," says the archbishop, as if he's just made the discovery, adding, in order to seem impartial, "I like the way they chant."

I liked it too. It was somehow part of us. Despite my protests, Monsignor Elias saw me out, quoting from *The Thoughts of Saint Apollodorus of Tralles,* his bedside reading. I went out into the gathering darkness. A gentle sea breeze stirred in the fig trees.

Behind me was the bent back of the old basilica. It had been forbidden to stand up straight; the edict of Sultan Sun-of-Religion had held it down from the day of its birth. Christians may not build higher than the roofs of the Muslims! They had had to make the parvis below street level. Then the architects of the thirties had replaced the surrounding houses with tall buildings, and our mother church had ended up at the bottom of a pit with a hundred windows, from which the neighbors shot cherry stones on spring evenings.

I wended my way toward the poorer parts of the town.

8

Doors that had been closed all day were now ajar and I glimpsed a murky light, a corner of a mosaic, a talisman in the shape of a Greek cross or a fish. Like an owl startled by the light, I hurried across brightly lit avenues. Without realizing it, I'd strayed into different territory: the sprawling, secret, convoluted suburbs of Esh-Shaffa, Bab-el-Qamar. I only like cities where you can get lost.

Kids were playing cowboys on bikes without lamps. The shadow of a coppersmith was still hammering a tray. A sybarite was being shaved while having his shoes shined.

A threat hanging over Marsania? Come, come! I wished nobody ill. Nobody wished me ill. I was intensely, profoundly where I belonged.

It was pleasant slipping back into the old ways in our house on Salt Street. The family on the ground floor got up first. Then Mark could be heard leaping downstairs to get to school on time. Our mother called greetings from the balcony to our neighbor across the courtyard. The joyous din of the street vendors came in through the windows. As I usually worked late into the night, I rose last of all, like a pasha.

Nobody had made any measurements before building our house. It had no sharp angles, only curves. After my years in America, I took a strange pleasure in walking up our crooked stairs, caressing the beams that sagged under the weight of years. Perhaps it would be my mission to breathe this art of living into my newly acquired science.

The cat had just had a litter. In our country we don't drown kittens—for fear of reprisals—because cats have nine lives. The building swarmed with kittens, skinny and charming. "All we can do," our mother joked, "is pray God to create plenty of mice."

9

On my return she had apprised me of certain realities. Our tenant in Qasrum sent hardly any money. My sister Ilena worked as an interpreter at the Foreign Ministry. It was a prestigious job, but poorly paid. And my brother Saad, instead of supporting the family, had buried himself in a monastery in the South. In short, there were lots of expenses and not much money.

At this point our mother began counting up the "useless mouths": old Katrin, our nurse, who was no longer good for anything but telling stories; my younger sister, still a child; little cousin Mark (Morqos in Arabic), who had lost his parents and couldn't possibly be taken out of the Lazarist School; the cat and her brood; the flies, the woodworms.

I'd been spared these details while I was in America. Our mother was taking in needlework. Through our parish priest, an anonymous neighbor had offered her an interest-free loan. Pride had made her turn it down. Instead, she had pawned her big silver cross, and the interest was mounting up. My first fees would go to redeem it.

My job was waiting for me in the office of Ibrahim El Souss, the doyen of the country's architects. Of Mozarabic stock like us, he was a "Christian hajji," with the date of his pilgrimage to Jerusalem tattooed on his hand. Feeling the onset of old age, he had wanted me back. A heart attack had left him unable to supervise his building sites properly and the Nasr Tower was badly behind schedule. In a word, he was offering me a partnership. His prestige and clientele in return for my enthusiasm.

His offices occupied a whole floor of a white building across the street from the De Gaulle Men's Clothing Shop. As I entered the lobby, I caught sight of a bilingual nameplate to which the name of a certain Gabriel had just been added. What interested the street urchins was the elevator— they took rides in it when the doorman's back was turned. In upper-class apartment houses, you needed a big five-pataka coin for the elevator, of a kind now only used for that purpose. We weren't so stingy.

There was no written contract of our partnership. Among fellow Mozarabs that wasn't done. For overseeing El Souss's jobs I got a share of the firm's profits. I was free to build up my own clientele, provided I gave the firm a percentage of my earnings.

With almost alarming ease I was getting used to my country again. It no longer shocked me to see a man in a city suit drinking orangeade out of the bottle, or a big brown roach climbing up the sides of the tub in our bathroom.

The wheels of my mother tongue were beginning to turn again. It was a most civilized language, full of codes and rituals and strictly ordered processions of responses:

"Morning of happiness."

"Morning of light," and so on.

Every turn of phrase bore the mark of the sacred. Even bus tickets were bought in the name of the Lord, *bismillah.* And nobody, not even we Mozarabs, could mention the future without adding a "God-willing."

I rediscovered the charms of our script, its springy stride, the letters that reach out to one another, expressing, perhaps, a curved vision of life. How childish your neatly lined-up Western letters seemed by comparison.

As soon as I could, I went to inspect the site of the future mosque. A promontory covered with old warehouses, jutting out into the harbor. The demolition gangs were already at work; steel girders were falling in a shower of sparks.

El Halwani had vowed long ago that a sanctuary should be built on this promontory. He'd been a vendor of sweetmeats, trundling his rickety cart around the port. And a saint. After his death, the government finally decided to honor his promise. As you might have expected, the project had been called *The Prince Regent's Mosque.* But the locals, still respecting El Halwani's wish, called it *The House of the Prophets.*

Islam recognizes four prophets: Abraham, Moses, Jesus and the Man of Mecca. Plus those who are not on the list but are revered nonetheless. Isn't there a Nebi Daniel Mosque in Alexandria? The Bible recognizes ten major and a dozen or so minor prophets. I'm willing to bet that the list is not closed.

May The House of the Prophets have room for them all!

This stone fortress of prayer, dominating the harbor, will be the first thing travelers see when they come into the bay. It will be on all the postcards. No, I really can't let it be built without me.

The Ministry of Religious Cults, third floor, left-hand corridor. I cool my heels for several hours. In the end I get the application forms; the photocopying comes to twenty piasters. The clerk has certainly guessed my religion; people have a nose for such things in Marsana.

"What is the name of your person?" he asks in neutral tones, opening his register. I tell him the last name of my person and the first name of my person. He can no longer pretend to see nothing odd. He puts the cap back on his ballpoint and stares at me without speaking.

It doesn't matter what people think of me.

It doesn't matter what I think of myself.

Twenty more piasters—under the counter this time—enable me to learn the names of the other competitors. First of all, Fannawi and Jaffar Hebbaz. I'm not worried by those two; they designed the latest vermicelli mosques. Then there's an unknown from Cairo. Thirdly, Rashid El Kholi, a famous architect, but who has never done anything of this kind. I've come into this late. Luckily the maquettes don't have to be in for another three months.

It's an expensive folly to build a mosque on this spot in place of the warehouses and customs sheds. The Prince Regent has promised to compensate the owners. The construction costs will be financed by a Saudi gift, and by public subscription. Nothing is too good for our religious fervor.

Now listen here, you Muslims. With this mosque, which I already carry in my heart, I set the seal on an alliance between our two peoples.

I might have guessed that Ilena had things to confide in me. Since my return, she had just smiled but hadn't said anything. Now, this evening, she makes up her mind. The whole house is asleep, but I'm drawing in the lamplight.

"Can I have a look? Are these your plans?"

She's grown more beautiful over the years. Her face is fuller, more serene. Her eyelashes are quivering.

"You'll win the competition, Gabriel."

"Don't be such a chauvinist. Wait and see what the others do."

The stool creaks as she sits down.

"You can't accuse me of chauvinism. I'm going to marry Ruwan."

"But Ruwan's married!"

For a moment I can't think of anything else to say. And my objection is meaningless since Ruwan is a Muslim. I congratulated him on his marriage three years ago: an arranged marriage that has not yet produced any children.

"Ruwan's just got divorced," my sister tells me.

In plain language, he has repudiated his wife on grounds of sterility. So now he's free.

"Has he proposed to you?"

"Yes, knowing I'd accept."

Confidently, she awaits my verdict. I take apart my compasses.

"My dear Ilena, it's a wonderful idea."

13

"Thanks, Gabriel."

Now I'm torturing my eraser—a precious eraser brought back from the States handmade of a substance unobtainable here.

"And what about our mother? Does she know?"

"Of course. You can imagine how she's taken it."

In the eyes of our people, it has always been worse to have a daughter marry a Muslim than to have one's cattle stolen. Families that happens to get fingers pointed at them.

"My only reproach, Ilena, is that you never mentioned it in your letters."

"It was too hard to write about. I thought I'd explain when I saw you."

But she explains nothing. And there is nothing to understand. Ruwan likes Ilena and Ilena likes Ruwan. It's the same the world over. I take a few steps in the small room, stooping to avoid the beams.

Ilena could have married just about any young Christian of a good family several years ago, for in our country girls marry young. Instead, she had waited for Ruwan. Maybe they were meeting in secret—in so far as it's possible to do anything in secret here.

"And now it's up to you to decide," she says.

Her shoulders are slightly hunched, her arms folded.

"Why up to me?"

"You've been the head of the family since our father died."

"What do you want me to decide? You've already decided."

"I need the family's consent."

Does the son's opinion really carry more weight than the mother's? I'd have to consult a specialist in Mozarabic law. But I wouldn't dream of doing so. While I'd been in the States, our mother had shouldered the burden of the family. She is respected and admired. I will not set myself above her.

14

"Ilena, you're of age. You don't need permission. You can make your own decisions."

Of age! Foreign notions like that don't go down here. The realities are different. She leans against the flaking, whitewashed wall, avoiding my eye.

"I was hoping for a different attitude from someone who'd been to America," she said.

"Exactly. In America, you don't need your family's consent."

She ignores my remark.

"Who introduced me to Ruwan? Remember?"

Obviously, if anyone's to blame, I am. Ruwan used to come to the house. My brother Saad, the future monk, swapped marbles with him and my sister Ilena—little Ilena —scribbled pictures on his hand. One day, we were playing a stupid native card game. Ruwan pretended to cheat, and she laughed till she cried. We often went to the beach. Because of him, Ilena would get dressed without taking off her bathing suit.

Ruwan was handsome. Still is, I daresay.

"Let's stop this discussion," I say after a while. "I won't stand in your way."

Then it occurs to me. I'm going to build a mosque. She's going to marry a Muslim. Doesn't that really come to the same thing?

"So how has young Gabriel shaped up?"

"He's said to have ideas."

"So he should, he's just back from America. It won't take our good old Marsania long to wear him down."

"In the meantime, have you heard? He's been given the Tower to finish."

"Rather him than me."

"It won't help him to win friends and influence people!"

The old crocodiles gossip in their swamps. What they don't yet know is that "young Gabriel" is going to take their mosque away from them. But all in good time.

Right now, my only ostensible activity is finishing off the En Nasr—or Victory—Tower. What victory? There's no shortage of them in our annals. "The victory over poverty and ignorance," says a minister, unplagued by doubts. The skyscraper will contain an international trade center that will restore Marsana to the place it occupied before the Suez Canal was opened.

But the difficulties encountered along the way have been as great as the project itself. The eminent Japanese architect supplied a set of plans and then went back to Japan, leaving the builders to get on with it. The ground is unstable and the special foundations cost more than was foreseen in the estimates. Huge concrete piles had to be driven. The main contractor went bankrupt and another had to be engaged on unfavorable terms. To cap it all, the owners of the neighboring houses started a lawsuit.

When you arrive by plane, the first thing you notice is this tall, unfinished skeleton sticking up from the city. Humorists have called it The Monkeys' Peak.

"You'll just have to show them you're the smartest monkey," said my partner, El Souss.

I'm taken up in a makeshift hoist. I hang on tight. We get out in blazing sun.

"Watch your step!" shouts the site foreman. "There's wet concrete."

Antar, the crane operator, sits alone in his cabin in the sky. He's spotted me and graciously moves the arm of his crane in my honor. The whole thing sways in the north wind.

The sea sparkles. Above the jumble of the port, I can see the hillock that will become a holy place—God, and the

16

architects' jury, willing. Antlike cars crawl along the cor-
niche. Beyond the city, barring the horizon, loom the hard,
purple Zeujitan Mountains.

"Hello, Ruwan speaking."
"Ruwan who?" I joked.
There's only one Ruwan. That unusual first name dates
back to pre-Arab origins and is handed down in his mother's
family from uncle to nephew.
"Well, Gabriel, have we forgotten our old friends?"
He's right. I'd been putting off seeing him and he knew
why.
"I'm picking you up at twelve o'clock," he announces.
Just like him to take all the decisions. You don't argue
with Ruwan.
As arranged, he turns up in my office, cordial and inso-
lently at ease. He's wearing a loose robe and has grown a
thin, brown, jawline beard. His presence makes me feel
awkward and a bit guilty. He pushes me over to the window
and pretends to scrutinize me:
"Okay, you'll do. The Americans haven't done too much
damage. Your cheeks have filled out a bit, that's all."
"All those damn cornflakes."
"If you get fat, I'll never speak to you again."
Hell! I may not have his figure, but if it came to a fight,
my muscles would get the better of his sinews.
He leafs through my copy of *Concrete Technology in Hot
Climates*, looks vaguely at some plans and clicks his tongue.
The few premature gray hairs on his temples don't detract
from the youthfulness of his face.
"Do you have time for a bit of a detour?" I ask.
I take him down to the old harbor, via Ali-Pasha Boule-
vard. Huge mechanical beetles are working away on my

1 7

inspired hill. I swear him to secrecy and explain my idea to him. I know the mistake that Fannawi and the others are going to make. They'll stand their mosque on the leveled rock, like a statue on a plinth. But mine will form part of the breakwater; it will be a continuation of the seawall. I'll make it a ship, a huge, motionless prow cleaving the waters of the harbor.

"Great!" says Ruwan. "We'll all sail with you."

I'm told he has considerable influence in young Muslim circles, so his letter, telling me about the project, was almost an official order. But right now his behavior doesn't seem quite so forthright.

Give your sister to the Muslims and the Muslims will hire you as a builder. Is that it? Get thee behind me, spirit of doubt!

We take a cab—one of those two-tone Dauphines that inspired tinkering has kept on the streets for twenty-five years. He gets me to tell him my architect's anecdotes, pulls my leg and laughs heartily. His green eyes always used to contrast oddly with his olive skin. The new beard emphasizes the strangeness of his face.

A low arch at a turn in the street; Ruwan's door. We climb some steps. The familiar figures are at their posts. The old retainer, grown so bent he can no longer look me in the face. Ruwan's father, a retired colonel, wearing on his lapel the Prince Regent's golden decoration. He's now a cripple and walks on crutches. He greets us and withdraws with sad courtesy, like an usurped monarch. Ruwan has taken over his powers.

"So you decided to change everything!"

They used to call this room the *salon,* and it was full of fake Louis XV furniture, much admired in Marsana by those with a little education. The new master has got rid of the ornate armchairs and shapely commodes. There's only a

18

thick pile carpet and brass trays. You sit on the floor, leaning against the wall, in the traditional manner.

"The house likes it," says Ruwan. "It feels better this way."

It would. Corsairs used to live here.

"You don't have too many regrets about leaving the army?" In the family tradition, my friend had been sent to the military academy. Then his father had a heart attack and the young lieutenant had to get a discharge and turn real-estate administrator.

"I never have regrets," he replies.

He too wants to know about America. I tell him about my famous boss with his Slavic rages. About the sugar maples in the fall. And the pale seashore with its endless fringe of shingle. How can you live beside such a sea? There are things I don't tell him. Things I leave to his imagination. The sweet redhead who refused to think of me as an oriental, and swore she'd make an all-American boy of me.

"I'm back for good now."

"God willing," said Ruwan, in a strangely solemn voice.

The servant has brought in a platter. My friend serves me. We eat with our fingers. Seeing me hesitate, he smiles.

"Go ahead, we're not savages. You'll get a finger bowl with perfumed water."

The tea is perfumed too; they put cardamom seeds in it.

"And what's Islam doing in the United States?" he asks.

Yes Gabriel, the Black Muslims. One day, the Blacks will break away from Christianity. You can be sure of that. It hasn't done them justice. Islam is the only hope for their race. It's the same in India: there are a hundred million untouchables, potential Muslims, and they'll carry the country with them.

It's no good asking my opinion on such serious questions. Drawing plans is enough for me. Ruwan is steeped in politics. I suppose it's an antidote to all those mortgages and agricultural lawsuits.

"Nonsense, I'm only an amateur!" my friend protests unconvincingly and immediately launches into a vicious attack on the government, the official opposition and the unofficial opposition.

"What do you think of Doctor Samiel?" I ask.

"He's an old scoundrel. His trick is to seem enormously active and never to change anything."

"Do you think the Muslims must pay obedience to him? I don't have to remind you of the line in the Koran about the infidels: *Take no protector from among them.*"

"How knowledgeable you are, dear boy."

But he doesn't answer my question. The sovereign deliberately put a man of obscure origins in power. He trusts this foreigner more than his own brothers because the foreigner will not be tempted to seize the throne. An old tactic with this dynasty.

"And what do you think of Fawzi and Shafic?"

My friend makes a quick gesture as if to puncture these windbags. He thinks no better of the religious leaders, whom he also regards as politicians. The rector of the Koranic University is gaga. Monsignor Elias may be saintly, but he's a miserable helmsman. As for his Most Serene Highness . . . Abbas III, son of Tawfik, son of Abdul Hassan, Defender of the True Faith, Commander of the Roads of the South and Podesta of the Purpurary Islands. His moonface with its timid little beak inherited from distant Turkish ancestors. His everlasting uniform, though he had never commanded so much as half a company. His only known quality is modesty. Our princes are called regents because, for a long time, they reigned in someone else's name. It was the same in the neighboring countries: the regency of Egypt, the Berber regencies, as well as the regency of Marsania. And when Constantinople degenerated

20

into a republic, our leaders, instead of proclaiming themselves king, kept their former title like an old garment. The end of an era, the end of a race.

"Stop it, Ruwan! You'll get us thrown in jail."

"They wouldn't dare. They know we are the future."

In front of us, there's a bowl of assorted camels' and gazelles' eyes. Don't worry, they're two kinds of almond.

"I gather you're working toward a renovated Islam, my friend."

"No. Purified, fined down."

How thoughtful he's grown all of a sudden.

"We were talking about the Turks just now," he goes on. "They tried to build a state without Islam. Look at the result. It speaks for itself."

"And what becomes of the Christians in your scheme of things? Do they pack their bags or order their coffins?"

"I'm surprised at your listening to such tales. The police slander us."

A creaking in the old beams seems to echo his words.

"Some Christians," he says after a pause, "have made the mistake of becoming lackeys of the West. It's true, they present problems. The others have nothing to fear. We'll see they get their fair share in the new society—as the Book commands."

He punctuates his words by tapping on the metal tray. Out in the courtyard, the hibiscus is already over.

"They say you're getting foreign money."

"Who is?"

"The splinter groups."

"Arab money is not foreign money."

It never occurred to him to deny the fact.

"Aren't you afraid that in demolishing the existing order, you're paving the way for Marxism?"

"Another cliché," he snaps. "Shall I tell you what Marxism is? Quite simply, a Christian heresy. It fed on the failure of Christianity. And it has no hold on Islam."

I say nothing. What's the point in these discussions? Each person's beliefs have their roots deep down in his history.

"Promise you'll come to my wedding," he says suddenly.

He's finally come to the point.

"I promise, Ruwan. I'll come even if my mother forbids me."

Two short sentences and we won't mention it again. In fact our whole encounter is so much froth around those two sentences. I should have played harder to get.

He bounds over to my side, lithe as a cat. His face lights up with merriment.

"As for you, old buddy, I understand that things are well under way. The name of a certain Eudoxia has been mentioned."

"We'll see."

"It's all settled. The archbishop wants you to have a fine wedding in memory of your father. Sarun has let himself be won over. To top it all, the girl is willing. She likes architects. Lucky girl!"

His jokes can be barbed. I've ensconced myself in a corner.

"Congratulations, my dear Gabriel," he goes on. "A wealthy family, a little *nouveau riche,* but you can't have everything. A mother-in-law who will put up with all your caprices. Sarun himself—well, he's the good sort of bandit. He'll be admitted into our society provided he's kept in check."

He's carried away by his own eloquence. Still, he may envy me. His in-laws are on their uppers and their only hope lies in me. His future mother-in-law won't allow his name to be mentioned. His future father-in-law is pushing up the daisies in the Babeluq Cemetery.

The servant has brought in the promised finger bowls.

We sit there, not talking, just as we did in the good old days, and all's well between us. One last question occurs to me.

"Have you still got your key?"

The key without a lock, handed down from generation to generation in Ruwan's family. The fetish-key they brought with them from Andalusia, like many other exiles now scattered along the coastline.

"If I showed it to you," the present owner says, "you'd take me for a disgusting revanchist."

I walk away down the little street. When I look back, there's Ruwan waving to me in the fragile winter light.

Turn, turn, Eudoxia. Turn in the cone of soft light. Strike the ground with your bare feet.

"I love dancing," she says. And the dance loves her. No matter where. Even in this nightclub, a bad imitation of Soho or Saint-Germain-des-Prés. Unseeing, she revolves, with the terrible seriousness she puts into all she does.

Eudoxia's father has insisted on picking her up. He's too shrewd a businessman to expose his daughter's reputation—his capital—to the slightest risk. His name is Sarun. Huge, sallow, enigmatic. A scar runs the length of his chin. It might be an old saber cut. He's dressed up, bow tie and all, just for this short car ride.

"Will you dance, papa?" asks Eudoxia.

Sometimes Sarun dances. But this evening he's not in the mood. Side by side we go out into the pungent night. He plays heads and tails with the Maria Theresa thaler he always carries with him. Their car is waiting for them on the street corner, insolently parked with two wheels on the sidewalk.

"Last time you had a Lincoln Continental," I say.

23

He smiles, pleased. The new car, of course, is in no way inferior.

Out of politeness, I ask about his business. He says a word or two about import licenses, the Ministry of Foreign Trade, the complicities bought and sold there. It's all a game and he excels at it.

"I like giving *baksheesh,*" he says in English, as though the foreign language added to the savor of the thought.

Let's go on dancing. Dance forever. But that's another evening, later on, at the ball on the Street of the Winds. It's one of those ill-famed places where there are four boys to every girl. At the door police are checking pockets, confiscating knives, so the evening passes off without too much trouble. And as the police are good-natured, they return the toys when it's time to go home.

"You won't tell anyone we came here, will you?" Eudoxia begs.

Turn, turn under the 500-watt bulbs.

Frankly, I didn't recognize her after my years abroad. But even when younger, she had those amazing, enormous eyes. Eyes that swallow up the face like the eyes of the twelve apostles in the frescoes of Deir-es-Safsaf.

The old folk in Marsana can remember the Sarun brothers coming down from their mountain hamlet with one secondary-school diploma between the four of them. The eldest looked like a nobody, but appearances can be deceptive. The second brother, known as Sarun the Great, was Eudoxia's father. Then there was Sarun of Abidjan, the toughest in business, who looked after the family's interests in black Africa. And finally, the youngest, who met his death in the prime of life at the wheel of a sports car. Success did not bring the Sarun brothers the respect of the honorable families. My father had no wish to be invited to their receptions. He preferred to look after the business of the Mozarabic community. His dedication earned him much goodwill, which I, undeservingly, have inherited. In a word, the Saruns had the moneybags but we had the good name. In these uncertain times—Monsignor Elias *dixit*—these two heritages should join forces.

The idea of this marriage did not come from any one person. It was the will of our dead, of our walls, of the whole city. And in addition, these rich people may have grown a little tired of themselves. Rather late in the day, they had started sponsoring the arts. As the brother of two businessmen and the father-in-law of a third, Sarun could legitimately aspire to someone of a different class. Why not someone in the arts? And, while he was about it, why not an architect? When all's said and done, architecture is more concrete than poetry.

Eudoxia had no reservations. She saw our union written in the stars. She liked to remind me of a tiny incident I had long forgotten. It happened in my last year at the Lazarist School. My father was already ill and couldn't bear noise in the house, so I was sent to board at school. Our only outing was a supervised Sunday walk along Princess Othmania Boulevard, also called the *Quai des Calèches*. White, or rather pale yellow, villas. Overflowing bougainvilleas, decorative palm trees that have never produced a date. Vendors of roasted almonds. A reassuring, rather misleading, facade. We schoolboys, correct in our dark blue uniforms, but with flowing ruby-red cravats—a refinement whose origin I have never known—which turned us into a kind of aristocracy.

A large car was parked in front of the old fort, its engine idling. The driver's seat was empty, but through the smoked-glass windshield we could see a very young girl with a flower in the neck of her dress. The glass distorted the colors and made her look unreal. She was smiling absently. At us? Perish the thought! "Lincoln Continental," observed one of our classmates who was car-crazy. We all stooped and glanced at the passenger. The master in charge made us hurry on. The shoeshine boys were splitting their sides.

"Say 'Good day' to the little lady!" cried Ruwan. His idea of a joke. He grabbed my wrist. I shoved him off. A tall man came out of the garden of a neighboring villa and took the wheel. I was too embarrassed to look at his face. With a roar of its engine, the car slid away.

"That's Sarun," said one of the boys. There was a buzz of interest. Sarun the Great, a man who had started from nothing and today entertained cabinet ministers. Speculator, said his detractors.

Later, I noticed I'd lost a cuff link. It must have fallen off in the scuffle. A white metal disk of no value. But it was precious to me, as my name was engraved on it in very small Arabic letters.

"I found it on the hood," Eudoxia confesses with a teasing smile, "and I still have it." She read the inscription: *Jibril.* Who is Jibril X in the graduating class at the Lazarist School? They soon identified me. He's the future architect. Ever since I was old enough to hold a pencil everyone knew I'd be an architect.

"I hated being a girl," says Eudoxia, "because it meant I couldn't go to the Lazarist School like you."

Those good Lazarists! They'd been driven out of France around 1880, by some absurd law, and had transferred their services to the youth of Marsania, Christian and non-Christian alike. Anyone who amounted to anything in the city had passed through their hands and thought like a Lazarist. In the Parliament, deputies educated by the holy fathers clashed with other deputies educated by the holy fathers, using rhetoric taught by the holy fathers. The Prince Regent's own brother . . .

The Sunday after the incident, no reason was given but we were taken on a different walk. Princess Othmania Boulevard had become too dangerous.

I had to wait till the Easter holidays to revisit the scene: the large villa the color of milky tea—a little tea and a lot of milk—with its Ionic columns and stone balustrade. Not a soul at the windows or in the garden. Behind the house I was delighted to see washing strung between two trees. So these proud folk were just like everyone else. They too had to hang their shirts out to dry.

Then the school sent me out into the world and I had to grow up. But its memory has stayed with me. The austere facade, the easygoing interior. The great monkey-puzzle trees in the garden that looked as if they had come off a drawing board. The drum that summoned us to classes. The sound of Ping-Pong balls in the torpor of a summer Sunday.

Ruwan, always the tease, told me that Christians are half-men, since they have only one guardian angel. Whereas any self-respecting Muslim has two—one on the right and one on the left—who are also spies, and have to note his every word.

The school has been nationalized, the cross taken down from over the door, the Pre-Raphaelite frescoes in the chapel daubed out. O Marsania, old land of toleration, drowned in the sea. . . .

Often, during those weeks of hard work, I'd tramp the narrow streets of the old city, pad in hand, sketching the delicacy of an arch, the sober lines of a buttress. I wasn't trying to ape the work of centuries. The Mosque of the Prophets would be modern, resolutely modern. But it would capture and reflect the essential beauty of the old metropolis.

I saw a great white ship, all sails set, breasting the water, gradually taking shape at the end of my pencil.

The old city may since have been gutted to make way for automobiles. If so, I don't want to know. In those days, no four-wheeled, or even two-wheeled, vehicle invaded this stronghold because of the narrowness of the streets and the incredible numbers of stairways. It was a city inside the city, and had been built like an onion, walls within walls. Its trade with the low-lying quarters was entrusted to donkey caravans, which plied their way endlessly through the steep alleyways. And sometimes, when an overloaded mule pinned me against the wall, its tattered lord would look down from his lofty perch and let fall a disdainful *"Balak, balak!"‡*

I'd give all the music in the world for the braying of the donkey behind each door, the sound of these invisible creatures all ready to work in the soft dawn light. Two classes inhabited these high places: the masters, a humble class of coppersmiths, idlers, Koran readers; and the servants, a four-legged, iron-shod proletariat, endlessly carrying life's daily burdens.

Of course, this little world had its well-known characters. There was the fat woman who waited for a horse to go by, then took hold of its tail and let it pull her up the street. The madman who walked past the cafés holding a tin can from which incense billowed out over the customers, *gratis pro Deo*. Driss, the cripple, who crawled through the traffic on all fours showing his fine teeth in a wide grin. Farez, the peddler, who impressed the simple countrywomen by throwing his unbreakable bowls on the hard ground, until one day, when drunk with success, he tried them on the paving stones and was laughed out of the neighborhood.

In the morning, mothers kneaded dough. Their children took it to the bakery and came home in the afternoon carrying on their heads warm, fragrant loaves wrapped in cloths.

After much scouting and sketching, I visited a house of prayer. There are said to be ninety-nine of them in the up-

‡ The plodding translation is "Watch out!" The real meaning is "Your wits!"

per city, one for each of the names of God. And if some people claim there aren't that many, don't listen to them, it's pure malice.

The Mosque of the Brasses, with its widthways, rectangular prayer hall and exuberant chandeliers. The Tidjaniya, robed in tiles of the rarest turquoise. And the Mosque of the Blind, curled around an aged tree which all year round sheds its silver-gray leaves into a fountain like tears.

Prostrate on his mat, the lone worshipper murmurs, "Oh, my God, separate me from my sins, as You have separated West from East."

The winding Alfaïn Street is the local Champs-Élysées. Two loaded donkeys can just about pass on it. It gets its name from the two thousand shopkeepers said to have once traded there. As you know, we've always thought big. But there are enough of them left for your pleasure. Vendors selling by the yard figs threaded on strings. Olive sellers, sellers of fragrances, squatting in their little shops like theatergoers watching the comedy of the street. At closing time, they grasp the cord hanging from the ceiling to haul themselves over the counter and mingle with the actors.

It's just a step from this street to the tomb of Ahmed Shibani. But you have to know where the entrance is. You Westerners place your monuments on a parvis. Ours, in the bend of an alleyway, show themselves only to the deserving. Pass without seeing, all ye who hurry by. Marsanians prize this tomb chiefly for its narrow opening in the wall, a slit like that of a letter box, but edged with lead. The faithful, desirous of the saint's blessing, put the tips of their fingers into it. But woe betide all liars; Shibani grabs their fingers and they can't get them out. This ordeal was common in the Middle Ages, but is rather less so today; the law may prefer not to put the saint's prestige to the test.

"Put your hand in Gabriel."

I'm about ten years old and I'm watching my two Muslim

29

friends do it. Of course I have no desire to risk the tiniest bit of myself in that dangerous hole. But they make me, the bastards. I see myself dead, or maimed for life. But no, nothing happens. We look at one another, laughing. Maybe Christians aren't such liars after all.

A few steps farther on, the street begins to go downhill, dropping precipitously from stairway to stairway, from the pious upper city to the corruption of the port.

"You'll be repudiated," cries our mother.

Dismissed out of hand like Ruwan's mother and his first wife. It's only too obvious. All well-to-do Muslims get rid of their wives as soon as they're bored with them and make a new life with a younger woman. My sister Ilena goes on turning the pages of her book and doesn't answer.

"You'll be repudiated," the little woman in black repeats, "and your children will be brought up by another woman."

Which is exactly what happened to Ruwan's mother. Muslim children stay with their father, and the repudiated woman has no choice but to go back where she came from. Ruwan was hardly allowed to visit his mother.

"I wish you'd stop saying 'Muslim' and 'Christian,'" says Ilena. "I'm not marrying 'a Muslim.' I'm marrying a man, leave it at that."

I refuse to take sides. I came back to Marsania to build something, not to get embroiled in family quarrels. Disappointed by my attitude, the accuser calls our late father to the rescue: "Look at him, Ilena. He's watching you. He disapproves." Our parents stand side by side, smiling in their black frame. They've only been married a short while. He is already somewhat detached from worldly things, she lively and winsome. Yes, our mother was once happy. Our mother was once pretty. It gives me a pang.

Carried away with indignation, the lady of the house goes on: "You were born into a family without blemish. Now you're the blot on our name."

Ilena gets up, tears in her eyes. A final blow hits her in the hallway.

"Every time you think of that boy, it's written all over your face. I forbid you to think of him, do you hear?" And that's how love stories end in Marsania.

"As you're my friend," he says, "I'll show you our key."

His name is Ruwan. Even though he's a disciple of Muhammad, he's my best friend. We're still in short pants. We're creeping down the hallway because his father has forbidden us to touch the famous key. And here it is, huge and corroded with rust. I can't help putting in a word of advice: "You should rub it with emery paper."

Ruwan gives a superior smile. "It's no use, we've lost the lock."

Normally, it's the key that gets lost.

"What lock?"

"The lock of our house in Seville."

His family was driven out of it, he says, by my Christian brothers. I withdraw with dignity and look up Seville in a dictionary. How can he blame me for things that happened so long ago? The injustice brings tears to my eyes.

"That key's of no importance," my father explains, in his gentle manner. "You know that house in Seville was pulled down years ago."

Keys which no longer open anything, but which are kept as armorial bearings by the Muslim and Jewish dynasties of Marsana, Tunis or Fez. Out of snobbery, some families that aren't entitled to them go so far as to have them made.

Night has fallen. Ruwan, in a pointed hood, is walking the streets of Seville. All the shutters are closed. He stops in front of a low house that's very old but still solid. Grass is growing on the

31

doorstep. Out of his pocket, he takes a long key, fits it into the keyhole and turns it with all his might. The door creaks open. Ruwan gives a shout of triumph. In he goes. I'm about to follow when the door shuts in my face.

Marsanian figures from the happy years: let us open the album at the letter S.

His Excellency Doctor *Samiel,* precious court dwarf, hair still black and brilliantined as though lacquered. I don't know whether the color is artificial or comes from some extra energy deriving from his tiny stature. It's said that to compensate for his own appearance, the doctor only likes big blondes. He frequents nightclubs, but only abroad. A man who knows how to live.

Safia was separated from her husband. He was a dealer in precious stones who plied from Rome to Bombay, from Anvers to Tel Aviv. Not long ago, he got his throat cut between two planes. But she had nothing to do with it: just common thieves. Indifferent to glory and even to money, Safia is interested in people and objects. She is determined to grasp their truth. She waits for them to show her their rarest, truest outlines and hastens to capture them on canvas, on a clay tablet, on a piece of stained glass. From her past, she has kept a taste for sapphires and turquoises. Sometimes, just for the pleasure of it, she goes to see Benoliel, the jeweler with the black skullcap. With the help of optical instruments, she shows me what she calls the gem's garden —grains of foreign matter which heighten its color and add to its price. Then she imprisons a ray of light and makes it dance. The old man is moved. "Anyone can see you're a painter," he cries.

Finally *Sarun,* his long arms, his muted voice, his horror of the sun. When I see him padding silently into the room, with his dark gray elegance, he makes me think of the bats that hang in their hundreds in the grottoes of his country estate. Only the other day, to save his fruit crop, he decided, despite Eudoxia's protests, to smoke them out. Dressed in fatigues and bush hat, he directed his workmen in person, curiously aroused by this act of fratricide against his totem animal. He brought us one of the creatures which had bitten his finger. By evening his hand was so swollen that he had to consult a specialist. "It's the cave virus," said the doctor, delighted to meet with such a perfect case.

While immersed in my project, I got a call from Bedros Napoleon Pasha, one of my poor father's best friends. "Come and see us, Gabriel. Next Sunday we'll be talking about mixed marriages."

The "we" referred to the *majlis-el-milli,* a lay community council, whose function it was to help the Exarch Elias and to settle disputes between Mozarabs. It was a carefully preserved legacy from the days of the Ottoman Empire. But why this invitation? Who had spoken to him about Ilena? It was in our mother's interest to hush the matter up.

On the appointed day, I went to the meeting. Bedros was in the chair. His was a well-known name; his father had been prime minister, the only Marsanian Christian to have held that office. In fact he didn't hold it for long; he was assassinated soon after his appointment. But our Bedros did not exploit the family aura. He considered himself a man of peace.

On his right, the distinguished and emaciated archaeologist Magda K. writhed on her chair. What's this? A woman in the club? Yes, to show we were more progressive than the other side. New members were co-opted, with the help of the Holy Ghost. Sarun had never been able to join because his wealth was too recently acquired, too flashy.

The meeting began with the *report,* delivered by the editor of our little Mozarabic newssheet, *En Nur* (the light). It itemized all the conflicts, great and small, between Christians and Muslims. All the stories the papers couldn't print. A Muslim had killed a Christian's dog which had touched him with its nose, putting him in an unfit state for prayer. Rotten eggs had been tossed into a church. In a number of places, stones had been thrown at shops that opened on a Friday—despite the tradition whereby the shops in the old city closed on Friday and those in the new city on Sunday. Mozarab students had been made to put up with insults. Can these be called incidents? Such things have always happened. Incidents also occur between Christians and between Muslims. All neighborhoods have their problems. Why single out these in particular? The reporter, carried away, goes on to mention the case of an unveiled girl who had acid thrown in her face while she was waiting for a bus. "Irrelevant," someone interjects, "it was a Muslim woman." But troubled looks show that these people feel concerned.

To restore a sense of proportion, Bedros Pasha recalls an instance when the activists had to give in: the quarrel over numerals. As you probably know, we orientals are rather perverse; we write everything backward, except our numerals. Letters run in one direction, numerals in the other. One fine day the splinter groups decided to attack this anomaly, which was obviously of Christian origin. "We'll turn the numerals around," they proclaimed. There was an outcry among tradesmen, accountants and businessmen. "Do you want to drive us crazy?" The agitators beat a retreat and let the matter drop.

Bedros goes on to point out that their actions are not always harmful. The other day, in the street, they thrashed a boy who had stolen some sandals from outside a mosque.

They also beat up men who urinate against walls. The elegant lady archaeologist keeps her blue-lidded eyes lowered, like one of those pre-Islamic queens whose tombs she so cheerfully violates.

"I should like to know," puts in the aviator, "what progress has been made toward modifying Article One of the Constitution." That's the article stating that Islam is the State religion. President Bedros throws up his hands: "Now, now, my good friend!" This former pilot, who was badly burned during the war and whose face is disfigured by a great patch of red skin, has to be humored.

"We are governed in the name of an alien religion," cries the aviator, hammering out his words. "I'd rather be ruled frankly by the devil than by those who usurp the name of God."

Hubbub breaks out. "I demand that my statement be recorded in the minutes," he says firmly.

Of course it won't be. Supposing the minutes were to fall into the hands of the Minister of the Interior! On the other hand, I'd be willing to bet the room is bugged. The Minister of the Interior pretends to know nothing, and the *majlis* pretends not to know that the Minister of the Interior knows everything. How delightful to live among intelligent people.

We finally get around to the main topic: marriages. The brilliant Magda is given the floor: "Here's a case that came to my knowledge. A Mozarab woman wanted to get rid of her husband, likewise a Mozarab. So she converted to Islam. Automatically, the marriage became null and void." Which is only normal: according to their law, a Muslim woman cannot be the chattel of a Christian man.

"But that wasn't the end of it. The husband was foolish enough to love his wife. So he converted to Islam. The marriage immediately became valid again, since both parties were Muslims. Needless to say, the husband lived to regret his action. 'Sorry,' said the cadi, 'we Muslims do not tolerate backsliding.' Two conversions for a failed divorce. Can you beat it?''

Everyone has some little story to tell. Woe betide those who marry outside their religion. "We can't change the rules of Islam," acknowledges the chairman good-naturedly. "Nor can we change our own. The main thing is honesty on both sides. I knew a woman who wanted to convert out of self-interest. I spoke to the sheik and he wouldn't allow it. He said she wasn't sincere."

"So," the aviator breaks in ironically, "the woman found another sheik who welcomed her with open arms."

When they'd all had their say Bedros Pasha closed the meeting and signed to me to stay behind. He's a tubby, lively little man with thick eyebrows that he's always pulling.

"Well, my son, now you know the lay of the land."

As if I hadn't always known. He tugs at his right eyebrow waiting to hear what I'll say.

"Ruwan's my friend. He has the right to marry my sister."

"Of course. But would you have the right to marry his?"

Certainly not. Muslims are not allowed to give their daughters to Christian dogs.

"Begging your Lordship's pardon," I say, "the question does not arise. Ruwan's sisters have all been married for some time."

Ruwan's the baby of the family; he comes after a long string of girls. His parents awaited his coming like that of the *Mahdi*, the Islamic messiah. Which explains why he's a bit of a spoiled child.

"People will always find good reasons for resignation," Bedros replies. "Every case is special, but the result will always be the same: a mixed marriage and Muslim children." Now it's the turn of the left eyebrow. I hadn't bargained for such an offensive.

"If we allow many more of these marriages," he goes on, "Islam will swallow us up. There will never be any give and take. We're doomed."

He dons his raincoat and an antiquated hat.

"It won't help us to act like mollycoddles," I reply softly, "crying persecution at the slightest pinprick."

"Of course not, my boy. I've always said as much myself."

"So instead of protesting against a decision that's been made, I'm saving my energy for the harbor mosque."

In the vestibule, I find my friend Eudoxia talking to the aviator while waiting for me. Our little meeting had aroused her curiosity and she had come to get a whiff of the atmosphere. Bedros Pasha is a gentleman; he smiles at her, despite the words he's had with her father. He knows the Saruns are too wealthy and powerful and that one day they'll have to be admitted to the *majlis.* All he can do, in this as in other matters, is put off the day.

The aviator thought he'd end the evening with a funny story: "Last week, some French tourists tried to change a 100-franc note. The cashier refused. Do you know why? Because of the bare-breasted *Liberty leading the people.*"

We laugh heartily.

"Believe it or not," he finishes, "these skirmishes are all organized. There's somebody behind them."

My partner, El Souss, took me gently to task for neglecting the tower site. And to think I'd been brought back from America for the sake of this monstrosity, which is as out of place in our city as an elephant's tusk in the mouth of a beautiful woman!

"Whatever I do it will always be just as ugly," I remarked, somewhat unjustly. The En Nasr Tower had a kind of terrible beauty. But it had been built in the wrong place.

Ignoring the advice of his doctors, El Souss went to the site to make up for my negligence. The elevator got stuck at the fifteenth floor. When they got him out, he was on the verge of a heart attack.

I put most of my energy into the House of the Prophets. I went down to the jetty to get an idea of how it would look. One evening, a sentry barred my way in front of the Kapudan Pasha Fort. He was a young fellow in black fatigues, with a big countrified face.

"I'm going to build a mosque. I'm the architect."

"Blessings on you, man of God." I had got through on false pretenses. This country bumpkin hadn't guessed my Christian taint. Before my eyes, minarets and spires stood up like ninepins. Houses climbed right to the foot of the Jeblasan, more properly called Jebel Hassan, after some conqueror who may never have existed. Obviously the new mosque would sit too low against this horizon. It would have to rise above the tangle of masts, chimneys and cranes. A great upsurge of whiteness. Yes, I'd alter my drawings, and hang the expense. In any case, I didn't know how much the Ministry of Religious Cults and the Saudi backers had decided to put into the project. As we like to say here, the Lord knows best.

I went back up to the boulevards. Night was falling. I couldn't find a single seat on the terrace of the *Palais des Gazelles* (written in French on a cream-colored ground). The old streetcars, unchanged since the days of the first Baron Empain, clanked along the shore, festooned, as always, with people. Passengers fought for a place on the running boards. "You should try it, it's cooler," young Mark had said to me.

Despite the fact that images were forbidden—which incidentally does not come from the Koran—every intersection in the so-called modern part of the town was adorned with a bronze statue of a stout pasha in a fez. One of them was pointing imperiously at an imaginary crowd. Another, a fellow architect, I suppose, carried rolls of plans under his arm.

On the Avenue of May 22 there was a screeching of brakes as two cars cannoned into each other. One of the drivers, who had a gash in his forehead, advanced on the other pouring out abuse. He didn't seem to notice that he was walking on splinters of glass. A crowd gathered.

"Have his blood!" cried someone.

"Bash his head in!" shouted a street urchin.

Suddenly I sensed that one of the men was a Christian and the other a Muslim, and that the crowd *knew* it.

"Kill him! Kill him!" yelped the kids. I stood on tiptoe, hoping to see a policeman. But the police were already beginning to keep out of ticklish situations. The man with the gashed forehead was hammering on the hood of the other man's car. His adversary, a slender figure in a very white shirt, had taken refuge behind his car while pretending to fight back.

"Coward! Coward!" taunted the spectators.

Two parties began to form. People crowded onto balconies, they, too, gesticulating. Suddenly a woman appeared from nowhere, screaming. She took the assailant by the hand and led him away. Once again, the genies of the city had proved compassionate.

Carrying a small suitcase, Ilena crosses the living room. She is very pale. She's wearing her best dress to show us that this departure is a special occasion. Our mother puts down her needlework, watches her and says nothing. Nothing. We hear Ilena opening the front door. I follow her out. I'll call her a cab. Ilena is going to stay with Ruwan's mother, a divorcée living alone, who has agreed to put her up. It's in her house that Ilena will make her long preparations for the wedding. Tomorrow I'll send on the rest of her clothes.

"Well," says our mother, when I get back, "are you pleased with your good deed?"

My papers are still on the table. I have to work out the exact curve of the arch that will be the entrance to the House of the Prophets. Perhaps the most important decision I have to take. The East cultivates a mystique of the entrance, from the man who said "I am the gate" to the metaphors of the Sufi poets. Enter the sanctuary on the right foot, oh believer, and when you leave, let it be on the left.

But our mother takes no notice of such details:

"I don't know if you realize, Gabriel, that your sister's marriage will make your own impossible."

"How come?"

She's eager for me to marry the rich Eudoxia. Once we're part of the Sarun clan, there'll be no more rainy days.

"You'll see soon enough. The Saruns are in a position to pick and choose their son-in-law. Why would they want one from a tainted family?"

I break my pencil lead.

"I didn't ask to marry Eudoxia. It's just too bad if they don't like me anymore."

"You give up very easily, my son."

Her profile looks hard against the white wall. Hard and full of suffering.

"What's more," she goes on, "you're not playing fair. You're letting Eudoxia compromise herself with you by not telling her what's happening in our family. Poor child! Watch your step. The Saruns will wake up."

There are days when I wish I had no past, no family, no memory.

40

"Come to the baths with me," says my father.

I'm scared of the baths. Katrin says they're no place for Christians. What's more, we don't need to go there as we've installed a bathroom in the house.

"Every Marsanian should know the baths," says my father, firmly.

A fat sheik is undressing in the changing room. He takes off baggy trousers, a knitted singlet, long underdrawers, short underdrawers and a cloth wound around his waist. If he goes on, there'll be nothing of him left. A firm hand has led me into the steamfilled room. Bodies are lying around. The masseur steps up on one of them and massages it with his feet while leaning against the wall. Stop!

I bang my fist on the desk. The draftsmen jump.

"This time we'll apply the penalty clause."

I'm talking to Red Truck, the contractor in charge of the main work on the Nasr Tower. Not satisfied with the delay he has already caused, he's had the nerve to pull out his men this morning and send them off on another job. "It was urgent," he tells me. Meaning: your tower has dragged on so long, it may as well wait a bit longer. He listens to the voice that shouts the loudest. His nickname dates back to the time when he was always to be seen at the wheel of a two-ton, oxblood-colored Dodge. He started out in a small way, but a lot of cement has flowed through the cement mixers since those days. I draw up a provisional breakdown of the penalty payments and send it to him by messenger. That will give him an idea of what to expect. I'm fed up with this negligence, these excuses and the endless petty skullduggery. And, of course, I have to vent my personal problems on someone.

A little while later, I get Red Truck on the line:

"There must be some mistake."

"No, no. Article 23 of the contract."

"What's got into you? You know very well those clauses are never applied."

"If they were applied occasionally, Marsania wouldn't be in the mess it's in now."

I can hear the guy choking on the end of the line.

"You wouldn't do that to me!"

He's the uncle of one of my schoolmates. His daughter married the princesses' doctor. Worst of all, he thinks that because he's a Christian he can take liberties with me. I stand my ground and he hangs up spluttering.

In the evening, some large cardboard boxes are waiting for me when I get home: the labels show them to contain hi-fi equipment. Just the kind of thing people would give their eyeteeth for, with import licenses so hard to get. Our mother doesn't know whether to be pleased or not. I tear open the envelope that comes with these wonderful things. A visiting card drops onto the rug: *Habib Sebtawi* (alias Red Truck, emperor of the building sites).

Young Mark, who's music-mad, dances around the room, clapping his hands. He'll soon change his tune. I tell him exactly what I think. I call a cab and, with the help of the driver, dump the whole caboodle in Red Truck's hallway.

It wasn't even a good make.

When I get back, Mark starts to insult me. Then he bursts into tears and kisses my hand. God! That kid!

"Mark's getting impossible," I say to our mother. "We'll have to send him to board."

"Remember what you were like at his age." And adds, as an afterthought, "It's no joke being fifteen these days."

These days? We've seen worse.

The following morning, Red Truck is back in my office. Arms folded, mealymouthed. I offer him one of Sarun's cigarillos, which he pushes away without a word. There's trouble brewing.

"So now you're the watchdog of the banks!"

"What banks?"

"The ones financing your precious tower."

"It's not just banks. The Tower has twenty-four backers: private individuals and corporations."

"A few pennies more or less won't make any difference to them."

"That doesn't concern me. I've got the job of finishing that tower, on the best possible terms. And finish it I will."

"Sure, my boy. But you don't have to overdo it." He spreads himself on his chair. Those folds of skin, those heavy features. We weren't made to get along.

"I've been asked to try and speed things up a bit," I go on stubbornly.

The messenger boy comes in with something for me to sign. Instead of sending him away, I read the letter in front of my visitor. But my eyes are clouded by anger and fear.

Red Truck pretends not to notice the insult. He crosses and uncrosses his legs, and starts in again as soon as I look up.

"Incidentally, your breakdown's wrong. You left out the allowance for bad weather."

"The what?"

"Article 24 of the contract."

"But the weather has been fine all autumn. And most of the winter."

He winks. He's offering me a way out: the bad-weather card.

I clear my throat: "Five days at the very most, and that's pushing it."

Red Truck shrugs. I haven't been very smart.

"Listen, Gabriel," he says, in one last attempt to help me. "This is the East. There are no individuals. The individual is

43

a Western invention. Here, there are only families, clans and tribes. You and I are members of the same clan. We have to help each other. That's how you survive. The fact is, I've got problems in the business. If we don't stick together, there are others who will and we'll be crushed. Don't you forget it."

His eyes are smoldering.

"I know your head's been filled with all sorts of ideas," he goes on. "Free competition, healthy rivalry and all that. Each for himself and may the best man win. That's all very well. But what does it lead to? An unlivable society where people are lonely and terrified, where they drink and take drugs. Tell me this: how many suicides have you seen in Marsania?"

The fact is there haven't been many.

"I'd rather have our arrangements and compromises any day," he says. "And if you ask me, helping a friend, even if you have to stretch the law a little, is an act of humility. It's an admission you're just a small part of a whole. You're too damn proud, Gabriel."

He stands up and makes a great show of holding out his hand to me.

"No hard feelings, I trust."

High time he left; he was beginning to win me over.

"Don't worry about your . . . What did you call it? 'Penalty clause'? I'll pay up. Little things like that don't frighten me."

I try to open the door for him, but he gets there first. He looks back and lets me have one last home truth:

"Gabriel, my boy, you won't go far with those principles. You'd better catch the first plane back to the States."

Fever. Fever from the south. With chattering teeth, I get out of bed to jot down some inspired sketches that I won't even be able to decipher tomorrow.

My mother was right. She was nearly always right. It would be better to tell Sarun. It would be better to get him moderately mad right away than to get him ripping mad later on.

I'd never seen his lair on the top floor of his tobacco factory. He'd bought the old place when he was very young and it was on the verge of bankruptcy.

I'd made my appointment by telephone, just like any customer. Sarun came out to meet me; his cordiality seemed a little forced. It was the beginning of what you people call spring; and the sun, shining through the big windows, was already overheating the atmosphere.

"Well now, young man, do you have a secret to tell me?"

His office was cluttered with packing cases and files, just as it had been in the days when he was starting out. In town, the Saruns made a show of their wealth; in the office they were puritanical. The only luxury was an almost abstract painting by Safia, a blue wash-tint on a light brown ground, titled *The Cigar Smokers.*

"We have always been an honorable family," I began, by way of a lead-in. I didn't have to remind him of my father's career. Instead I chose to mention an ancestor who had been hanged in our village under the Mad Sultan for refusing to convert to Islam; a great uncle, the "doctor of the poor and needy," whom thousands of people had escorted to his last resting place; and, for good measure, my own brother, a novice in a desert monastery.

"Excellent," said Sarun, not quite seeing what I was driving at. Tall, wary, slightly stooping. Fullface, he had a mel-

45

ancholy expression, but the profile was rough-hewn. Oriental mystic or great nocturnal predator?

"And now, I'm afraid I have to tell you that my sister is going to marry a Muslim," I blurted out.

"That's a fine how-do-you-do!"

His face relaxed. It was the first time I'd witnessed Sarun's silent laughter.

"Did you really imagine I didn't know?"

On the wall above his desk was an old photograph of him receiving the "Best Business" award from the hands of the sovereign. Sarun eager, almost obsequious, the Prince Regent rather absent-looking, with a faint smile on his pale, round face.

"Your sister hasn't made such a bad choice," he said. "Ruwan has prospects. He'll be a useful relative."

"Yes, I know he's related to the whole military aristocracy."

"I wasn't thinking only of that."

He'd spoken English in front of his secretary. I couldn't believe my ears. Ilena's marriage, far from being a liability to me, was being counted as an asset.

"We have to move with the times," Sarun concluded banteringly. What a priggish idiot he must have thought me. He had risen to see me out. The walls reeked of tobacco.

"What about you, Gabriel? When are you going to get married?"

To spare my feelings, he hadn't mentioned Eudoxia's name.

"I haven't done anything yet. I'll get married when I've built something." A remark calculated to please him. The elevator arrived, sweeping its iron shaft.

"You mean the Nasr Tower?"

"Yes. But I was really thinking of the mosque."

"My boy, you haven't chosen the easy way."

Down below, someone was hammering impatiently on a

46

door to hurry us up. Sarun continued to hold on to the gate of the elevator.

"May I give you a piece of advice? We must have grand designs, but we must also know when it's time to change them."

Full moon over the white city. The roofs bear their burden of sleepers. I hear some of them, not far away, stirring in their dreams. Streetlamps on the Promenade trace the curve of the shoreline all the way to the pale sweeping beam of the Ras Elassi lighthouse. Beyond this frontier lies a vague, dimly phosphorescent zone. I alone, at this late hour, know it's the sea.

I draw without respite, and without stopping to see what I've done. Tomorrow, of course, I'll check. I'll have our engineer calculate the thrust on this arch, the load on that column.

I scribble on till sleep takes my pencil out of my hands. At last I've found out what was wrong: my parvis. The mosque looked out on an empty space. I'd forgotten the lessons of my great predecessor, Camillo Sette. Never let a monument stand alone, Gabriel. Like a cake on a plate. It must form part of the city.

Well then, I'll fit the stern of my ship into the harbor quarter. No matter that there's nothing but warehouses there now. Sooner or later, they'll all come down. We'll build a salient of houses, and the ship of hope will spring from them. We'll build a town in the shape of a prow. So I'll submit to the jury an overall plan for the neighborhood as well as the plans for the mosque itself. Once these have been accepted, they will serve as a guide for future architects. No doubt my tall buildings will be accused of ob-

47

structing the traffic. But a few details more or less don't bother me anymore. With intrepid pen, I dig a tunnel.

We have an engineer in the office who measures the resistance of materials. Nahas, a Muslim. I give him the revised plan. After a week's checking, he okays it.

"You'll drive yourself crazy," warns my old partner, seeing me so hard at work. I remind him of the deadline. He smiles. No one in this country has ever met a deadline! People make allowances for eleventh-hour, and even for thirteenth-hour, architects.

My life is made up of buttresses, architraves, timpanums and stalactites. A prayer of white stone will surge up from the heart of the city.

Gap-toothed Katrin tells a story:

"One day, the cobbler saw a donkey walking all alone in the country. A fine donkey. And he felt like getting on its back. Of course, he wasn't going to steal it. He just wanted the pleasure of riding such a splendid beast.

"No sooner had he climbed up than the donkey rose spinning into the air. Abu Amran hung on to its mane and shouted at it to come down.

" 'Serves you right!' said the donkey. 'That'll teach you to steal masterless donkeys.' "

"Naughty donkey!" cries little Ilena.

"It wasn't the donkey's fault," explains Katrin, "it was the fault of the jinni inside it."

She knows a thing or two on that subject. She knows the story of the jinni that loved stewed pears, and the jinni who asked for the hand of Ali's daughter.

"There are no such things as jinn," says young Gabriel.

"Wretched child!" cries Katrin, spreading her fingers to ward off evil. "Khamsa on him!"

Jinn can't bear being laughed at.

48

Rejoice oh inhabitants of Marsana, for Ilena is getting married.

But I am the only member of the family to go to the wedding.

Local custom has it that the groom should present himself at the bride's door and ask for her hand. The first time, the father refuses, and the second time too. The third request is granted.

I ought to have acted as head of the family. Ruwan has been kind enough to spare me. We simply pick up Ilena at Ruwan's mother's house, where she's been living for the last two weeks.

The musicians are there too, wearing ceremonial turbans. Ilena is riding on a mule and Ruwan, radiant, walks beside her. No one will deny they make a handsome pair. The local women deafen us with their shouts. They don't know yet that the bride is a Christian.

Yesterday it rained. Today the city is washed clean. The colors are new. Happiness is cavorting in the sky.

But in our house, I know the curtains have been drawn and voices are lowered. The cat and her kittens hug the walls. Our mother is fasting by way of atonement.

Ruwan's father has come on his crutches to meet the procession. His servants fire a volley of shots into the air. The old corsairs' house is decked in streamers. Normally, a second marriage is a quieter affair. But my friend's first wife is forgotten: she gave him no child.

Neither imam nor mufti has been invited. In Islamic countries it's not necessary. Any good Muslim can pronounce the words that join a man and a woman. A friend of Ruwan's will do it. One of those bearded young men in tunic and leather belt that he goes around with.

49

I exchange a few words with the bridegroom's mother, a woman who was once beautiful, and whose age allows her to go unveiled. She has the same green eyes as my friend. It seems that Ruwan adores her.

"I like your sister," she says in a rather odd tone. "But she'd better watch out. My son burns everything in his path."

Safia: I feel she has always haunted our city and my imagination. And yet, when I think back, I recall one particular day when I looked up at her and when she uttered my name in her dusky voice. Perhaps, without knowing her, I had sensed her presence in the narrow white streets and cascading gardens. Perhaps she had left the imprint of her lips on my glass at the *Casino des Paradisiers.* She claimed that the soul of our city could be explained by the stairways that ran down on all sides to the docks. Marsanians, she said, never think on the level. There's always a floor underneath. Their spirit is full of corridors, blind alleys, vaulted passageways. And in the end, you always fall into the sea.

I'd heard about her at the Saruns'. There was an aura of scandal about her, for, in our country, it wasn't the done thing for a woman to have a trade. But in the end, polite society will always forgive success. Safia was a painter; she also worked in ceramics, mosaics and stained glass. She had studied in Europe. There was some doubt about her exact origins, which is unusual in a country where everyone is labeled from birth. According to malicious gossip, she was Jewish and the Prime Minister's niece, which might account for certain public commissions.

Every spring, the Saruns held an at home, to which the cream of Marsana was invited. Trained from youth to be good hostesses, Eudoxia and her sisters meted out to each guest the exact amount of consideration due to him. A black servant handed round a bland, slightly nauseating drink, the recipe for which I've never known. Tailcoated musicians, playing in one corner of the room, made the crystals of the great Napoleon III chandelier tinkle in rhythm.

You had to elbow your way through an aviary of generals, ambassadors' wives and ecclesiastics. Even in those days, the mistress of the house suffered from bad circulation in the legs, and lay curled up on a sofa, as lusterless and plump as a gray quail. And now and again you caught a glimpse of Sarun's tall cadaverous form, with his bow tie spread out like a bat.

I'm sure that was the occasion when *she* came up to me without waiting for Eudoxia to introduce us.

"So you're the famous Gabriel."

To which I immediately replied, "And you're the famous Safia!"

Whereupon we both burst out laughing.

She was tiny, sheathed in cerise silk, her hair done in a heavy coil. Her wide, tawny-yellow eyes made her look like a well-behaved little lioness. Was she pretty? The question did not arise. She was Safia, and had the world in her pocket. Eudoxia thought her a genius.

She was full of questions. Was I really a student of Ned Halperin? What did I think of the new Chicago concert hall? Then suddenly:

"I hear you're going to build a mosque."

She spoke casually, as if it were just a whim of mine.

"I know it will all be splendid," she added kindly. She must have found me slightly ridiculous.

"The trouble is, Safia, that I'm not a Muslim." Of course this was public knowledge. But I felt that by mentioning it myself, I somehow made it less dangerous—like taking the lid off a saucepan to let the steam escape. And besides, this woman, who was neither Christian nor Muslim, was a sort of arbitrator.

"Keep on drawing," she said. "And don't listen to anyone." Insolent advice, but just what I wanted to hear.

Safia's cavalier attitude to what we call the foundations of our society was notorious. "Religion," she used to say, "is simply a cause of strife."

The following day, if I remember rightly, she showed Eudoxia and me her studio: a little white house in the upper part of the city, which had just been hooked up to the water-supply and sewage systems. She lived alone, with a maid she had brought back from one of the countries she'd lived in. The poor thing was like a piece of furniture. I have no doubt she had chosen a foreigner specially, in order to keep her at her mercy.

At the time, Safia was painting strange, fragile landscapes on marble plaques. On a shelf there were rows of old coins, eaten away by verdigris. Despite her lack of belief, she claimed to read prophecies from them.

When she visited me in my office, her elegance and self-assurance caused quite a stir. She wanted to see the plans for the House of the Prophets; I'd shown them to hardly anyone. Much to my surprise, I agreed.

Without going into the architecture, she found fault with me for neglecting the decoration: "How do you see the prayer hall? What sort of flooring?"

I'd been thinking of tiles in a carefully chosen arrangement of white and turquoise. The color so much admired in the Tijanes Mosque. But it was too subtle a shade; delicate, impossible to capture.

"Leave it to me," she said firmly. "And what about the walls?"

"I'd thought of leaving them bare."

"You want mirrors running the whole length of the

prayer chamber. Panels two and a half meters high edged with a narrow cornice."

"But that will destroy the impression of convergence."

The prayer chamber converged on the sacred niche. I was very proud of this arrangement.

"It will be reinforced," Safia replied. "As the worshipper moves toward the *mihrab,* he'll see two other selves walking beside him."

I held out a few moments longer against this inspiration that was not my own. But it was the ideal way to widen the area. The mirrors would increase the numbers of pillars, arches and chandeliers. We'd get something as spacious and exuberant as the Great Mosque in Cordoba within a much smaller compass.

For the ablutions court she had another idea: a frieze of Kufic characters—that was an early Islamic script, massive and powerful. She knew a marvelous blind sculptor who had spent his life on Kufic script and worked by touch.

I was fascinated, three-quarters convinced.

Then Safia bought an island and we didn't see her for some time.

That spring of hard work was also a time of rumors. Of political events whose implications I somehow failed to grasp. Those in the know said that the El Andalus brotherhood was behind it all. Refugees from Spain had founded this institution long ago and today's members were their descendants. In the course of time, it had become an aristocratic club, chiefly concerned with charitable works. Now, more active elements had taken it over, eager to revive it as a shrine of memory and revenge.

There was also talk of the Salafiya, or revivalists, and of the Murabitin, or oathtakers, whose name recalled the Almoravids and the Marabouts. The Forty Brothers, whose members, needless to say, far exceeded two score, had deemed it expedient to adopt a number firmly rooted in Eastern tradition (the forty days in the wilderness, the forty martyrs of Sebastia, the forty intercessors of Islam). Certain people claimed that all these groups were mere facets of the same movement.

It was Archbishop Elias who found them their nickname. Despite his failing health, he held a question-and-answer session in Saint Mark's basilica every Friday—Sunday being a working day. There was quite a crowd. Someone mentioned the mounting threats:

"When the Demons of the South pass by," he said, "everyone holds his breath and prays silently."

The Demons of the South, that was what we called the desert winds, which come blowing over the lagoons and put our nerves on edge. Now they had taken on human form. To tell the truth, we Mozarabs had always had a strong taste for demons. We attracted them as milk attracts flies.

Keeping their faces hidden, these new devils recruited in all levels of society. You'd hear the lady of a Christian house saying to a Muslim guest at a May reception, "My dear, you wouldn't happen to be a Demon of the South?"

A campaign was launched against signs written in foreign languages: the tradesmen in the new city were visited by very polite but very insistent young people who invited them to take down all non-Arabic signboards from their shopfronts. Christians were no more singled out than anyone else, but they complained more.

I went on calmly preparing my maquette, with the help of two draftsmen.

"You don't imagine it's easy to make it in the shape of a boat," they grumbled.

I knew all about mosques: the blue domes of Persia, the white minarets of the Turkish valleys, the red fortresses of the Niger basin, the twin towers of the Cape Verde Peninsula copied from Portuguese churches. Domes on squinches, octagonal tambours and pendentives held no mystery for me. But I did not know what my rivals were up to.

One day, my curiosity got the better of me; I called on Yunis (Arabic for Jonah). I'd met him at an architects' conference; he'd been the best of the lot. He worked alone, and went in for cheap housing of the not-so-bad kind. For him, too, the House of the Prophets was a chance to prove himself. It goes without saying that he was a Muslim.

Yunis lived in a 1930s building whose staircase had seen better days. His office was in his apartment. He welcomed me with some surprise, but warmly. He was only a few years older than I, and already had four kids and was going bald. A nice round face lit up by lively eyes.

His project? Hmm, one didn't talk about such things before the maquettes were in. A good idea is soon copied. But out of friendship for me, he'd reveal the essentials. (Friendship, he said, and I felt touched.) He'd studied in Cairo with the famous Hassan Fathy and was planning a pisé building for Marsana. The houses he had built of this material in villages in the South had been a success; the unbaked clay kept out the heat much better than concrete or brick.

I expressed mild reserve. I too had heard about the advantages of adobe in Arizona and New Mexico. But beware of our damp winters!

We went on talking and Yunis asked me to stay to dinner. The kids played around under the table. "O God, portion out our food," he said, "not too much and not too little." I hadn't noticed the incipient callus on his forehead. This hallmark of a pious Muslim is caused by his prostrations. We call it the raisin.

The next day, in return, I invited Yunis to visit my little kingdom. He went into ecstasies over the building, the flooring tiles, the mirrors and potted plants. The maquette was not quite ready, but the plans drew a sigh of admiration from him. As he was leaving, he had tears in his eyes. Shaking me heartily by the hand, he said, "You deserve to win."

According to the rules, I still had to work out the overall cost.

"When in doubt, underestimate," advised old El Souss.

"What about Article 17? If the real cost exceeds the estimated cost by 5%, the architect's fee will be reduced by 10% and so on."

"Whatever happens, you won't make your fortune with this project. What matters is to make a name for yourself."

But that was the whole point. I didn't want to make a name for myself. I envied those old master builders who merged with their work and have not even bequeathed us their faces. If one day the Marsanians were to say, "the *giaour's** mosque," that would be my reward.

In spite of everything, my scheme would be less expensive than Fannawi's. My spies told me that my rival had taken it into his head to air-condition his mosque instead of letting the drafts cool it.

In those days Marsanian architects handed in disgustingly messy plans. Nobody seemed to mind. I went to the other extreme. The secretaries had to type and retype my report and supporting documents till they dropped. Each sheet was put into a transparent folder. The folders were held together in a binder specially imported from Nuremberg. It was all there: the overall plan at 1/200th scale, the drawings of the three facades, and the sections. . . .

Entries had to go to the Ministry of Religious Cults in a double envelope. This odd little rule was designed to preserve anonymity. But it did not prevent candidates being called for interview later on.

* nonbeliever

56

Sometimes, at the end of the day, I'd put on a burnous and attend collective prayers. Certain mosques had a dome with a ring on top, as though to enable the Lord of the Worlds to put his finger through it on the appointed day and lift it up. I had a weakness for the smallest oratory in the city. It was a tiny place over a grocery store where the old sheik, all alone, read the same ancient manuscript over and over again beneath a station clock whose hideous red figures flashed on and off.

The House of the Prophets would be unique of its kind, but would have strong links with the city's other sanctuaries. At least that was what it said in my preamble, one of these lyrical come-ons so dear to architects' hearts. El Souss says it's not unknown for bad juries to be influenced by this kind of literature.

When I went to deliver my entry, I was told the deadline had been postponed for a month at Fannawi's request. He'd had a last-minute idea and wanted Marsania to benefit by it. Oh well, you can always improve on your vermicelli!

Sometimes, Eudoxia came to the office to encourage me. She was a spoilt child—Sarun's own, rather odd, way of indulging her was to choose her dresses—and she could perfectly well just have taken it easy at the yacht club and the *Alliance Française*. But not a bit of it! Miss Eudoxia wants to be useful. Miss Eudoxia is burning to help others. She registers at a school to learn about pus, blood and ulcers. Every morning she can be seen catching the bus, a touching sight in her uniform skirt and without even a purse, as she's afraid of being robbed in the crush.

The day Eudoxia starts a course at the Berthome Bey Hospital, Sarun sees what she's put over on him. A daughter of his living with half-naked patients! The whole family

57

is pleading and weeping. I think I may have wept too. A friend points out that the experience will be useful to her when she has her own children. In the end, the satrap gives in.

Eudoxia in the wards, in the operating rooms . . . If you know what a hospital in Marsania is like!

This one was built a century ago by a supposedly Swiss doctor called Berthome, a Saint Simonian caught up in Islam. The outside is still imposing enough, but the inside is more like skid row.

Instead of giving my name at the gate, where I'd be asked my business, I walk in head high, putting on a confident air. Smells of formalin, pus, and urine, made worse by the heat. Ward orderlies spraying the corridors with chlorate-of-something-or-other. Patients in nightshirts dragging their mattresses out onto the patios as soon as the shadow hits them.

"There are some great consultants here," Eudoxia tells me. "Mirit, for instance. He'd earn four or five times as much abroad. He stays here out of patriotism."

And we're puffed up with pride because Mirit is a Mozarab.

Eudoxia takes to heart everything that happens in this little world. One day, she proudly announces that she's going on the night shift. Her schedule becomes irregular and our meetings less frequent. Another time, I find her in tears, because of Yussef, the old fellow she feeds with a spoon. He never speaks. The doctors say a tumor has destroyed the speech center in his brain. But Eudoxia, without thinking, feeds him a spoonful of soup that burns him. All of a sudden the old guy starts swearing at her.

"Got our speech back, have we, Yussef? Congratulations."

In reply, the old fraud simply turns his face to the wall.

I pull the curtain and there sits the three-master, ready to set sail.

"Well, well!" cries Ruwan, somewhat surprised. "I never thought you'd do it."

"But you gave me the idea. You dared me to do it."

"I was joking. You know me."

My head swims. I lean against the wall. Somewhere, far off, a machine hums.

"At least tell me if you like it."

"It's unusual."

I pull myself together. I stare at the strange green eyes, which stare right back.

"It's beautiful too. Truly. Bravo."

"Do you think I'll win the competition?"

"That'll depend in part on the other competitors. I wish you well."

"Does it at least make you feel like praying?"

"Hard to judge from a maquette, old boy."

He hesitates a moment, stands there in his long, loose shirt, deep in thought.

"Yes, I think your work brings us close to the essential."

Suddenly, he's gone, without taking leave, like the wild cat he has always been.

The child and the old negro.

The Sidi Yahia Mosque, twenty years ago. Yahia is John the Baptist: yet another rehabilitated Christian. The mosque is one of the most modest in the city, and does not even have a Government-paid priest. But the child knows it because he lives next door. The old negro is the caretaker. He has snow-white hair, and two teeth

*missing on the lower jaw, which means, so they say, that he was
once a slave. The child calls him grandfather.*

"Look," says the old negro.

*He doesn't show this treasure to everyone. It is a marquetry
panel, made of marble and exotic woods. A pattern of squares and
rectangles, black on white, white on black.*

"Can you read?"

"You bet!"

"Even Kufic?"

"Kufic's hard."

*"Look carefully, Gabriel. These designs are letters. M H M D.
Now, bend your head. What can you see? Again M H M D. Bend
farther. . . ."*

Four times Muhammad's name, turning clockwise.

*"Remember this, my son. The ignorant see only black and white.
But I know."*

How does this old serf know Kufic?

*"Everything has a meaning," says the big old negro. "Even
when you think it hasn't. You look for the meaning, and one day
the meaning finds you."*

So Ruwan had backed out. And El Souss was to follow suit
the next day.

My partner was a likable old fellow, with humor enough
to sport a flowered shirt; he took special pleasure in pouring
sour milk on his couscous. I couldn't believe he'd let me
down.

"I've been thinking, Gabriel. I can't take responsibility
for this project."

"Of course, uncle Ibrahim. Our agreement is quite clear.
I pay you a fee for the use of the office facilities, whether or
not my project is accepted. The profit and loss are entirely
mine."

El Souss sat down, quivering with emotion:

"That's not what I'm trying to tell you, my friend. What I mean is that your project cannot carry the signature of the firm."

"Whyever not? If I enter the competition on my own, they'll call me a young upstart."

At best, an architect begins building at thirty-five. Up until then it's forced labor.

"Your references are excellent," says El Souss. "But I've had no part in the project."

"I've listened to your advice."

"Very little. Quite honestly, one can't tell you much."

His short laugh pained me. He undid a button on his flamboyant shirt:

"I thought you'd guess my reasons, Gabriel. One Christian in a venture like this is already a lot. Two Christians . . . imagine! One jolt and the boat will capsize."

He could say that again, seeing it was a stone boat! I turned to the window to hide my tears.

"Isn't some Italian supposed to have built mosques in the Gulf States?"

El Souss agreed that this is true. But that was several years ago. Would it be possible today?

"What's more," he went on, gasping for breath, "the Gulf States are not a good example. No one will accuse those people of heresy. That's not the case here. Whatever the Government does, it's suspected of being lukewarm toward the Koran."

His tiny gold cross quivered in the neck of his shirt. Old Ibrahim had started out at a time when all architects were Christian. And all doctors, all lawyers. But every year, breaches had opened up in this secure family circle.

"If you like," he offered, "I'll write a note to go with your entry explaining that I couldn't participate because of my health, but that you have my full backing."

A sop. I nodded gratefully. At that hour the office was taken over by charladies, who were shouting to one another from end to end of the corridor and sloshing buckets of water.

"You knew, didn't you," he said, "that the Prince Regent offers a special reward when he's pleased with a public building? Well, here's to your success."

He raised an imaginary glass.

I decided to forget my disappointment and immerse myself more deeply than ever in my adventure.

The deed is done: I've taken my entry to the Ministry of Religious Cults, three days ahead of time, and been given a receipt. A square of yellowing paper, scrawled on with pale ink. I'm not letting it out of my sight.

All I should have to do now is wait for my just deserts. But my attitude makes the Saruns smile. Talent, so they claim, always needs a helping hand. The city doesn't know me yet. It needs to see me, and learn to accept me. Then the jury's decision will be automatic.

"You have to create the right climate," added Eudoxia, with an authority I wouldn't have expected of her.

In our country, money has always carried social obligations. Madame Fuad Bey, for example, patronized the arts, and Princess Meissun went in for pedigree cats. Madame Sarun and her daughters, who were more ambitious, chose to give an Islamo-Christian soiree in honor of my project.

I had never seen their country place above Kfar Eden, a village of round tiles. It was an absurdly magnificent 1930s Graeco-Roman villa that Sarun had rescued from the developers. From its terrace, you could see the whole valley all the way to the blanket of warm mist that from June onward covers Marsana.

That evening I arrived late and hid behind a potted palm. In the garden, someone was holding forth on the Trinity in front of several rows of chairs. For a moment I was panicked by his vocabulary, then I found his vision interesting. The three "Persons," he told us, were simply three successive faces. First of all God showed us his face of power—Yahweh —then his face of love—Jesus. As for the third face, his face of light, Muslims identified it in the Koran, whereas Christians were still awaiting it.

The people applauded politely. Clearly they were afraid of falling into a trap.

And I too distrusted those who kept repeating: God, God. As a character in Molière said: *Friendship needs a little more mystery.*

Eudoxia plucked at my sleeve: "We're thinking this evening. Move closer."

Her role was limited to handing around petits fours. But this meeting of minds, in her home and at her instigation, put her into a state of jubilation.

"I'd like to say 'good evening' to your parents."

"Father has been detained by a supplier."

That's a relief! The idea of being observed and sized up throughout the evening had been preying on my mind all day.

Out of consideration for the Muslims, no liquor was served. The guests were drinking orange-flower water, sometimes known as *café blanc.* All this sobriety had not kept "the best people" away. A literary general, a purple cassock, a couple of bankers. . . . Bankers, in particular, adored theology.

Eudoxia introduced me: "Gabriel, he's an architect."

"An architect?" cried the Christian ladies in astonishment. For them there were only two respectable professions: business and holy orders.

An elderly gentleman, as bent as a weeping willow, was

63

in conversation with the lady of the house. Eudoxia steered me in their direction.

"It's Amor Pasha, of course."

He was related to the ruling family, hence a Muslim, and was shortly to chair my competition jury. The crafty little minx! She wanted to advance my cause. No one in Marsania would have taken it amiss. But I had my principles.

In another little group, the best-selling novelist was telling malicious stories against the chief of police, Turqi Pasha, butt of the intellectuals of the day. Having noticed that his servant picked his rough drafts out of his wastebasket, the writer took to embellishing them—going so far as to put in flattering phrases about the government and the police, which had no chance of ending up in the finished work.

"Late one night, there was a hammering on my door. Who should be there but Turqi in person, buttoned up in his uniform and carrying a bunch of flowers. 'My dear fellow,' he said in French, 'I'm enthralled by your next novel. Won't you do me the favor of telling me how it ends?' "

The story got a big laugh. Needless to say it was pure fiction, but the unfortunate chief of police would have trouble living it down.

The evening ended with a reading by El hajji Ayub (Arabic for Job). He was a teacher of Islamic religion at a secondary school and was well-liked for his broad-mindedness despite his one little oddity: he persisted in calling himself *hajji* in a city where most former pilgrims to Mecca had stopped using the title.

One day, he began, *Jesus saw a young man working in a garden.*

The reader was somewhat short in stature and no platform had been provided. But his opening words put a stop to the chatter.

"Give me a grain of your love," the young man said. *"You couldn't bear as much as that,"* Jesus replied.

64

"Then give me half a grain."

"Very well, half a grain."

A little while later, Jesus was back in those parts and asked after the young man. Jesus was told that he had gone mad and was running about on the mountains all alone.

You see, many years have passed, but I've remembered those lines. Much will be forgiven the Muslims because one of their number wrote them: Algazel the mystic philosopher.†

He could have found many other examples, Ayub added, wiping his forehead. Jesus used to be *persona grata* in Islam. Then came the Crusades, and the colonial expeditions. Jesus was enrolled under the enemy flag. No one dared to reject him, since he appears in the Koran, but a conspiracy of silence grew up around him. Children were no longer told about him.

Fireflies were flashing in the gathering darkness. I've always wondered what drove these insects to be so prodigal of energy. Amorous display? Messages to be decoded?

A monk in a cylindrical toque appeared on the scene. He hadn't been expected. Eudoxia nudged me: the Archimandrite Lukas.

"The Prophet," he began, "condemned Christian doctrine, though not always in the same terms. But how did he know this doctrine? What kind of Christians could he have met in his oases? Outcasts, heretics being driven southward, such as the mysterious monk Bahira, who appears in the biographies. What would the Man of Mecca have said if he had known true Christianity?"

There was a short silence, broken by the fall of a teaspoon.

"The Prophet knew so little about Christianity," put in

† El Ghazali

the livelier of the bankers, "that he thought The Trinity consisted of The Father, Jesus and Mary."

There was only one possible conclusion: we Christians had been wrongly condemned. It would all work out in the end.

The Muslims protested loudly: how could the God-inspired Prophet have made such a blunder?

"Islam must rediscover Jesus," declared the worthy old gentleman after a pause.

Several people went back into the salon as it was getting chilly. Farther down the hillside sharp cracks could be heard at regular intervals. Sarun had installed an automatic scarer in his orchards to frighten off the bats that came out of the neighboring grottoes at night like a legion of devils.

"They're pleasant, don't you think, these high-level get-togethers," says the aviator, who has joined me. "But what do they represent, these people who drink the Saruns' lemonade? Nothing whatsoever. The masses, with their inherited prejudices, remain below."

Eudoxia had insisted on inviting him, despite my reservations. You never knew what he'd do next. His face is disfigured by a reddish flame-shaped patch of skin, and a tuft of wiry black hair sticks out of his well-cut collar. Handsome or repellent? I guess the girls find him handsome.

"Not to mention the imbalance," he goes on, coming right up to me as if he'd suddenly grown shortsighted. "There is no shortage of Christian specialists on Islam. But do you know any Muslims who have specialized in Christianity?"

He's called Jirjir (Gregory if you prefer) and he's hardly a day over thirty-five.

"The guests are delighted," put in Eudoxia. "There's been real progress toward understanding."

Across the room we watch her curtsey to the general,

curtsey to the archimandrite, like a debutante with exaggeratedly good manners. I can't help smiling to myself.

"Aren't you hungry?" asks the redoubtable Gregory. "Try one of these meat pasties."

No thanks, the heat has taken away my appetite. I look for a way to escape. Of course I run straight into the master of the house: Sarun himself. He is shaking a few hands. How long has he been there? How long has he been watching me?

"My husband has come back specially from Marsana," says Madame Sarun in her cooing voice. "He simply loves spiritual matters."

I might have guessed as much: the richer they are, the more . . . And I haven't said anything intelligent all evening!

"Cigarette?" he says, in a bored voice. They're his own make, Hamdullah (God be praised) brand. Even our poisons are pious.

Turning our backs on the big house, we lean on the balustrade. Darkness has spirited away the flaws in the decor—Highway No. 4 and the outlying villages. All we can see are the constellations of little lights dotted about the mountainside. While far below a sudden breeze has dispersed the mist and the city is sparkling like Harun al-Rashid's treasure.

The morning takes me unawares. The city is half asleep. Now and then a bus with a few yawning passengers in it. Even the doorman, who decides which visitors may take the elevator, is missing.

The great Ramadan has spread its fiery wing over the country. I'd been so absorbed in my scribblings that I'd forgotten the date.

When Ramadan falls in winter, it isn't too hard to bear; the day is soon over. But in summer, how can you wait till dusk without drinking a drop of water? We Christians keep off the café terraces; we don't want to offend or be provocative. In our houses, though, we favored ones can do as we please.

El Souss has installed a small icebox in a corner of the office. He gets drinks out of it. For the first few days I do likewise, when none of the Muslim employees is looking. Then shame gets the better of me.

Noon, the hour of the white demon of our legends, so white you can't see it, but its breath burns your face.

In the street, stoical bakers are loading up their metal trays before carrying them to the oven. Long filaments of flour, molasses, cinnamon: tonight there'll be the dessert we used to call "hair" when we were kids.

Imperturbable Ramadan. Time has eroded other rules of Islam, but this one seems to grow stricter from year to year. A whole people does violence to its body to show respect to God. And to show the Christians what it can do.

We too, of course, have our times of abstinence: the Great Fast of Lent, the Fast of the Apostles, the Fast of the Ninevites commemorating Jonah's sojourn in the belly of the whale. If we observed them properly, they'd take up half the year. But they are only privations, whereas Ramadan turns life upside down. No cigarettes, no women in bathing suits. Don't swallow your saliva, that would be breaking your fast.

Oom Nidal, our fat neighbor, even makes her cat observe Ramadan.

As night falls, I go out into the old quarters to watch for the end of this long wait. Men are sitting at tables outside little restaurants, only men. Their glasses are filled, their tomatoes seasoned. In silence they are listening for the cannon shot that will deliver them.

68

As our proverb says, "All good things must be waited for".

Sated and refreshed, the city starts coming to life. The sound of transistors grows louder: Warda, Farid El Atrash. Sometimes a passer-by, hugging the walls of the old city, is lucky enough to catch the liquid notes of a reed pipe, or the voice of a real woman, accompanied by iron castanets.

Then every Muhammad and Fatima make for the suk, where they'll go from stall to stall till past midnight. Their fast ends in festivity every night. Yes, I know, they spend as much in these four weeks as in four ordinary months. I don't hold it against them. Ramadan is not a time of mourning, but a time of communion. It's the one period in the year when habits are banished and madness takes over. On the edge of the old city, an open-air prayer chamber, consisting of hangings and rugs, has sprung up. There, grave family men sway backward and forward for hours on end repeating the name of the One, *el Ahad.*

At last, worn out, our heroes go to bed. But not for long. Half an hour before dawn, the watchman passes through the sleeping streets beating his drum. He even comes down Salt Street, since ours is a mixed neighborhood. I know that hoarse voice: "Gather your strength, ye faithful." Those who are too exhausted simply turn over in bed, wishing him a long life. Others manage to get up and swallow a biscuit and a glass of tea before the fateful moment.

One of these nights is more important than the rest: the night of the 26th, also known as the night of destiny. A mysterious glow appears in the sky, and anyone who sees it has a wish granted. I can remember watching for it as a child. Then I mentioned what I'd done, in confession, as though I'd committed a sin. To my surprise, the priest refused to condemn me. We Christians, he said, are also entitled to the light.

But it was also in the month of Ramadan that the

69

Mozarabs used to pay their tribute to their masters. One after another, the married men knelt in front of the tax collector, handed over the required sum and received in exchange a slap in the face that was not always symbolic. Sometimes, in order to identify those who had paid, a lead seal was hung around their neck on a string.

I could not hope to get on with the En Nasr Tower during Ramadan. Nor to appear before the architects' jury. Inaction weighed on me.

Eudoxia did not spare herself; she went right on with her hospital duties, because germs don't observe Ramadan. She looked pale and drawn. Every evening her father's chauffeur picked her up at Berthome Bey and took her out to Kfar Eden for the good air.

"I know it's ridiculous to slave away all day looking after those poor creatures and then ride home in a Cadillac. But what can I do?"

She urged me to take up summer quarters. A room had been set aside for me in the Graeco-Roman villa. "Anyway," she said, "everybody's in the mountains right now." "Everybody" meaning the thirty-odd families that mattered.

We'd tried, in various roundabout ways, to get in touch with our friend Safia. She'd taken some tubes of paint and was playing Robinson Crusoe on her island, the first person to live there since the Phoenicians. Something about this woman's sacrilege appealed to me.

Safia's answer came back to us via a naval officer. A borrowed launch would take us there.

The day before we were to go, Eudoxia telephoned. She was sick.

"What rotten luck! Getting flu in July!"

She asked me to get the Harbor Command to tell Safia we couldn't make it. But I had decided I'd go, with or without Eudoxia.

70

Summer weighed on the city. Like a giant sitting on our chests. The air was full of moisture from the sea, and the wall of the Jeblasan stopped it from blowing away inland. We waited till nightfall before trying to live a little. When I came home, round about midnight, along the ill-lit avenues of what used to be the modern quarter, all the concierges of Marsania would be sitting silently in their darkened doorways, like so many ghosts ruminating on their former lives.

For several days, the south wind had drawn a yellowish veil across the sky. The air was strangely heavy, with millions of grains of sand suspended at such a height that they couldn't come down. "It's the Demon of the South," said the good folk. At night, through the open doors, I could hear our mother tossing on her bed, mumbling to herself. "Family without honor," she seemed to be saying. And in the morning, we'd find on our windowsills a little light-colored dust that had come from afar.

Our younger sister went to Qasrum to stay with our cousins. And Mark went to the mountains with the Scouts. I stayed on alone with the little woman in black. She had grown even thinner; her bones stuck through her threadbare dress. Nothing was left of her but a bundle of memories and pride.

Some of the people in our neighborhood had got to hear about my plan for the mosque. One morning, as I passed Star-of-Religion's stall, he gave me a couple of pomegranates. He was just an ordinary grocer, except that he happened to be a descendant of the Prophet, a sharif. On Fridays, he put on a green turban. The rest of the time his only privilege was to sell his watermelons for a quarter of a piaster more than his neighbors. In our city, as a result of

71

polygamy, there were too many great-great grandsons of Muhammad for them all to amount to something.

"He gave them to you?" our mother asked in surprise. "I must do something in return. I'll shop at his stall tomorrow."

She hated the idea of being beholden to anyone.

Once or twice I ran into Ruwan. He was fasting. So I fasted. We spoke very candidly of God. The God of Islam inspires awe, fear and wonder. But is He a God of love?

"God doesn't need our love," Ruwan replied. *Allah is independent of all creatures.*‡

All the same, perhaps He will accept my stone offering.

We also exchanged a few risky remarks about the country's young people.

"I have no illusions," said Ruwan. "If you opened up the brain of any boy, you'd find in it the desire for a car. But that'll change. We'll see to that, and quicker than you think."

He was sitting on the guardrail of the old harbor. The heat rising off the inert water was so thick you could almost touch it.

A day or two later, sulfureous shapes appeared in the sky. We wondered what these vaguely threatening chimeras would spew out. And some people questioned these faces, claiming to recognize the head of a long-dead prince regent.

Then, one morning, I woke to find terraces, trees and sidewalks covered with a film of dust. The sky had emptied out on us.

The launch heads for the promontory: a tall, bare, over-hanging rock eaten away at its base by the sea. At the last

‡ Koran, III, 97

72

moment, we catch sight of the sandy strip where we'll land. This is Safia's island.

"Watch where you put your feet, or you'll be blown up," the owner jokes. Korben was once used by the fleet for target practice. Shells fell thick and fast, but did not manage to sink it. Now passing sailors pick up the unexploded shells. They save the powder for fireworks to celebrate a circumcision or a wedding. This is how one of them blew his head off last year.

Safia keeps her belongings and her drums of fresh water in a little tent. The local fishermen, who are notoriously rough customers, have had every chance to rob or rape her. But she seems to inspire a superstitious fear.

There's an unfinished canvas on the easel. It's all blues and ocher, and it's called *Mélanges*. "I like a *mélange*," she said, "provided everyone retains his individuality."

A somewhat contradictory statement, but which encapsulates Marsania.

The mainland is blurred by the haze. The neighboring islands wallow in the water like huge aquatic beasts: Zerah, Manarf, and the one with the hump called the Camel. The pilot ties up the boat.

"Let's climb," suggests Safia, pointing to the summit of the island. "How do you like my kingdom? Will you build me a holiday home here?" She bursts out laughing: "Don't worry, I haven't got a penny to build with. I was just putting your virtue to the test."

There are no paths on the island. We're walking over stones. In spring, stunted flowers poke out of crevices in the rock. The sun has scorched everything. I'm sweating under my straw hat.

Safia questions me banteringly about what's been going on in town.

"What about your friend Ruwan?"

"Let's not talk about him, please."

73

"I'm told he's the up and coming man," she persists.

"Come off it! There are umpteen organizations like his. They'll crowd one another out like young plants."

Safia plays with her sunglasses. "That's one way of looking at it. But supposing all those organizations were just different names for one and the same reality?"

I shrug. I should have heeded the warning. This woman, supposedly absorbed in her art, has the entrée to ministries and knows everything that's going on.

At our approach, a snake glides away with a dry rasping sound. Who had the preposterous idea of bringing reptiles to Korben? The Phoenicians? They used to worship them in their temples. Safia's hand had been in mine; she withdraws it. Far below us, a diminutive pilot is wading in the cove.

"The day the Government starts bugging me," she says, "I'll raise my flag and secede. I'll make my living issuing stamps."

Her empire is shaped like a high-heeled shoe. We reach the back end of it, which is also the highest point. Across from us, lies Ghorr, the island with the wild goats. What is the sea brewing as it hollows out the caverns at our feet? We hear it slipping in and out, murmuring honeyed words. Now and again, an explosion makes us shudder.

I've disturbed the sea birds that nest on the stones. They're flying around our heads, deafening us with their cries. Instinctively, I protect my face.

In the midst of this tempest, Safia raises her arms as though to deliver a proclamation.

"I'm crazy about these moth-eaten kingdoms," she liked to say.

To get away from the interminable Ramadan, I take myself off to the country to deal with family matters.

74

I've slipped on the ocher-and-white-striped burnous of our region over my European clothes. In the gray of dawn, the little stallholders are already selling their sesame-seed loaves and sticky cakes. There's an iridescent patch floating on the water in the harbor. "Where are you going?" asks one of the sailors, seeing my suitcase. The ship's siren gives a feeble blast.

Between Marsana and the little port where my family comes from lie twenty leagues of cliffs and headlands. Today, it all looks lovely, but when it happens to rain, the wadis get angry and spew muddy water far out into the sea.

The coastline is covered with a dense thatch of vegetation, which climbs over the peaks and cascades down to the shore. I know every lighthouse, watchtower, every cove with its rotting boats. We pass the fort at Tidrirt, huddled on its tongue of land. It gives me a pang to see the crumbling battlements and grass growing on the roof. The Coast of the Wrecks; that's the name on the old sea charts.

The pale surface of the sea is broken by a few black rocks that look like flies floating on sour milk. Complicated light effects that can be taken as hints and signs. Drifting seaweed, tiny wavelets. And the long, fluting cry of the bird we call *el flehir.*

We've stopped talking the official language. We prefer our own Faranghi, which is used up and down the coast and in the poorer neighborhoods of the capital; a dreadful mixture of Arabic and Italian, with a dash of French, a pinch of Greek and a soupçon of Turkish.

One of the passengers, a young mechanic who belongs to the Latin church, has recognized me. He was on my side in the war games we played as children. We reminisce intermittently about old friends:

"George has gone to Europe with his sister. So has Daud. Fuad went to America, like you. But he won't be coming back."

"So Fuad's gone too! Pretty soon there'll only be the old folks left. Why? What's the matter with the place?"

"Our land is niggardly," he replies. His father and his father's father had expressed the same judgment in exactly the same tone. Then, seeing this doesn't satisfy me, he begins to hem and haw, says it's hard to find work in Marsana. Finally he comes out with it: "People are afraid nowadays."

Afraid of what? There's no way of knowing. It's as if we were surrounded by mist. My companion has raised his hood, as our menfolk do when they want to be left alone.

The boat calls in at the run-down asbestos mine. This would have closed long ago, if it had applied the wage laws. Workers grab the rope and catch parcels on the wing. One of them laughs, but it turns into a cough. Poor devils, eaten away by asbestos. The waste from the mine has formed an ice pack at the mouth of the little river.

The terminus of our journey is Qasrum (bad Arabic for the castle of the Christians). A Crusader castle, clinging to the hostile mountain like a limpet. One day, weary of this possession which had earned him nothing but hard knocks, the bailiff Robert de Guéménée sold us to the Muslims. They'd been our masters before. We were used to it.

Today, the little town lives by working cork. All the kids are lined up on the dock. All the dogs as well. We Christians keep them as pets by way of distinguishing ourselves from our neighbors. The old fort smiles through the palm trees. Rising up from the blue bay, the pink roofs smile too. We haven't built terraces here; it rains too much in winter.

The first passenger jumps ashore, and a little girl, as is the custom, throws a handful of rice over him.

"Saïda, Jibril," someone shouts. The Christian greeting.

Qasrum is a town on two hills, joined by underground passageways. The slender Latin church and the squat Mozarab church face each other across the square; but the old rivalries are forgotten. There's even a mosque, standing a little apart, among the poplars. As for the Nussaris, they don't need a temple; they make do with a courtyard or the back room of a shop. "When two men pray together," said one of their sheiks, "God is with them."

Samir, the indefatigable old philosopher who strolls around waggling his feathered rump, doesn't belong to any of these schools of thought. Some painter seems to have amused himself decorating his beak with squiggles of pale yellow, pale blue and a thin red line. He looks at me wearily, scrambles onto a mound, batting the air with his huge wings. Then his eyelids close like a shutter.

The pelicans are gradually leaving the coast. I don't know how this one came to be washed up on our shore. He must have got tired of earning a pittance in the neighboring coves, and developed a taste for our fishermen's scraps. Now he enjoys the attention of all, and meditates on the meaning of history.

A neighbor puts my suitcase on a donkey. We set out up the steep street. I see Paul has repainted his shop. The township has tried to tar the dirt road.

Our house is recognizable by its tangle of honeysuckle and our bread oven—still in use—with the black marks on it. This is our real family home. We've only lived in Marsana for fifty years.

Michael, pronounced locally Micallef, our shrewd, loud-mouthed tenant farmer appears.

"Sorry I didn't get to the boat. My feet are swollen."

He's limping in a very obvious way. I sympathize. I'm asked to admire some improvements he's made. Then he points gloomily to the roof:

"You'll have to call in a roofer."

The barley hasn't done well. Frost has killed the apricot tree. The chickens have died of some mysterious disease. In a word, disaster. Always the same old complaints. I've heard them so often they've become reassuring. I smile. Old Michael's a bad lot.

What's more, tomorrow he'll give me to understand that he's willing to buy the hovel. He's not rich, but with a loan from his brother-in-law . . . Get away with you, Michael! You're not going to ruin yourself just to make us happy!

I've been given a room with a reed ceiling; it's full of memories and old junk. I think of all I could do here with Eudoxia's money: change the tenant, build a separate house away from the workers, plant a vineyard. . . . But the fact is, Eudoxia's wealth weighs on me.

The bells are calling us to prayer. They ring longer than in Marsana, for here we can do as we please. It's the evening service. Worshippers come and go, barefoot peasants, or little girls playing mother with a baby brother balanced on the hip. Our church welcomes me, with its openwork screen, its wooden gallery running around the nave, its own inimitable combination of lightheartedness and devotion.

But what's going on? Whose back is that? It's not our usual priest. A frail-looking newcomer, with his head on one side, is reading verses from the Scriptures.

He turns around: under the miter, a small face swallowed up by a huge pair of glasses. Almost timidly, he pours forth words of peace. His beard looks as if it came from a property room. How young he is!

Our friend Nasrallah had always officiated in this church. But Nasrallah is dead and no one had thought to tell me.

The town whose priest is a child.

On my return from Qasrum, I found the whole town buzzing with talk of reforms. Dr. Samiel's government had taken advantage of Ramadan to draft its bills. The main one was a bill limiting agricultural holdings to one hundred feddans (some hundred acres).

In plain language, they were out to cut the grass from under the feet of the Forty Brothers and the other conspiratorial groups who were preparing to stir up rural discontent.

The Mozarab middle class saw this as one more case of persecution. The great Muslim landowners would suffer as much, if not more, but the Mozarabs felt that the measure was aimed at them. That was typical of the Christians. At the slightest pinprick they drag up age-old grievances. Remember Caliph So-and-so who made our fathers wear a blue turban? Remember, in the days of Ali-the-Bad, the little bell we had to ring when we went into the baths? And those horsemen who, not so long ago, made us get off our donkeys when we passed them?

Christians have long memories.

Luckily, Sarun takes a more intelligent attitude. We go and see him in his tobacco fields, surrounded by pink flowers. He shows us how to distinguish the rich leaves, which grow low down and will soon be picked, from the poor leaves, which will be left on the stem. Savoringly, he tells us about the blends of spices, the aromatics, the drop of honey that will be added. Even though he makes Marlboros under license, there's nothing like native cigarettes.

But all his doctors will let him put in his long cigarette holder is eucalyptus.

"What about this reform?" I ask.

"People have got it wrong. The limit is a hundred feddans per adult, not per family. That means a hundred for my wife, a hundred for myself, a hundred for my eldest daughter, a hundred for the second . . ."

Forgetting his education, he counts on his fingers. The second daughter is Eudoxia, of course.

"And a hundred for my little girl who'll soon be grown up, won't you, darling? That makes five hundred. Don't

79

worry, we'll get by. We'll just have to sell a few feddans under the counter."

He snaps his long hand shut like a fan. And curses that stupid elder brother of his for putting too much money into land.

"Yes, but you manufacture poison," observes Eudoxia, the nurse.

"If I didn't, others would. And I at least put money into the coffers of the Regency."

He starts to laugh, motions to his chauffeur and turns toward us:

"If you ask me, I was cut out for politics."

The great Sarun, the cold and melancholy wheeler-dealer, leans on the gate of his tobacco farm as though it were the column of some temple. What black angel engraved those shadowy lines on his cheeks?

He has opened up a little. But never again will he speak of himself.

Needless to say, this reform makes the intellectuals laugh. Their response is to go one better. Did you say a hundred feddans? You must be joking. Let's say fifty. And in no time it's scrawled on every wall, in chalk, tar and Mercurochrome.

In my immediate circle, Ruwan is likely to be the most affected. He and his father own heavily mortgaged estates, which they will have to sell off at a bad moment. I mention this on the telephone. Ruwan scolds me:

"You can keep your sympathy for others. I'm all for the fifty-feddan limit. And you don't have to worry about your dear sister. She'll have enough to live on."

He's almost scathing. But then his tone changes:

"And how about you? We haven't seen you in ages. Come and have dinner while we still have some money left. Don't forget, my house is yours."

Young Mark, who has overheard these last words, starts

repeating like a corncrake, *"Beïti beïtak, beïti beïtak.* What a hypocrite! What a hypocrite!" And he dodges the clout I aim at him.

With all these goings-on, of course, the authorities have no time to think about architecture. The jury still hasn't met. Or if it has, it's been in the greatest secrecy. On the off chance, I call my friend Yunis, the apostle of unbaked clay. He tells me he has withdrawn his entry. My scheme gave him an inferiority complex.

I give him a friendly scolding. Then I try Fannawi, the competitor who is most in favor. No, he hasn't heard anything, either. But he's a bit too insistent. Something's going on behind my back.

In the meantime, all I can do is fuss over the Nasr Tower. It has been laid down in the specifications that the glass robe is to be brown. I manage to get this changed to light blue, which will be more in harmony with our city. Well, well.

I may as well admit it. On our first visit to the island, the inevitable happened. We'd never said a word, but we'd known it for a long time.

Safia cut short any display of emotion: "Get this straight, once and for all. I don't believe in love."

We went down the hill. The pilot was waiting for us, motionless in the sunlight. "I fell down," she said, to explain her crumpled dress.

Safia, the only woman in this country who doesn't believe in love. Soon married, soon disillusioned. Or maybe she'd never held with such rubbish. On what planet was she born?

Skimming the wavelets, the launch sped toward the city. The pilot kept his eyes averted, as though obeying an order.

Safia spoke to me like a friend, "You'll marry Eudoxia. You're made for each other."

Obviously.

And the great Jeblasan rose slowly to meet us, towering over the dwellings of men.

Thus we lived and thus we loved, under the rock of Islam.

Summer was just drawing to an end when an ominous event took place: a group of European visitors was refused admittance to a number of mosques. The Tourist Office sent a complaint to the Ministry of Religious Cults, but received no answer. I talked it over with Nahas, our calm Muslim engineer:

"Intolerance is getting worse."

"No, Gabriel. Think of Mecca. Only believers are allowed in."

"My dear fellow, Mecca's Mecca. In Marsania, the mosques have always been wide open."

He nibbled his great sad mustache. I decided to consult an expert, the preacher who had helped the Saruns organize their ecumenical soirée.

El hajji Ayub told me to meet him in a little-frequented café. He arrived as I was finishing my first cup of coffee. White tunic, yellow slippers and black glasses despite an overcast sky. Before coming in, he looked around at the passers-by.

"I often come here," he said, "because the waiter's half deaf." And when I raised my eyebrows added, "I've had threats, Gabriel."

Yet the people around us seemed harmless enough. The waiter came running. He may have been hard of hearing, but he was full of goodwill. A customer, aged about fifteen, was sucking on a hookah, trying to look grown-up. The hajji motioned that he'd have one too. On the wall hung a portrait of the Prince Regent, young, bedizened, brilliantined, wearing the vague smile that the upper crust of those days tried to ape.

On the opposite wall, polar bears were drifting on ice floes. We all long for what we haven't got. European schoolchildren write essays about holidays in the sun. Little Marsanians begin theirs with: "It was snowing . . . ."

Ayub proceeded to list the decrees forbidding the infidels to enter mosques: Caliph Mutawakil's, Sultan Qalawn's. These decrees had soon been forgotten, but they remained in force, as nothing was ever rescinded in Marsania; we merely accumulated. If the matter were referred to a court, these old texts would have to be applied.

He stopped talking while the tripod with the glowing coals was being set up. With exquisite courtesy, the waiter put the tube to his lips to start the smoke circulating before handing it to Ayub.

"It's true," I said, "that the incidents of the past weeks have involved only Westerners. Our native Christians are not affected."

"God willing," replied my guest, puffing out a stream of bubbles, suggesting so many stillborn royal decrees.

And he left as he'd come—black glasses, yellow slippers, white tunic.

That very evening, I tried my luck at the Tijaniya, where I knew the caretaker, a cheerful little hunchback.

"No, *effendi*," he begged. "Not today."

"Why not? Is it a festival? I'll come back tomorrow."

"No, not tomorrow, *effendi*."

"Do you mean never?"

"We never say 'never,' " the little hunchback replied prudently.

I'd shaken him. He was almost in tears at seeing me so upset.

"It's insane," I said. "Has the Government issued orders?"

Obviously there had been no orders—at least no official orders. Word had simply spread from mosque to mosque.

"Have you been threatened? Have they said you'll be dismissed if you let me in?"

"Only believers may enter," the little hunchback replied.

"And I'm not a believer?"

He gave a strained smile. He did not want to get into an argument. I turned on my heel.

"Don't go, *effendi*."

A passageway connected the mosque with some dilapidated rooms where the imam and his family once lived. The hunchback opened a tiny wooden shutter. I looked down into the prayer chamber where a few men in white, on rush mats, were silently engaged in their ritual prostrations: a little world of deep peace from which I was to be excluded.

As if he had read my thoughts, the hunchback refused my tip and called down a hundred blessings on my head.

Outside, a young man, holding the hem of his robe in his teeth, was sweeping up rubbish. Some mothers of large families were waiting in line outside a subsidized grocery store (green tickets for flour, pink for oil).

We'd see who was going to have the last word. The very next day, I tried another neighborhood and went into the Mosque of the Ropes without the slightest difficulty. This mosque got its name from the ropes on which its lamps used to hang. Brown hair, olive skin; who could tell me apart from any number of Muslims?

I sat down on a step near the fountain. It was midday, people had come in to rest. Some students, lounging on rush mats, were leafing through their lesson books. An old fellow was fast asleep by the wall. A granny was curled up in a corner—was she really a person, not a thing?—a shapeless creature hugging a bag of groceries and a ginger cat. Apparently the new rule did not apply to cats.

"Our strength is that our places of worship are at the center of daily life," Ruwan had said one day. "They serve as courthouse, school, dormitory and public baths."

The House of the Prophets would also make for rest and peace of mind.

The interior would be all mirrors and turquoise tiles. There would be cypresses in the courtyard for pilgrims come from afar.

Nobody was bothered by my presence. The incorrigible architect in me noted the dome supported by ribs, the horseshoe arches. A dove was strutting along one of the beams. Its brown cap was shot with slate gray. Thrusting out its head, it peered anxiously about. It too was alone of its kind.

Suddenly the caretaker, who had seen me come in, approached with as martial a gait as his slippers allowed. When he got to where I was sitting, he stopped, then walked around the fountain, darting suspicious looks at me. After a moment, I turned around; his eyes were still on me. The student nearest me had raised his head and was also staring at me in a puzzled way. Even the old man, who had been so sound asleep a moment earlier, sat up.

I can't have made quite the right movements.

I put my sketchbook in my pocket, got up and strolled over to the door. Outside the mosque were the trestles of an open-air pharmacy. The apothecary—his hooded, bespectacled little face looked as if it had been shriveled by the study of learned books of magic—was counting the morning's receipts.

For a moment, I had the impression that all the inhabitants of the street were thronging round and pointing at me: "A Christian, a Christian."

I took the shortest way home.

"The joke," said young Mark, with all the wisdom of fifteen years, "is that they think we mind being shut out of their mosques. Well, we don't give a damn. They can keep their houses of prayer to themselves."

Nevertheless, I sent a note to a newspaper, where a school friend of mine was working:

For some days now, the mosques in our city do not seem to have been admitting Christians. Are Christians held to be further from God than the cats and birds, which still wander freely around these sanctuaries?

We are told that Islam would like to be better understood and better liked. Then why hide what's best in it?

I signed it with my initials and sent it off, despite a grimace from Sarun.

Ruwan, my *beau-frère*. Today, I get a bitter taste in the mouth when I chew over these curious French words meaning brother-in-law.

"How does it feel to be married?"

I hear myself talking, as if I were someone else. Only yesterday, we were running together through the alleyways of the old city. And now here's Ruwan, a responsible, respectable citizen. I can't help looking to see if he's wearing a wedding ring like a westernized Muslim. It would be no disgrace. Wedding rings come to us from ancient Rome, they're not a Christian stigma. He'd rather not. If he's married, that's his business. An impenetrable hanging shuts us off from his home.

"How does it feel to be married?" he repeats dreamily. "You'll soon find out."

Ilena comes in, smiling, calm. She too is wearing traditional dress. How like my father she has suddenly grown. The same sweetness tinged with humor, the same faraway

86

look. Unless the look is due to vanity that prevents her from wearing glasses.

"Happy?"

You don't ask a woman that in front of her husband. And I didn't. But the light in her eyes answers, "Happy."

No one seeing her could take her for what she is: an ingrate, a fallen woman, who has run off with a lover.

They tease me gently about architecture. Ruwan tells me one of my rivals has suggested an inflatable rubber mosque.

No mention has been made of the word he'll put in for me to the Muslim jury. That's taken for granted. And I'll have no false pride about accepting his help; it will simply make up for the disadvantage of having been born on the wrong side of the fence.

"Islam has its inconsistencies," I say. "It lets me build it a temple. It wouldn't let me marry one of its daughters."

Ruwan thinks this over for a moment.

"What seems unfair to you," he answers, "is only a principle of wisdom. A Christian can enter a Muslim household and he won't hear any ill spoken of Jesus. But a Muslim going into a Christian family has a good chance of hearing the Prophet's name insulted."

An ingenious explanation, I won't deny it. My sister has slipped away with the empty coffee cups. My friend sees me to the door:

"Ilena is expecting a child."

In the end, that's all he cares about. In comparison, my projects, my ideas, are soap bubbles. He only asked about them to be polite. Ruwan is blessed. Or thinks he is, which comes to the same thing.

Since our guilty expedition on her island, Safia had taken to phoning me at the office, after hours.

"Radio Safia calling. Bringing you the latest news."

This was always some comical happening, which she related with the utmost gravity. A fortune-teller on Wool Street had told her she'd remarry, and that her husband would be an old general. A large cat had taken up residence in her garden and refused to decamp; could it be a reincarnation of her grandfather?

One evening, she turned up in person, pretty upset.

"The red-light district has been sacked."

Naturally, not a word about it on TV.

"Take me there," she said. "This is something I've got to see."

Alguazils were barring the nefarious streets. But we looked respectable and they let us through. The ground was strewn with debris. Only the night before, the girls had been in their booths, simpering at clients, baring their fat, painted flesh. Then Genghis Khan had descended.

"I'll buy you a lemonade, over there," said Safia banteringly.

A long, narrow café known for pot smoking. There too, the windows had been smashed and the neon lights torn out. A carbide lamp on one of the tables threw a harsh light on this scene of destruction. The owner was prostrate in one corner. All I could get out of him was invocations of the Prophet's name.

"*Janna*," my friend spelled out, looking at the signboard, which was still just about legible. "Paradise. Or is it *Jahannam*, hell? They have almost the same name, so they must be very much alike."

That kind of remark was Safia all over.

A whore was sitting in the street, weeping. As we passed, she grabbed hold of our clothes: "Have pity on a poor, wretched woman."

Safia pulled her to her feet. Blood had run down her lip

88

and mixed disgustingly with her makeup. She was still young. Large eyes stared out of a ravaged face.

"Who was it?"

"Boys in white robes, with leather belts and clubs. May God blacken their faces!"

Only the night before, she—like the other girls in the trade—had been in her tiny observatory watching the crowd flowing past much as it did in any other part of town. The men expressionless, the boys making eyes.

"They've killed me," she said.

For a moment I thought of calling Eudoxia to get the woman admitted to Berthome Bey Hospital. But she wouldn't hear of it.

"They were as beautiful as angels," she added, unexpectedly.

Safia looked at her appraisingly, no doubt visualizing the portrait she might have painted.

"Tell me honestly, will business pick up again?" the poor thing asked imploringly.

"Of course it will," said Safia. "Business always picks up."

I took my friend to Atabekian's for a sherbet. She told me about two Jewish prostitutes who had donated a velvet curtain for the Torah, and the rabbi had courageously accepted their gift. She grew extremely animated and wanted to know how many times I had visited the red-light district, and what my impressions had been. When I swore I'd never set foot in it, she looked at me skeptically.

"I'd have come, if I'd been you. You're lucky to be a man."

Surprisingly enough, none of the people around us, sitting under the colored chandeliers, seemed troubled about the day's events. Safia saw this as further evidence that in the East, everything which happens is the work of secret societies. Ideas shun the light of day; they move covertly.

Not only was our artist interested in stairways, as I've said; she also went in for secret passages, vaults and cellars. For her, the world was a labyrinth on many levels, with its wells, crypts, catacombs, which explain the visible part of it. Any of her paintings would express this better than I can.

"All in all," she says in conclusion, "these Demons of the South are just jokers."

The following day, an envelope bearing the words "Ministry of Religious Cults" made my heart leap. I was all the more disappointed to read, "After mature reflection and a reappraisal of Article 21 of the specifications, the administration has decided to halve the architect's fee." I checked the original rules and found that, in such a case, an applicant could withdraw his entry. Big deal.

So that was their game. Faced with a difficult choice, the powers that be had decided to discourage entries. I showed this juridical curiosity to my partner, El Souss, who scratched his nose. Up till then, the undertaking had only been rash. Now it promised to be ruinous.

"The malevolence of government offices is boundless," he observed. "Woe unto him who depends on State commissions."

And he reminded me that we had decided to open a separate account for this job.

"Don't worry," said Nahas, the engineer, as soon as the boss's back was turned. "I'll forget to bill you for part of my work." As a Muslim, he believed in the Mosque of the Prophets.

But Gregory, the aviator, whom I ran into on Mulay-Abdullah Street, knew what was at the bottom of it: "My boy, it's scheming, rackets and rake-offs. Officially, everyone's fees are to be reduced. In fact, though, the Minister of

Religious Cults has promised one of the competitors an extra fee on the quiet. Which means that everyone will withdraw except the man they want to promote."

Ominous scenario, and quite plausible. I sent in my answer that evening: "Gentlemen, I am still in the race."

Colorless clouds were massing at the ends of the world.

My protests about the exclusion of Christians from mosques hadn't been published. I suspected Sarun of phoning behind my back to stop it.

Our mother was aging visibly, consumed by a grief that struck me as pointless. She'd show me the plants on our balcony, whose green tendrils hung down to the apartment below. She said that before he died, our father had named each plant after one of us, and that since then they had flourished when we were happy and drooped when we were ill. "Look at Ilena's," she said. "It's the only one that's fading." I shrugged.

Old Katrin sat in her corner all evening mumbling *ya Rebbi,*[*] though she herself couldn't have said why. And my partner, El Souss, kept saying at every turn, "The telephone's falling apart. The country's falling apart."

On my office wall, I pinned a big sketch of the town and the harbor, whence the Mosque of the Prophets set sail like a white frigate.

Sheep made their annual appearance on the balconies of our neighborhood. You could see them browsing between the clotheslines, unaware of what was in store for them. Soon the religious holiday would bring all life to a standstill. Three days of enforced idleness, except for those who took the plane to Mecca.

Taxis, decked with flags or children's balloons, come down from the mountains carrying old pilgrims clad all in

* Oh Lord.

white, beaming with joy at the thought of dying of exhaustion in the crush.

There are also many young pilgrims, some even taking their wives along. This year Ruwan has gone with them. Wearing a seamless robe—like the last robe of Christ—right shoulder bare, he will circumambulate the Kaaba seven times, then stone the devil's columns. El hajji Ruwan!

May I be forgiven, I don't like Aïd-el-Kebir, although it does commemorate Abraham's sacrifice and Moses' Passover. I don't like the stale smell, the blood in the gutters. "It's better to eat our dear Lord Jesus; it's cleaner," as I used to say as a child.

The break gives me a chance to visit Abuna Pierrot. Eudoxia has been urging me to do so for a long time. She claims there is a connection between my work and his. He's a silent prophet; the only kind allowed nowadays, so it seems.

I already know him slightly, having met him at one of the Saruns' soirées, where he'd looked out of place with his none-too-clean jellaba and his wooden cross.

"Forgive me, I don't really belong here," he'd said to me. "I'm one of Eudoxia's mascots."

"So am I, Abuna."

Pierre Pierrot, son of a Belgian engineer and a Mozarab schoolteacher. Known sources of livelihood: mathematics and French lessons. Hobbies: collecting abandoned children.

This evening, I push open his door unannounced. A young boy gets up on crutches. Another youngster, his leg bent under him, shunts across the floor to meet me, propelling himself with his hand. The cat jumps off the Father's knee and I see that it too limps—the hallmark of this little household.

"You'll eat supper with us," the Father orders.

I run out to buy fruit and bread. When I get back the table has been set. The boys are elbowing one another.

"We're eating the Aïd sheep," the Father announces, and in reply to my questioning glance, "Here we are all devotees of Muhammad, except Tuma and me."

"Was this your choice?"

"Not at all. I took what God sent me."

His eyes are burning in his pink face, in which two races meet.

"It so happens," he explains, "that Christians are a little better off than the others; they rarely abandon their children."

"Tuma's rich," says one of the boys. Half Tuma's face is covered with a purplish scab.

"I'm teaching Tuma his catechism. I make the others recite the Koran. Beshir, show us how well you can say the *Fatihah*."

He smiles impishly. Then dropping his voice, he says in French, "I could easily convert them. These children are at my mercy. But I won't let myself. They were born Muslims and it's not for me to change that. Later on, maybe, if they want to. Even then, I won't advise it. A Muslim who renounces his faith can expect all sorts of trouble."

In the glowing circle of lamplight, these unutterable thoughts seem strangely self-evident. He goes on for a while, talking about his joys and sorrows. Now and again, the eldest child put in his two cents worth, showing that he has followed part of the conversation. After the meal, they all sing the song he has taught them:

> *Au clair de la lune,*
> *Mon ami Pierrot . . .*

I can't help casting an anxious professional eye on the state of the beams and flooring. An old house that's never been repaired. The Father takes my arm:

"Did you know, this may be Raymond Lulle's house? He certainly lived on this street."

Raymond, the great scholar, philosopher, alchemist, who learned the language of the Saracens in order to convert them. Four times he came to these shores. Four times the sultan sent him back, politely refusing to cut off his head. Father Pierrot told me he had pried up some of the loose stones in the hope of finding a message from his predecessor. A man of Lulle's stamp could not have grappled with Islam for so long without learning a lesson. It's up to us to find it.

"Don't look too hard," I joke, "or the house will fall down on you."

He's too diffident to ask why I've come. I explain: our friend Eudoxia thought we should meet. Of course he remembers Eudoxia, a fine girl. He looks at me, expecting to hear more.

"Eudoxia and I are probably going to get married," I say. I can feel myself blushing. To get off this dangerous ground as quickly as possible, I tell him about the mosque. Of course, he knows all about it.

"It looks to me, Gabriel, as if you're doing the same as me. Working for the Fridolins."

"Fridolins?" That must be a Belgian nickname, a rough term of endearment for the followers of the Prophet.†

Behind us, one of the boys is sweeping the floor in the name of Allah, the Merciful and Compassionate. A habit the Father has got them into. "How can you pray while performing a lowly task?" ask the local people in astonishment. After which, the boys in turn kiss my hand and go out to watch television with the neighbors.

"I ought to hire a nanny to look after those kids," exclaims the Father. "I don't care what people say."

† Fridolins: nickname for the Germans during the two world wars.

94

Irresistibly, our conversation turns to Islam. Islam has borrowed our five daily prayers, spoken while facing east, which are already mentioned in Tertullian, the North African Christian. Islam has also swiped the parable of the camel and the eye of the needle, though in the process, the rich man has become an infidel, which makes all the difference.

But many bits of wisdom belong only to Islam, for example the astonishing passage where we see the assembly of genii accepting the Koran. And the one where the wicked angel is damned for refusing to bow down to man.

When Abuna Pierrot shuts his eyes, you see an honest Walloon face. Then he opens them, disclosing a passion from another source.

"You're on the right track with your mosque," he says. "Somewhere, far, far away, the two paths converge. Our imperfections prevent us from seeing where they meet. But we must keep going. Keep on going."

A small boy crosses Albacore Street carrying a cup on a tray as carefully as if it were the Holy Sacrament. There's a lingering fragrance under the arcades, the last jasmin of the season. And I return to my task buoyed up by this unstinting approval.

Keep going! Toward the southern territories, for instance, where my brother Saad is to take his vows.

My mother is too tired. She has deputed me to attend the ceremony in her place. Eudoxia suggests going in papa's car. I refuse with a burst of laughter. She takes no offense, but announces next day, "Gregory will take us."

The old campaigner likes the chanting of the monks. And his past protects him against accidents. He's already had his share: he was burned in the sky.

"My car's fine," he tells us. "Except that it won't go into reverse."

That's typical of him: he doesn't back away from anything.

Monasteries ought to be built of concrete in filthy suburbs. What's the merit of burying yourself in a place as beautiful and moving as the one we're going to? *Deïr-es-Sebaïn,* the Abbey of the Seventy. All we can see, in the evening light, are palm trees and spires rising from the hollows in the dunes of the Suat Desert. Beauty seduces a little too easily.

We set out before dawn. The endless road to the South, with its humps and badly patched-up wounds. On windy days, little tongues of sand form on it. You think they're soft, but they're hard enough to jolt the car off the track.

With her elbow half out of the window, Eudoxia claims she can see a jerboa, or even a wild saluki. I've been slaving too hard lately, sleep overtakes me. Around five in the afternoon, the driver switches off the car radio, and we start crossing the salt pans.

For generations, the monastery has been fighting a losing battle against the encroaching sand. The dune is advancing, piling up against the wall. It will soon be over the top.

Eudoxia rings the bell at the foot of the tower. We're late. The green sky is getting darker every minute. This is the hour—according to the statutes of the monasteries of the South—when the demons take flight. They too have their rule.

Up above us, someone is scratching away by the light of an electric lamp; a mason monk, filling cracks. Apparently, they don't want to hear us. Suddenly a voice calls out from behind the iron door: "Who goes there? Man, woman or demon?"

"Two men, one woman and no demons," Eudoxia replies

firmly, as though we hadn't been observed through a spy hole.

"After sunset, there are demons everywhere," says the monk. "Go your ways, creatures of the night."

Negotiations follow. Gregory scribbles our request on a piece of paper and slips it under the door. We hear the sound of sandals receding. By now, it's really dark. The sandals come back. His Grace the Father Superior will be pleased to let us in.

We meet this cerberus who for two pins would have left us outside. A shy, blushing brother hostler followed by a tiny fennec, which must be the monastery's mascot.

As far as I can tell in the darkness, it's not as idyllic inside the walls as outside. The abundance of novices has made it necessary to put up new outbuildings. Work is going on everywhere: repointing, patching, cementing. When the vine shoots have grown sufficiently, there will be an arbor where the brothers can take the air. Sacks of plaster block the entrance to the main bell tower.

"Next time, dear brothers," I say under my breath, "kindly consult me."

Saad is unrecognizable; his forehead is covered with eczema, and he has a tightly curled beard like the young king Ahasuerus. He serves us beans in olive oil—excellent, believe it or not—and takes us down to the crypt, where he shows us the skulls of the seventy founders of the establishment.

"You're going to build a mosque? That's absurd."

He hasn't even asked after our sister. Instead, in our honor, he reads some verses from *The Song of Songs,* accompanying himself on little cymbals and with clicks of the tongue.

Thy neck is as a tower of ivory, he recites. You in the West talk of ivory towers, but you've distorted the meaning.

We listen to this wild text, which a clumsy paraphrase has

made even wilder: *A garden enclosed, is my sister, my spouse.*
Somehow I feel that this eternally young poem was written
for Ilena and Ruwan. It tells the whole story of Islamic marriage.

Whereupon the reader wishes us refreshing sleep and dis-
appears through the wall.

"I hardly recognize the monastery," says Eudoxia.
"There are twice as many monks."

"That's not surprising," replies friend Gregory. "Young
Christians used to have a wide choice. All careers were open
to them. Now we're being pushed out of politics, the civil
service and the army. There's still business. If this goes on,
the whole of the next generation will end up in holy orders."

"Not at all," protests Eudoxia. "A vocation is a gift of
God. Dew in the desert."

She goes off to the women and children's wing and we
hear the door being fastened with heavy chains behind her.
And by the light of a lamp, we try to find our quarters,
thinking one last time of *the little foxes that spoil the vines.*

We're soon awakened by the sound of the simandra, a
metal bar suspended on a rope, being hammered by a face-
less brother. Shivering, we cross the courtyard under the
stars which have not even begun to fade.

"Let's follow the crowd," suggests a deadpan Gregory.
"They must know where coffee is being served."

In accordance with the custom of the Mozarab monks, we
take off our shoes at the entrance to the chapel, then grope
our way to a place on rush mats. All the lamps are out
except one, which is hidden behind the screen. But the
smell lingers, the smell of sweat and incense, telling us of
fifteen hundred years of masses and prostrations. And there
we wait, small and infinitely unworthy.

A light is coming toward us like a will-o'-the-wisp. It
looks as if no one were carrying it.

98

"He is the Light," intones a monk, who blends in with a pillar.

Other little flames follow, each accompanied by a new voice. A whole procession is now moving against the whiteness of the wall.

"He is the Light, the Light, the Light."

Yes, this is what we must tell Ruwan and his friends. Their Islam has remained on the fringes of the night, whereas these monks maintain a presence at its heart.

Hosanna in the great earthen church that is dressed in whitewash like a bride. Hosanna from the crooked pillars and misshapen dome. Hosanna from the cracks, a hundred times filled and a hundred times opened up again, like the stigmata on the bodies of the Blessed.

The last candle bearer is the Father Superior himself, Hegumen Basil, clad in his heavy vestments. He was once professor of philosophy at the Modern University of Marsana. Then he renounced all philosophies. Arms outstretched, he prays for the Patriarch of the Mozarabs, who holds the see of Damascus; for baba Boulos (Pope Paul); for our terrestrial master, that idle infidel who lives in the prince regent's palace. Tirelessly, he kneels and rises. At last he turns his imperious face, his huge night bird's eyes, toward us.

"Your faith makes a mockery of sickness. Your faith makes a mockery of politics and of war."

Gregory grabs my hand, crushes it in his. I scan these faces from another world, looking for the novice who is to be ordained. But he, prostrate in his cell, still has a few hours left to prepare himself.

We come tottering out into the gray dawn, which mysteriously contains the promise of heat. "Let's go to bed till the sun gets up," says Gregory.

Happy man. Despite my accumulated fatigue, I'm no longer sleepy. I wander along the rows of climbing vines, where the first birds are beginning to stir. Monks going

99

about their household chores pass me without so much as a glance. I have to admit there's something terrifying about them, with their youth, their martial gait, steel-rimmed glasses, black turbans, black beards. Gregory was wrong: they're not embittered down-and-outers; they're the soldiers of a beleaguered garrison.

In the early light, the monastery can be seen more clearly. An old covered well, a Saracen tower one can reach by ladders. Unfortunately, the main facade of the house has been cemented over and the chapel braced with iron props. But when rounding the apse I come across a poor, charming little thing that no one had thought of restoring: a mosque of all things!

No, it's not a mirage. It was built by the Jaffarid emirs, right in the middle of the monastery grounds, to serve the needs of the garrison they put there. Very simple, slightly lopsided, with doves nesting in it. The monks have had the diplomatic tact to whitewash it. But I suspect they're undermining it on the sly.

"Tell me who you are," I ask this chapel. "Tell me the secret of your toleration."

Not what's meant in the West by that word, which is only indifference. But that other toleration, which is a deep understanding of things.

Eudoxia appears, mortified at having missed the night worship.

"Shame on you, Gabriel. You visit this unique place and all you find to look at is this . . ."

Come let us rejoice! My brother Saad is going to stretch out on the paving stones. The office of the dead will be said over him. His name, his person will be taken from him. Saad dies. Saad is dead.

Leaving the monastery some hours later, ourselves slightly dead, we see some bedouins begging at the gatehouse. Once the scourge of the countryside, they are mere domestic predators now. The monks grow watermelons in the dunes roundabout:

> *The desert has fed the plants they have sown*
> *For the love of God.*

We see before us a line of flat-topped mounds, eroded hills. Caverns have been hollowed out in their sides by the hand of man. This is where the first hermits dwelt, before anyone thought of building. It's here that my brother Saad will make his retreat when he has been in the monastery twenty or thirty years.

I climb the crumbling steps leading to one of these caverns. I hear a whirring sound and something hits me in the face. I turn and see a hoopoe zigzagging out into the desert with its red crest and checker-patterned wings. It must have flown into the grotto to cool off and taken fright when I came in. Now I've got a bruise just below the eye.

"It was an angel," says Eudoxia in all seriousness. "You bear the mark of an angel."

Then, quite suddenly, I was summoned by the jury. So it really did exist. And knew that I existed.

I slept badly. This summons might be just one more move in the war of nerves. At the last moment, they'd find some pretext for turning me down. I cut myself while shaving and had to put a Band-Aid on my chin.

"Wait, I'll come with you," young Mark cried.

"What about school?"

"You'll write me a note."

I loved him for his childish devotion.

We take one of those little blue-and-white-striped cabs called zebras. Despite the Koranic mascot hanging from the rearview mirror, we get a puncture. Before I can stop myself, I've shouted, "You did it on purpose!" As if a huge plot had been hatched against my poor little plan.

"No, *effendi,*" the driver protests. "Give me a hand and we'll be on the road again in five minutes."

No time, friend. We set off at a gallop. Mark clears the way for me between the donkeys and the orange peels, and we get there ahead of time. He slaps me on the back and leaps onto a bus. He'll be a little late for his geography class.

The Ministry of Religious Cults occupies the former palace of the Beylerbey Ahmed. Today, I'm in no mood to admire its architecture. I'm bathed in sweat. Feeling in my pocket, I come across a small object that Mark has slipped in: a childish thing, a cross made of dried beans strung on wire. It had been blessed on Palm Sunday.

I'm shown into a large echoing chamber. The Minister is not there. Neither is the maquette, which won't make my explanations any easier.

Amor Pasha is acting chairman. He's the dignified old gentleman I met one summer evening at the Saruns', and today his face seems even more distinguished than it did then. But he's wearing a red scarf around his neck; he has a streaming cold.

Has anyone spoken to him on my behalf? Sarun promised he would. Maybe he decided not to in order to puncture my ridiculous project as soon as possible. Perhaps it's just as well. I'm fed up with intrigue and nepotism. Let my work speak for itself.

"You're very young," says Amor Pasha kindly.

I might have expected it. My file contains a brochure designed to counteract that impression: a copy of Ned Halperin's letter of recommendation; a letter of thanks from the Mayor of Baltimore; a bird's-eye view of the Du Pont de Nemours swimming pool, which I did more than forty percent of; a photograph of the Annapolis Pentecostal Temple . . . Very important that Pentecostal Temple.

"I meant no criticism," says Amor Pasha. "We're all for young people. Aren't we, gentlemen?"

The Saudi Ambassador makes little approving noises. He represents one of the main financial backers. I take in the other members of the jury. Which are my friends? Which are my enemies?

Turning his fine sculptured head, the chairman offers the floor to the man on his right, then the one on his left. Both decline politely.

"Very well. Then I shall begin. I gather you are putting forward the idea of a three-master."

To say the least. The bowsprit mast and the mizzen mast will be smooth and cylindrical, except for the narrow balcony running around the cone of the roof. The main mast will be octagonal, like the belfries of Languedoc—containing two very slender spiral staircases, which will coil into one another and join at the top.

"Don't you think the hollows in your sails might become dust traps?" Amor Pasha asks.

Each of the masts will hold up its sails: huge curved sheets of milky, toughened glass, which will reflect the sun gently like real sails that are wet with spray.

"If sand does collect in them," I answer boldly, "we'll hose them down."

I suppose it's traditional to begin with the more trifling objections. The faces around the table are expressionless. The Ambassador blows into his hand as if it were one of the sails we've been talking about.

"Let's get on to the decoration," says the chairman. "It seems very austere to me."

The outside will be bare, except for the portals. The flying buttresses will shoot out of the body of the building like four pairs of oars. They'll be beguiling enough to the eye, with no need of gingerbread.

In the prayer hall, however, the inside edge of the arches

103

will be of two colors. Not stone and brick, like the Great Mosque at Cordoba, but stone and mosaic. Safia has promised to help me find our beloved turquoise.

A plinth of the same mosaic will run the whole length of the ablutions court. And parallel to it, a frieze of Kufic verses, which the famous blind artist will make.

"Kufic?" says Amor Pasha. "Not many people can read Kufic."

That old black slave could.

"Your Excellency," I say. "The essential thing is to choose an architectural plan. We can reconsider the decoration later and change it if you wish."

What a sail-trimmer this Gabriel is. He knows very well that the decoration goes with the building. You can't have one without the other. But we must clear the hurdle of the jury. After that, we'll see.

Amor Pasha strains to catch what I'm saying. He must be hard of hearing. I find myself staring at the green lozenge on his lapel—the Regency's highest distinction. What has he done to deserve it, aside from marrying one of the Prince's nine sisters?

On his left, Sheik Talaat El Bisri looks daggers at me. Sharp nose, mean mouth. I've been warned about him; he's a tough customer. Thin, still young, he studied Koran at the El Azhar University in Cairo. His students regard him as a master.

"We need circular windows," says Amor Pasha.

"Stained glass or stone?"

"Stained glass would clash with the rest. Stone. I like circular windows."

And he folds his diaphanous hands, pleased to have exerted some slight influence on the project.

Then Rauf Effendi takes over. He is consultant architect to the Ministry of Religious Cults. A fat, greasy face. Dirty gray hair that doesn't quite go with his very black eyebrows. The half-closed eyes refuse to meet mine.

The file is spread out in front of him; my prose covered with remarks that appear to be unfriendly, but his manner is precise and fairly polite. We get bogged down in technical details. The Saudi takes notes but says nothing. Sharif Damuri dozes off.

"Your dome is too low," says Rauf. "The dome should be the symbol of the flawless firmament that the Koran speaks of."

My dome huddles at the foot of the main mast. Luckily, though, I've brought along some alternative sketches with a higher dome. Undoubtedly the change could be made, but it would spoil the proportions. The paper passes from hand to hand. Heads are shaken. In the end, I deem it politic to raise the original dome by a meter, and Rauf seizes on this concession—as if it were a victory for Muslim tradition over the presumptuous science of the West.

I know this character wants me to be turned down, but he has made the mistake of going into detail, a clear admission that my project is worthwhile. My boat is sailing before the wind.

Nudged from his torpor, Sharif Damuri voices a few naive concerns. Have I provided public toilets? Toilets are most important; such things show that mosques are superior to churches. I haven't forgotten them. I have put them discreetly in the basement. But I can't promise the jury that the basement won't flood with seawater.

So far, no one has asked the central, unanswerable question: how can a Christian design a mosque? How can the work of a Christian dog be acceptable to God? The extremist newspapers certainly won't fail to raise this point if my project is chosen. I'm a member of a long-despised species. They are my superiors by divine right. Yet, you might say, they're a little ashamed of this superiority.

"Your turn, Talaat," says the chairman, as though passing a ball. Faces light up. At last we're getting down to brass tacks.

Sheik El Bisri raises his pale eyebrows, puts on his glasses and looks straight at me:

"Isn't this Ned Halperin you give as a reference a Jew?" His nostrils flare with disgust.

"I don't know, O Sheik. We never discussed the matter. It may interest you to know he has built a basilica in Brazil."

Talaat makes a dismissive gesture: Christians may hire whom they please.

Chairman Amor signs to him to drop this subject: if we start tracking down everybody's Jewish connections, we'll topple the State.

"My second question," Talaat goes on somewhat testily, "is why have you put in a minbar?"

There's a gasp of surprise from the others around the table. A minbar is a pulpit. All important mosques have one. And my plans naturally include one—as, I imagine, do those of the other competitors.

"Explain yourself, honored friend," says Amor, vainly trying to undo the red scarf that's wound around his neck.

"The minbar was unknown to the first Muslims. Let me read you a letter from Caliph Omar the Great to the Governor of Egypt. *I understand you have erected a pulpit in your new mosque. Is it your wish to look down on Muslims? I order you to pull it down without delay.*"

That could be the first unapplied decree in the history of Islam.

"Forgive my saying so," cuts in Sharif Damuri—now fully awake—"but I've never heard of that text. We must check its sources."

"My sources are excellent," replies Talaat.

"Check them all the same. Caliph Omar was certainly illiterate. He dictated to secretaries."

"Christian secretaries," puts in Amor Pasha, with a duplicity I would not have expected of him.

The Saudi Ambassador is doodling on his blotter. You can see he's annoyed with Talaat for trying to give them all a lesson in Islam.

I clear my throat. "May I propose to the jury that we defer this question? We can remove the minbar, or we can put it back. It doesn't affect the structure of the building."

"Proposal adopted," says Amor quickly.

"A moment ago we deferred the discussion of the decoration," observes Sheik El Bisri, his face growing grayer and grayer. "Now we're deferring the question of the minbar. I can't help wondering what will be left."

I steal a glance at my watch. What other weapons is this man holding in reserve? I pray for lunchtime. But I fear that these men of riper—or overripe—years won't be hungry.

"If I'm not mistaken," Talaat goes on in a neutral voice, "your prayer chamber comes to a point."

"Your" prayer chamber with a touch of disdain. Of course it comes to a point. The site has dictated that. It will be the prow of the ship.

"But in that case," says Amor Pasha, who has just become aware of the problem, "the colonnades won't be parallel to the end wall."

"No, they won't, since there won't be an end wall. The colonnades will come to a point. They'll converge on the mihrab."

The mihrab is a niche, framed by columns and topped by an arch. It will point in the direction of Mecca. It is a door to the unknowable.

"Can't we have a straight wall instead of a point?" asks Sharif Damuri in surprise.

"You'd waste the end of the site, and the prayer chamber would be too small. Unless, of course, we took some space

107

from the courtyard. But then the courtyard would be too small."

Not to mention the fact that we'd have to give up the idea of the boat. I hand a sketch around. El Bisri doesn't even deign to look at it:

"In the mosques of Islam," he says in his musical staccato, as though reciting a poem, "in the mosques of Islam, the prayer hall is rectangular. The rows of columns run parallel to the end wall, or are at right angles to it."

He's right in principle, but he's forgetting all the mosques built as trapezoids, parallelograms, or worse, because of the street layout.

"You are speaking only of custom, O Sheik," I say softly. "As far as I know, no doctor has condemned the triangle. I defy you to find one who has."

He gives a start, lowers his head and begins scribbling. I'm sure I've gone too far. He's capable of ferreting away for days till he finds a quotation that will crush me.

As I see it, the convergence of the two walls symbolizes the convergence of our two faiths. But I can't tell them all that.

"What about the mirrors?" asks the Sharif in his quavering voice. "The elderly have poor sight. They'll bump into them."

"No, they won't. I've put in a projecting plinth. That will stop them."

This was the first time anyone had criticized the mirrors.

"My friends," says Amor Pasha somewhat anxiously, "I presume you are all now quite clear about this business of the triangle and we can get on."

"Just a moment," says El Bisri, raising his gun-metal countenance. "If we're going to have a chamber that comes to a point, how shall we pray in it? We won't be able to line up in rows." He sounds triumphant. What will become of

108

those long rows of prostrate worshippers you see in the mosques on a Friday evening, all facing the east wall?

"You'll pray in a triangle," I say boldly.

"In a triangle!" El Bisri raises his arms, appealing to all present.

Yes, in a triangle. And everything—the walls, the colonnades, the worshippers too—will move toward the focal point. I wait, confident that there is no jurist capable of proving that this is not Islamic enough.

Amor Pasha sees me as far as the entrance hall; a signal honor for a young puppy like myself. He has a fine head of white hair, and a slight twitching in his cheek.

"Well now, my son, that didn't go too badly! Luckily for you, Talaat was too harsh. He antagonized the others."

The morning isn't over yet. Maybe my rivals, Fannawi and the man from Cairo, are waiting in some corner. But I see no one. Has the jury met just for me?

"I have to admit," Amor goes on, "that your being a Christian does not help matters."

Here we are at last. I have any answers down pat.

"Your Excellency, did the Arab conquerors know how to build? No, certainly not. Who did know how to build at that time? Christian architects. Who knew how to sculpture and ornament? Christian craftsmen. The first mosques could never have been built without them."

He interrupts gently, "It's not your fault that you were born into a Mozarab family."

I appraise the aristocratic architecture of his face. Whoever designed those plans, bravo! He sighs, places his translucent hand on the banister. Marble on marble.

The final dart strikes home as I'm going through the door: "Perhaps the designer of a mosque is a Muslim at heart, though he may not yet know it."

Outside, in the autumn wind, two kebab sellers are arguing like Homeric heroes.

Ruwan, who played soccer in those days, had begun to read Ibn-Khaldun in the school library. I laughed at him.

"Go on, admit it. You don't understand a word."

"Yes, I do. It's perfectly clear. Arab energy is in the South. In the desert. Periodically, the south wind blows on the North, and an Arab kingdom or empire rises up. After a while, the energy abates and the empire falls into decay. Then the south wind blows again."

Interesting idea, you can't deny it. All around us people were deploring the decadence of the powers that be. Perhaps a force from elsewhere would breathe some life into them.

One day, I introduced my friend to young Ilena:

"This is the handsomest boy in the school, Ruwan ibn Abd-el-Karim ibn Sabah-ed-Din ibn . . ."

My fanciful pedigree was cut short by a dig in the ribs.

He took Ilena's hand and, to impress us, made us climb to the top of the minaret of the Andalusian Mosque, which he rather considered his family property. He pointed out the little courtyards of the old city, in many of which—on that late autumn day—stood trees of gold.

"I shall protect you all your life," he said, "in memory of the Angel Gabriel who saved the Black Stone from the Flood."

Usually, for obvious reasons, I didn't see Safia alone, but with Eudoxia. And Eudoxia, far from minding, was glad to give her friend the chance to shine. As for Safia, she seemed unaware of the wrong she had done Sarun's daughter. She considered that the act which had taken place on the bare ground of the island was simply a brief episode, a sop to the flesh, with no strings attached. She was probably right.

"Every day, one must create a little beauty," she would say. Then a mild play on words. *"Jamâl,* beauty. *Jamal,* camel. Are we to infer that the idea of beauty originated in the idea of a camel?'' Eudoxia laughed and clapped her hands.

Sometimes the polyglot Safia liked to tell me off about my French. "You've got a good vocabulary. But oh, your accent!"

Despite the years of exile, I still have it. It's a pity you can't hear it. On the telephone, I immediately give myself away despite my past subjunctives.

Early that winter, she asked us to attend the Feast of the Fountain Makers, in other words, the water-supply and sewer workers' guild, one of the city's most closed corporations.

"Do you mean you've been invited? How did you manage that?"

She gave a mysterious smile.

The Feast of the Waters! I'd heard about this ancient ritual, with its Islamic tinge, that was held every year in honor of the River.

The Wadi Marsan had given its name to the city, and still supplied its drinking water, but it hadn't been seen for centuries as it was buried beneath the buildings of the old quarter. Just occasionally, a dull rumbling behind the wall of a house, and an abrupt hump in the street informed you of its presence.

I had a sudden desire to see this hidden water, which gushed out of the mountain as if through a wound.

"The architecture of the underground galleries is magnificent," said Safia, as if I still needed persuading. "It'll be good for your mosque."

Thousands of prisoners—thieves, schismatics, factionalists, Christians captured at sea—are said to have perished building those vaults.

Eudoxia had already accepted. She was an all-round believer. She believed in God, in her father, in medicine, in

111

Gabriel, in Safia—and threw herself into every undertaking with an enthusiasm tempered just occasionally by a brief attack of despair. She was the exact opposite of her friend, the teasing gambler, who was entrenched in her art as in a heresy. However, it was Eudoxia who had made the salons of Marsana accept this divorcée of uncertain origins, somewhat older than herself. In a word, this adventuress.

On the appointed day, a man was waiting for us outside a tumbledown house on the edge of Esh-Shaffa. He was somber-looking, like most of the fountain makers. The guild, recruited from father to son, had its own code of honor, its own tribunal.

"Is that you, children of the earth?" he asked.

"Hark to the song of the river," Safia replied.

An exchange of passwords. In different circumstances such precautions would have seemed ludicrous. But the gravity of the personage, the alarming state of the building, the remoteness of the neighborhood cured us of any desire to laugh. The man opened a little door, lit his lantern and signed to us to pull up our hoods. He himself looked like some sort of monk of the nether regions.

At a bend in the passage, the roar of the wadi could be heard, and a stale smell filled our nostrils. The walls were oozing and there were little puddles to be avoided.

Another light appeared nearby. It looked as though we would meet the other group. But these nocturnal figures were on the opposite bank. We were walking parallel, each group on a sort of ledge. By the light of the lanterns, I glimpsed the massive courses of masonry built by the slaves; time had hung mosses and grown grayish stalactites on them. We had to step over pipes, the damp touch of which made us shudder. Below us surged the dark water.

"Remember," said our guide, pointing to a walled-up passage, "that's where the victims of the Great Plague are buried."

112

Half an hour or so later, the men on the far bank crossed a bridge and joined us. Their faces were all hidden, except for a venerable mulatto whose white beard blanketed his chest. The air now smelled fresher, healthier.

Our guide put down his lantern. We were on a little platform that overhung the river. I could just make out the mountain wall ahead of us. The water gushed and bubbled out of it. Stone pillars, on either side of the opening, suggested a portico.

"You can see it rained last week," said Eudoxia.

Someone began beating a tambourine in a slow, persistent, rather terrifying rhythm. We were sitting on our heels. Two men tried to light twigs of thuya. Eudoxia took my hand. A deep bass voice began to intone the liturgy:

"Ansur."

Old Katrin's fifth secret.

"Ansur," came the reply.

"Ya fum-el-jebel,"‡ sang the bass voice.

*"Ras-el-ma,"** a nasal voice replied.

Voice answered voice, in the half darkness, with changes of tune, held notes and slight variations.

The rhythm of the tambourines quickened. The men let out a long, modulated shout. A tall, swarthy devil got up and overturned a basket, out of which tumbled three terrified hens, tied together by the feet: one white, one black and one of seven colors. This was the gift, demanded from time immemorial, by the jinni of the waters.

The hulking fellow seized his knife. It was then that the ceremony was interrupted. Firecrackers, animal cries, whistle blasts. For a moment, I thought it was all part of the ritual, but then a confused scuffle broke out. Someone extinguished our lanterns. A small person, brandishing a blazing branch—could it have been Safia?—confronted one of the

‡ O mouth of the mountain.   * Fountainhead.

assailants. Then a Bengal flare lit up the scene with a sinister red glow.

Like us, the invaders had their hoods pulled up. I didn't have time to count them. One of them seized the sacrificial chickens and flung them overboard. Another tripped up the big swarthy fellow, and pushed him into the river. A third fired a pistol at me. I screamed. I felt no pain, but a strange substance got into my eyes and up my nose. I saw I was covered with flour.

Then our assailants vanished down a side gallery, shouting slogans with a megaphone, "Down with idolaters," or *"Tariq wahid,"*† which made a strange din in the echoing vaults.

One of our number, armed with a knife, wanted to go after the intruders.

"Let them go, Othman," said the old mulatto.

The lanterns had been relit, and the man who had taken the forced dip climbed up the wall, from crampiron to crampiron. More frightened than hurt.

"I expected to be killed," confessed Eudoxia. That got a big laugh from Safia, who seemed delighted by the adventure and was handing around a few more tips.

The experts put their heads together. Should the ceremony be started over again the next day? The chickens had not been sacrificed according to the rite. But the jinni of the waters had swallowed them up all the same.

Before we broke up, our guides in chorus cursed these boys who'd dared to disturb such a solemn ceremony.

"They're saying it was the Demons of the South," Safia explained.

That was my first encounter with a secret army, which I had thought to be a popular myth.

† One way.

114

One day, out of the blue, the eminent Yamamura remembered that he had begotten a child on the shores of Marsania, and paid it a visit between two planes. He was surprised to find the tower still unfinished, and stationing himself at its foot, looked it up and down through his powerful binoculars. He condescended to acknowledge that the work was well done, then took off again for some distant destination, a sawed-off genius with a derisive laugh.

Yes, I still had plenty of work to do on this skyscraper. But I could not help going back to the port, where a far more important task awaited me. The ground had been cleared. When would the plans be approved?

Not a word from the jury. They must be in a fine quandary. The weeks went by. We were sinking gently into the bad season.

I tried to get news through Sarun. Unfortunately, the matter was outside his sphere of influence. What about Ruwan? He knew what was going on in Muslim circles. No, Ruwan was the last person.

In the meantime, I planned every detail. I'd come across a photo of a chandelier made of hundreds of little crystals and weighing several tons. Just what was needed for the House of the Prophets. But such things, I was told, could only be obtained from the West, which would lay me open to more criticism.

Safia went with me to see the famous carver of letters. We watched him tracing his festoons and ornamental leaves, which grew out of one another in splendid contempt of nature.

"I long to start your work," said the blind man, striving to perceive me in his darkness. "You have the voice of a just man."

I'd resumed my wanderings through the old city. Houses with flights of steps adjusted to the steep slopes. Bluish doors under porches of glazed tiles. Hanks of steaming wool hung up in courtyards with two or three tiers of galleries. Flaking plaster, huddled forms, where palaces once stood.

A venerable plane tree fanned out over the wall, its russet leaves miraculously spared as yet by the onset of winter.

Sometimes I passed an apprentice baker, his hair gray with flour. Or a little girl carrying a box of Vache-qui-rit cheese (one of the main vehicles of French influence in our country). I might see a woman waiting under an archway with a bundle on her head—it would never have occurred to her to put it down.

Then, as night was falling, I'd end up in one of those little cafés where the walls were painted with dreams. I loved those winter evenings, peopled with pointed hoods which zigzagged from door to door like phantoms.

One Sunday, Mark persuaded me to go to a Scouts' meeting with him. He attended them regularly. The Scouts met at a place in the suburbs called The Bitter Oranges, a large villa that had been vacated because of a lawsuit. A kind of obstacle course, with ditches and hurdles, had been laid out in the derelict garden. "That's how we keep in training," my young guide explained.

His buddies were toting equipment. Some of them, God knows why, knew my name. Various kinds of tackle were hanging in the entrance. There was a vaulting horse in the middle of the drawing room.

"Good Lord, are you Scouts or gym champions?"

"It's not just gym," said Mark, pointing at some trees. The sound of shots could be heard coming from that direction. I went pale.

The pine grove concealed a shooting range. Wooden

fences had been set up to stop stray bullets. A paper cutout had been nailed to the execution post.

"It doesn't cost much," said the boy placatingly. "We save the cartridge cases. We even save the bullets and melt them down."

In the shed I see a small crucible and a crimping tool. The only real expense is the powder. He takes a tommy gun from a "supply sergeant" hardly older than himself and lies down between two sandbags. On the stock of his gun there's a tracing of the Virgin. Mark fires slowly and deliberately in bursts of two or three shots. One of his pals jumps up to count the hits.

"Eight out of six. You're improving."

"What about you, Gabriel? Come on, give it a try."

I refuse. There's a lump in my throat. Our little Mark, who was wearing short pants only last year. Now he's learning to kill. When he was shooting at the target just now, he was out to kill.

"The day the Arabs attack, we'll show them!" cries another of his pals.

The Arabs! These boys should just take a look at themselves in the mirror. I'm overcome with rage:

"Where's your Scoutmaster?"

"What can I do for you, Gabriel?" says a familiar voice behind me.

It's Jirjir, the aviator, very much at ease in his battle dress.

"Yes, I'm here. I haven't been able to fly since I was wounded. I had to find something else to do."

"Are you crazy? Doing these things with kids?"

"Which is more crazy? To open your eyes or to close them?" His own are only too wide open; the pupils fill them almost entirely.

"What's more, they're not kids anymore," he cries. "They're boys who'll have to fight for their beliefs, for their families."

A large gold medal gleams in the fleece on his chest.

117

"How you do go on, Gregory. Marsania is not a violent country. It's an old country of compromise, a patchwork of communities."

"Marsania will be what the devil wants."

For a moment his assurance shakes me. Am I on the wrong track with this mosque of mine? A lot the Muslims care about what I'm trying to do. They've always had right on their side. And God and the prophets. Islam's incredible clear conscience.

Jirjir puts his hand on my shoulder: "Take your sister. She decided she'd set foot on the other side of the fence. And now she's completely lost. Her children will learn to read the Koran. It's intolerable."

Instinctively, he knows where it hurts.

"What about the police?" I say, to change the subject. "They must have got wind of what's going on?"

"Of course they have. We make a bit of noise sometimes. But you know our Regency's police. They pester you about little things; with big things they look the other way."

Jirjir is fiddling with the scabbard of his dagger.

"If you want peace, prepare for war," he goes on. "You were such a grind at school, you probably know how to say that in Latin."

"You're wrong. Fear will just build up on both sides. Ready to explode."

Mark has joined us, visibly unhappy that my visit should have turned out so badly. He runs his fingers through his fair hair, which seems to single him out for a different destiny. As a child, he was quite blond. When a Mozarab baby is born with blond down on his head, people are very proud; they say he's descended from the Crusaders.

"Think it over, Gabriel," says the aviator. "One day you may be sorry you didn't side with us."

He held out his hand. I think I may have shaken it, in spite of everything.

From its gaping windows, the big house watches me leave. Oneiric ruin and garden of traps.

Someone's running down the drive behind me. Mark.

"Are you furious? Tell me, are you furious?"

"Get your bike and come with me. I forbid you to set foot here again. Understand?"

The other day, at nightfall, an old gentleman recalled himself to my memory. He died long before I was born, but everyone has heard of him. His name was Bedros Pasha, and he was the father of our famous Bedros Napoleon Pasha.

December 1936: the Christians are celebrating. Bedros has just been appointed Prime Minister. What, have they actually dared hand over the keys of State to an infidel?

June 1937: the inauguration of a school. A young man steps forward in the crowd and stretches out his arm. No one has heard a thing. But a red decoration appears on the Prime Minister's lapel. He is rushed to the Berthome hospital. He dies without regaining consciousness.

June 1937: to avoid trouble, the Prince decides that the Prime Minister shall be buried in the mountain village where the Bedros family comes from.

July 1937: after an inquiry—would you believe it—the murderer turns out to be, not a religious fanatic, but an ordinary mental defective.

November 1937: the accused was so mentally deranged that he killed himself in his cell the night before the hearing.

But we, who are children of a better generation, will settle our affairs at less cost.

Rain over Marsana. Thousands of white frogs are hopping about on the street. Ponds form at intersections, and shouting schoolchildren jump across them.

Rain for the coast, but not inland. The mountain stops it. The Nasr Tower against a winter background. Workmen huddle around a brazier. The huge looming skeleton is just beginning to sheath itself in glass. I've reduced the delay. But we haven't caught up.

Re Tower:

Opinion No. 1 (The Government, the official newspapers, a few forward-looking businessmen): Marsania can be proud of itself for building this skyscraper.

Opinion No. 2 (the intelligentsia): Ghastly!

Opinion No. 3 (I fear I may be the only one to hold this opinion): if we counterbalance it with other, rather more modest towers, it will reveal its beauty.

Opinion No. 4 (the masses): the tower stands in a direct line with Mecca; won't it block the path of our prayers? Nonsense, say the ulemas. Absurd, says the Koranic university. Prayers can pass through concrete, glass and steel.

All the same, certain local prophets mark shaded areas on the town plan. There are good mosques and bad—those whose prayers are occluded by the tower. And, like it or not, attendance at the bad ones begins to fall off.

I slosh through mud to the basement entrance. Workmen are getting on rather halfheartedly.

"Where's your hard hat? Put it on at once. You too."

What's the point of all those safety notices we put up? I fly into a rage. I take the freight elevator to the fourteenth floor. Perched over the void a young worker is welding. He's held back by a leather strap. Thank God he's put his goggles on. But no hard hat. What's got into them all?

As I approach him, I'm overcome with dizziness. But that doesn't stop me from bawling him out.

"What about your head, you fool? On a building job you never know what's going to fall on you."

The young welder stops working and pushes up his goggles. He smiles: "We're all going to die one day, *effendi*."

120

A frail emblem of peace appears in the sky.

One evening, I returned from the site to find a strange character in my office. He introduced himself as private secretary to the Minister of Religious Cults. Stunted, flabby-looking, peering over the tops of his glasses, he made me think of Tartur, the spirit who guards the treasures of the earth.

He was one of those petty potentates who summon their victims, leave them rotting in waiting rooms, and when finally they deign to see them, demand a remuneration (justified perhaps by the meagerness of their official salary). Which made his visit all the more remarkable. And alarming.

"Your scheme has much in its favor, young man. Most original. Rather too original for Marsana, I might add."

I cracked the joints of my fingers.

He had brought along *The Architectural Code,* a monument copied some years previously from European models. Article 47 stated that if a jury turned down a project of real merit, it could—in recognition of the architect's talent—reimburse his expenses. It goes without saying that this clause, designed to encourage the fine arts, was never applied.

"Certain members of the jury favor this solution. They admire your work."

"I didn't get into this affair for the pleasure of being reimbursed for my pencils."

"Of course not. But your expenses would be calculated generously, if you follow me, my young friend."

In other words, I was being bought out. That would give El Souss, my mother and Mark something to smile about.

"How many competitors are still in the running?"

The man made a slight grimace and I had the impression he was about to tell a lie. He thought better of it, realizing that I would learn the truth from someone else: "Two in all. The others have dropped out."

No doubt because of the fee being reduced. My only rival was the vermicelli king!

"Thank you for coming," I said. "And to hell with Article 47."

At bottom, Ruwan was right. What with kowtowing to special interests and conciliating factions, the political machine had ground to a halt. Diversity was killing Marsana. But who would have the strength to put a stop to that?

When I described the scene to Eudoxia, she clapped her hands:

"You're doing all right, Gabriel. If they're trying so hard to make you drop out, it's because they know they'll have to accept your scheme."

I was rather embarrassed at the fanaticism with which she espoused my cause.

"If you weaken now," she added, "I'll take over. You've told me so much about this mosque that I'm sure I could build it."

What's more, she meant it.

Sarun, on the other hand, remained skeptical. He moved about silently and you'd suddenly find yourself confronted with his tall stature, his amused air, his somewhat intimidating benevolence.

"What exactly are you expecting to get out of this caper? Wealth? Glory?"

I mumbled wretchedly, "This mosque could bear witness to a . . . an alliance."

"An alliance. Aren't you going a little too far?"

He sat down and took a paternal attitude.

"I don't think there has ever been an alliance in Marsania," he said after a pause. As was his wont, he spoke slowly, giving the impression that he was groping for the words to express his deepest thoughts. "There have only been deals."

And he swallowed a mouthful of mineral water—the only drink his doctors allowed him.

We were on his veranda, a kind of conservatory where hothouse plants intertwined in wild exuberance. It led to a number of private rooms into which I had ventured only once. Chancing to open a door, I had found myself in the Saruns' bedroom. From the wall paneling, a portrait of the youthful master of the house gazed insolently down at visitors.

"No," said Eudoxia, "that's not my father. It's my youngest uncle, his favorite brother, the one who was killed in an automobile accident."

So it was here, in this far corner of his home, that Sarun kept the undying half of himself, forever reduced to silence.

"There's a golden rule in this country," continued the other half of Sarun, watering the plants with what was left in his carafe, "respect the secret garden of the other party. You're trampling it with your projects."

"God isn't a secret garden," I said. "He's our common possession."

Sarun gazed at the backs of his long, manicured hands, mapped with veins, tendons and freckles. Then he laughed his silent laugh:

"I'm not so sure God would agree with that. For a long while he was a Christian. Nowadays, I can't help wondering if he hasn't become a bit of a Muslim."

And no doubt I would be lumped together with

> *Those who built a mosque from mischievous motives*
> *to spread unbelief and disunite the faithful.*‡

‡ Koran, IX, 107.

123

"If I were you," said Sarun, taking advantage of Eudoxia's brief absence from the room, "I'd negotiate my withdrawal from the competition in exchange for a firm offer of another project. For example, a low-rent housing development. There's a great need of them."

"It's not the same ministry."

"That doesn't matter. Would you like me to arrange it?"

He bent his long, hollow face toward me—his archduke's face, as Safia liked to call it. There was no money for working-class housing. But an appeal was to be made to the Islamic Development Fund.

I shut my eyes and saw the port, with Fannawi's mosque going up: a great upside-down meringue, with swirls of cream and candied fruit.

I would fight, fight and hang the consequences.

That was my frame of mind when Safia appealed to me for help. She was calling from a phone box; she had been crying. Safia crying! I could hardly believe it. She had such a gift for laughing at those who'd wronged her, and for turning their weapons against them.

I had to pick her up outside the El Hosn Cinema. Boys were studying the chicks on the posters. Even emancipated women didn't behave so rashly in Marsana. Safia saw me in the distance and came toward me. She was on time. What was the world coming to?

She led me at once through those passageways that crisscross the old quarters. I noticed that she had twice looked over her shoulder, whereas normally she walked down the street as she walked through life, heedless of what anyone would think or say.

"The Sephardic cemetery has been desecrated," she told me. Her eyes were red from weeping.

Never before had she referred to her origins. She was so independent, so unlike anyone else, that up until then I'd thought of her as if she had been born by her own resources.

I knew the way, which led through the most unfrequented part of the old city: long alleys, getting narrower and narrower, at the end of which there would be a pile of rubble or a little boy playing a solitary game of marbles. We came to an iron gate. A sign indicated the visiting hours. I had never been through that gate; I had been deterred by a barely conscious superstitious belief that air breathed by dead Jews would not be good for live Christians. There were still many people in the city who were convinced witchcraft took place there.

The gate had been padlocked. It was a bit late to be taking precautions. Safia hammered on the sheet metal with her little fist and then it was my turn to look over my shoulder. An old man shuffled up in his slippers. He was intoning, or rather whining, a kind of psalm for the Days of Wrath. Safia addressed a few words to him that I could not understand.

The entrance to the cemetery was shaded by old medlar trees, the yellow fruit of which was formerly eaten only by Jews and today was given to the poor of the city. Inside, tombs shaped like half-cylinders were crowded together with no space between them. The more recent ones bore names and dates. The others, which were merely white-washed, huddled like unbaked loaves ready for the oven.

"Look! Look!" cried Safia.

A saraband of inscriptions ran across those white bellies. I went closer: "One way," "Allah is the greatest," "Let us worship his name."

"It isn't all that serious," I said. "The God of the Koran is also the God of Jacob."

Her smile was pained. No, manifestly that was not what they were telling us. And their moderation only made the threat more menacing. They had refrained from using obvious slogans like: "Death to the Jews." They were disciplined and thoughtful. They were spelling out the future.

"This cemetery is our memory," she said in a changed voice. "We came from Spain, driven out by Queen Isabella, and we were buried here, our hearts full of sorrow. Then our brothers of the black jellaba and plaited hair came from the oases of the South, and they too lie here. And the money changers of Salonica, the goldsmiths of Persia, the rabbis of Babylon. My mother's grandfather rests here. My mother's father. And my mother herself."

Her voice rose and fell as though in a litany. I tried in vain to decipher some of the inscriptions.

"The only one who isn't here," she finished, "is my poor father, who wasn't even Jewish."

That was all I ever learned about her father.

She took her handkerchief and tried to rub the marks off one of the tombs. After a while, she gave up and set a stone on it, as was customary. I piously followed suit. "Maybe our stones will be the last," she said grimly.

A tiny kitten had come running across the tombs. We happened to be barring its way. It sat down and its pink mouth split from ear to ear, as it set up a pitiful miaowing— a little Jewish animal, voicing a ritual lamentation. Woe unto thee O Israel, the gentiles have come, they have sullied the dwelling of thy dead.

It may be that all religions will pass away and be forgotten. But even if the heart of man turns away from them, the most ancient and the most secret of them will remain: the cult of the dead.

"Don't leave me alone," Safia pleaded. "Tomorrow, if you will, but not today."

Her little car was parked on the edge of the old city. She asked me to drive. Her hands were shaking.

126

"God forbid," she said, "that it should be the turn of you Nazarenes tomorrow."

Without a thought for the spying neighbors, she took me to her little white house—the house of happiness—at the foot of the Jeblasan. The servant had gone into town. Blue and brown snakes writhed and twined on a canvas that was still wet.

Taking off her embroidered jacket, she sat down on a rug and began to sing in her wonderful nocturnal voice. Slow, husky singing that rose from deep down in a well. I think I caught some words of old Spanish, the Sephardic language. Her mother, or grandmother, must have taught her these laments. She was Jewish affliction, invincible, intractable, turned in on itself and heavy with the weight of years.

"You think I'm Safia," she said, "but I'm someone else. When I was little, I fell gravely ill. My mother used a remedy that's allowed only in desperate cases: she called in the rabbi to change my name so the angel of death would not recognize his victim."

"What was your name before?"

"If I told you, the angel of death would find me instantly."

Whereupon she burst out laughing like a madwoman and pulled me into her arms.

Random jottings of an evening:
> *Said the jackal to the cock: "Come pray with me."*
>> *Flexible sealing gasket.*
>>> *The suffering common to Jews and Christians is not, ladies and gentlemen, an Islamic virtue.*
>>> *"My camel," he said of his large beat-up car.*
>>> *These almost transparent plums, which were once the pride of the orchard.*

127

In winter, the old negro put on his indigo greatcoat and his fez of the same color; he cut a fine figure.

When the holy man arrived in the wicked village, the villagers, to mock him, served him roast cat.

Awaken, Ismael!

I've been accused of duplicity in connection with my engagement. There was nothing calculated about it. That I swear.

The truth is, I hadn't the strength to hold out. Eudoxia wanted this engagement. Sarun wanted this engagement. Monsignor Elias wanted this engagement. As for me, I no longer knew what I wanted.

The battle for the mosque took up all my energy. Sometimes I wrote down the jurors' names on a piece of paper, and tried to award them marks, from naught to ten, for their degree of favor to my cause. Perhaps I'd be saved by the Saudi Ambassador, who said least and financed most. Unaffected by local quarrels, he had no reason to be anti-Christian as there were no Christians in his country. That should enable him to concentrate on a single criterion: the beauty of the project.

"Think about us a little," said Eudoxia gently when she saw me immersed in such thoughts. "We love each other, don't we? So what are you waiting for?"

"I'm waiting to prove myself. To gain recognition as an architect."

"But I never asked you for that."

This mere child was demanding the solemn promise that we Mozarabs call the half-covenant. It could always be broken; that's the nature of engagements. But everything is brought into play to avert such a calamity: the blessing by

the priest, the songs of fidelity, the ring on the right hand
that will be transferred to the left on the wedding day.

One evening Eudoxia came home very excited.

"It's all arranged. The ceremony will take place a week
from Wednesday."

"Let me at least consult my mother."

"It's done, she's given her consent."

As though to crush any lingering resistance, Monsignor
Elias in person had been mobilized in his cathedral. I felt
too much alone to protest. Moreover, I had thought up a
new argument in favor: as a fiancé, and to all intents and
purposes, a husband, I'd look more respectable to ministers
and members of the jury.

Eudoxia's happiness was a joy to behold. She confessed
that one of their maids, who was something of a geomancer,
had advised her to get engaged on a Wednesday. I laughed
at her. I shouldn't have. Why wouldn't the Lord reveal his
secrets to an old servant?

My mother's happiness was a joy to behold.

Everyone's happiness consisted in putting fetters on me.

The ceremony took place by the light of two candles.
Eudoxia looked pretty, standing alone in her white caftan.
On the wooden gallery above us, invisible children sang
psalm after psalm: songs of minority peoples, songs of light
and shade, with their sinuous melodies and melismas—their
joy tinged with aloes.

In accordance with a recent custom, the fiancée read a
text of her choice. This consisted of boring bits of advice
from *The Book of Tobit*. Eudoxia reeled it off like a frightened schoolgirl. But then came the spark, which cut
through the half-darkness:

For alms deliver from death.

What had made her think of that?

Mar Elias now entered the narrow circle of light. Almost

totally crippled, shrouded in a gold chasuble, he was holding on to one of the servers. But his voice was still strong:

"If there is any couple I am happy to bless, it is this one."

The lights came on again, revealing the Mozarabic arches of the old basilica. Behind the screen stood a canopy topped by a cupola, like a church within a church.

"The West has lost the sense of the sacred," I remember Abuna Pierrot saying. "But Islam has kept it. And the Christians of the East even more so."

I had imagined that Safia would come. But she had not wanted to join in this alien liturgy. She stood waiting on the steps outside, smiling, holding a few flowers.

She kissed Eudoxia and paid me some suitable compliment. I hadn't seen her since the scene in the cemetery. She was trying hard to act as if nothing had happened. But I knew that a rift had come between her and the rest of us. While the guests were piling into the cars, I took her aside.

"You're so intelligent, tell me, is it true that alms deliver from death?"

Straightening the chic little hat she had donned for the occasion, she said, "Only art, Gabriel, can deliver from death."

The people in the cars are getting impatient, the driver is blowing his horn. Damn it, Gabriel's just got engaged. Can he be talking shop again!

"Look at that old girl," says Safia, pointing at the basilica. "She's been giving death the slip for more than a thousand years."

Yes, she's beautiful, the old hussy, huddled in her ditch.

The Saruns are now welcoming their guests. I've asked for things to be kept as simple as possible, but for them simplicity means at least fifty guests. Bay windows, orange wine and potted plants.

Mark has seen fit to come in his scout's uniform. Eudoxia tells me not to be hard on him. Well, I suppose I should be glad the scoutmaster hasn't been invited too. The Saruns believe in keeping connections in all camps.

It'll be a lot worse on our actual wedding day. Eudoxia and I will be standing on a dais, gaped at by the crowds, while the country's most famous danseuses file past with lighted candelabra on their heads.

Toward the end of the evening, Ruwan makes his entrance, perfectly at ease among all these Christians. Our mother catches sight of him and winces, as if she had stepped on a snake. But she can't say a thing, as she's not the mistress of the house. Very pointedly, he beams a big smile at her as he goes by. What a man!

"All alone?"

"Ilena has stopped going out because of her condition."

Her pregnancy isn't that far advanced. But better not pursue the matter.

Slender, elegant, Ruwan is wearing a suit and tie today: quite a concession on his part. I introduce him to Safia, who's been wanting to meet him. She immediately corners him in the most scandalous way. It's only too obvious that she's taken a shine to him. They appear to be talking about painting.

A horde of kids are wandering around the room, strumming on the piano, which should have been locked. Eudoxia pulls up their pants and stuffs them with petits fours: a prefiguration of the big brood she's no doubt looking forward to—for that too is a way of giving alms.

Mark is sitting at her feet like a page, trying to interest her in the workings of the Kalashnikov. This 7.62-caliber miracle weapon can be dismounted in a matter of minutes, whereas its American rival, the M16 takes an hour. Eudoxia laughs as if it were a game.

Safia has at last released Ruwan. I go over to her.

"Have you found the man of your life?"

"Don't be jealous, angel, it's vulgar."

She is airily smoking a *Vizir* (Sarun Brothers Ltd.).

"However," she adds, "it's not the private individual that interests me, it's his political side."

She's overdoing it. This leader of some mini-sect!

"Incidentally, he's even more dangerous than I'd thought."

"How do you know? You did all the talking."

"Tut, tut. You were watching?"

A Mozarab portrait of Christ has been placed in a niche at the end of the room. The face is the color of sleep. Jesus of Galilee, your sufferings for this worthless world are over. Before you're laid in the earth, your eyes, according to the custom, will be closed with pieces of silver, the very ones you wanted to render unto Caesar.

"Have you heard the latest?" Safia goes on. "Berrebbi's quitting. He's liquidating."

He's the richest Jew in the country (the brewery, the esparto-pulp factory).

"Where's he off to?"

"He's retiring, to the Lake of Geneva."

Hell, Berrebbi isn't that old. And he must have sons or nephews. If he's selling out cheap, then he's afraid.

"Guess who he's offered his business to. The Sarun brothers."

"The Saruns will refuse."

She looks me up and down ironically, as if to say, just as well you've got me to keep you in the picture.

"Don't you believe it, Gabriel. If need be, they'll borrow from the devil to buy it. It's too tempting."

She enjoys these odd stories. She may even exaggerate them. A waiter is handing around glasses of a dark liquid called *karkadi*.

"But wait till you hear this. According to the chief of police, it was the Saruns who sent their thugs to desecrate

132

the cemetery. The idea being to terrify the Jews and buy them out cheap."

For us, Easter is not just a holiday. It's the day when we take stock of ourselves, when we remember that we are different. Easter is the life-giving wine that we lay in for the whole year.

You Westerners like to paint the Agony of Christ. We, I believe, are somewhat ashamed of this episode. We prefer to depict the glory of Easter.

Not so long ago, we had our own date for Easter, different from that of the Latin church. But the situation became untenable. "Do you resurrect your Christ twice?" the Muslims asked. A synod unified the calendars. The monasteries of the South wrote "Easter or death" above their gates. Then they gave in.

The ceremony is even more beautiful in the country. I can remember the office of the *Tenebrae* at Qasrum, with old Nasrallah handing the fire to the horsemen on the steps of his church. Each one would gallop off, torch in hand, to a Christian village in the mountains to relight the lamps.

"This year," say the people, "there will be no singing for Easter. There will be no Easter presents. No Easter Masses. Pass the word around."

This is Mar Elias's way of reacting to the growing numbers of incidents: the flogging on El-Tor Street, the three wounded Christians in Manzil-el-Jedid. For the first time since the desecration of the basilica by Sultan El Mostansir, the Christians of Marsania will wear mourning on Easter Day.

And the Minister of Religious Cults needn't bother to come at eleven o'clock to the basilica to pay his compliments to the archbishop-exarch, as he has done each year

133

since 1124. And the provincial governors needn't bother to pay their compliments to the senior clergy. We want no more of your smiles.

His Excellency Dr. Samiel immediately summons the influential liberals of our community in the hope that they will get this stupid old archbishop to change his mind:

"I regret to inform you that the Government regards this as a slap in the face."

Good Lord! When we were only trying to remind them that the Constitution recognizes certain rights: the right to fresh air and sunshine. . . . And tell me, what business is it of the Government what Christians do, or do not do, in their churches?

Little Samiel brushes these objections aside. Freedom of worship is not the issue. What worries him is the country's morale. The archbishop has spread alarm and despondency. What exactly are these threats he's going on about? What are these famous "incidents"? Have you read about them in the press?

"The Government," he goes on imperturbably, "through the instrumentality of the Ministry of Religious Cults, is the guarantor and enlightened protector of all recognized religions. Its duty is to safeguard all religious freedom. And cancellation of the Easter ceremonies is a serious offense against the freedom of your Church."

An outrageous statement, worthy of this grinning little cynic, backed up as he was by a long tradition of meddling in our affairs. It's true, the State is the big brother of our Church. It pays our priests a salary (in compensation for confiscated church property). It can oppose the election of a bishop, close a temple . . .

The assemblage sits down. Dr. Samiel sends for the inevitable coffee, with green nougat, and begins cajoling and flattering. Yes, my friends, you can count on the protection of the Palace against all violence, from whatever source.

134

"Thank you, your Excellency," replies the most courageous of those listening, "but the terrorists of February 11 are still at large."

"No police force in the world is perfect. We are pursuing our inquiries."

"On El-Tor Street, you arrested a couple of terrorists, but you let them go."

"Nothing was proved against them," murmurs the Doctor. "But for the Manzil-el-Jedid crime, we are holding someone."

"An illiterate stooge. Nobody bothered the leaders."

"Ah, so you know who they are? That's interesting. Tell me their names?"

When Bedros Napoleon Pasha described the scene to me, there was a catch in his voice. He had tried in vain for a reasonable compromise.

The next day, we learn that the Latin archbishop will be celebrating Easter after all—the dear man had promised to stand by the Mozarabs—moreover, he had good reason to do so, for Latin shop windows had been broken on Nebi-Moussa Street; a Latin cyclist beaten black and blue behind the Fish Pools. Suddenly he has changed his mind. All it took was a phone call from a minister. Ah Samiel!

Two prominent Mozarabs even agree to go to Damascus with a letter from the Government. Damascus, the seat of our spiritual leader, His Beatitude Meletios III, patriarch of Antioch, Alexandria, Jerusalem and all the East. The letter invites him to depose his unworthy son, Elias, for offending against the dogma and traditions of our Church.

In our homes, we hold our breath, we lock ourselves in, we count the days to Easter. Rumor has it that on the morning of the Resurrection the Army will open the churches by force. And what will Mar Elias do then? He'll probably pronounce the anathema on the two messengers. Not a bit of it; he orders public prayers to be said for them. Which is more insulting.

There was a new softness in the air and the flowers in the gardens had burst into bloom. Spring had come.

"Why don't we take a trip to Broad Bean Hill on Sunday," Eudoxia suggested. I owed her at least that much.

Harlequin Hill would be more like it: a Mozarab village on one hilltop, a Latin hamlet on another, a handful of Muslim houses in the valley. The people lived on reasonably good terms, except for an occasional boundary dispute or private quarrel.

The driver of our bus, a member of the Latin church, had stuck a Sacred Heart on his dashboard, framed in the words: *Et verbum caro factum est.* But this didn't protect us against a white-bearded preacher, who got on the bus before it started and extorted our small change in the name of Islam. Then, as the engine roared into life, most of the passengers crossed themselves. It put one in mind of a pleasant Sunday-school outing.

The bus wound its way between the burgeoning foothills. Not an inch of land was wasted: terraces of almond trees, squares of the purple medic, or alfalfa, beloved of agronomists, in the most inhospitable corners prickly pears and, standing out from the rest of the vegetation, the bluish skeletons of the fig trees, always so slow to put on their plumage.

In the Muslim zone, men were sowing spring seeds. In the Christian sector they were celebrating the Lord's day smoking and drinking coffee in front of their houses.

Huddled on her seat, the old woman next to us was burning incense sticks—against bus-sickness, I presume. When she moved her arm, I saw she had a watch tattooed on her wrist: less expensive than a real one and every bit as esthetic.

We continued our expedition on foot. Eudoxia cried out in delight at everything she saw: here a henna mill, there a little girl swinging herself, who shouted a greeting at us; farther on a group of white herons in a field, as motionless as votive stones.

In among the poles, we could see the pods of peas and beans. We are apt to disparage this humble food. As the proverb says: *Beans are the emir's breakfast, the farmer's lunch and the ass's dinner.* But our mother knew how to prepare them. She'd cook them all night in a crock under the ashes and serve them to us with butter and salt.

Minarets rose up like candles from the greenery. The countryside was dotted with whitewashed marabout tombs, and small Mozarab chapels, each with its modest icon in it. A landscape marked and fashioned by men's faiths till it too became a prayer.

"You don't say anything," Eudoxia protested. "All you can think of is your architecture."

We had come to a small square house. An enormous mimosa crowned it with a cap of gold, which almost hid the wall on our side. Below the house, the slope grew steeper, but was cultivated all the way down to a colorless sea.

"This is where I'd like to live," she said. "You'd go into town every day. Shall we buy the house?"

I shook my head. The peasants in these parts are especially unwilling to sell. The sun tried to break through. We felt the heat in our damp clothes. Three or four storks flew lazily inland. But we were not Roman enough to interpret the oracle.

"Let's explore our property," she suggested.

The other side was defaced by large, clumsily written black letters. *Tri . . .* or *Tari . . . Tariq wahid:* one way.

Eudoxia looked bitterly disappointed. She sighed, went

up to the stone. "Hatred is powerless against prayer," she said. "Hatred is powerless against love."

Poor little girl, caught up in the games of men.

A messenger has left an envelope. I turn it over and over. *Prime Minister.* What magic vapor will escape from it?

His Excellency, Dr. Samiel in person, asks me to come and see him. That can only mean one thing: he himself wants to tell me I've won the competition.

A rap on the knuckles for the Christians, then a pat on the head for one Christian. A standard ploy. So standard I'm surprised I didn't see it coming.

To me, Samiel is a name rather than a face. He holds that the limelight saps power and is seldom seen at functions or on television. But he is not averse to conversing with his humble subjects when, as in the *Thousand and One Nights,* his agents bring them to the palace. A shrewd politician: twice fallen from favor, twice restored to favor. He manages to please both monarch and Parliament. He is widely thought to be a convert to Islam. And, to top it all, a patron of the arts, and it's in that capacity that I had the honor of meeting him.

The soldier at the gate waves me through. For some time now, the so-called *white* and the so-called *black* regiments have alternated on guard duty. The sentry today is a *white,* sporting a black beret and black Sam Browne belt.

His Excellency withdraws his hand with a laugh when I make as if to kiss it. The first thing about him that strikes you, aside from his diminutive stature, is his ears; they're too big, though delicately shaped, and seem to tremble with a life of their own. They, perhaps, are the real seat of his intelligence.

138

"I've heard about you," the great man begins amiably. From Sarun, no doubt. Perhaps from Safia as well.

I decline the proffered cigar. He lights one himself, crosses his plump legs. Ruwan says he's an oriental Metternich: brilliant talker, but devious, always finding good reasons for maintaining the status quo. Once you tear your eyes away from those ears, the face too is interesting: shrewd, despite a certain puffiness, sallow, pierced by intense little black eyes. Like his niece, or alleged niece, Safia, he looks as though he'd come out of the workshop of a proficient miniaturist.

"Now then," he says, as if he were talking to a child, "are you really set on building this brotherly mosque?"

I don't think he believes in brotherhood—or in freedom, justice or any such moonshine. He sees the people as a huge beast, docile and dangerous, which able dwarfs are leading down a slippery path. Now and again, one of the dwarfs gets gored. Samiel, it's plain, has no wish to be the next victim.

He pretends to consult the file that has been prepared for him, puts on his glasses, but takes them off again with an impatient gesture.

"Certain ulemas object to the shape of your building, which would oblige the faithful to pray in a triangle."

"What would they say if I made them pray in an octagon?"

I spread out a plan of the Dome of the Rock in Jerusalem. The prayer chamber is indeed eight-sided, and the whole of the center, bordered by a balustrade, is taken up by the sacred rock. The worshippers can't even see one another.

"Well played!" Samiel comments, snapping his fingers. "I hope you'll soon be asked to rebuild the Dome of the Rock to a more orthodox design."

Since the quarrel about Easter, which still holds our little world in suspense, the Prime Minister has become a bogeyman for the Christians. Others call him amiably "the gnome." But neither of these nicknames quite suits him. He's more of a maestro. And, come to think of it, what is he a doctor of? He has never been known to treat a patient.

The soldier brings in coffee with ginger. Samiel barely touches his. I can see why; it's the end of the day and this must be his fifteenth cup. Maybe they keep warming the same one up.

"I shall be perfectly frank," he says, raising his doll's hands. "Your scheme is the best. The others aren't worth a fig."

So he's taken the time to form an opinion of his own, in defiance of his advisers. Perhaps, like Safia, he worships only beauty. It's rumored that he has a superb private art collection.

"However, my friend, talent is not enough. The circumstances must also be right. Your project comes at the worst possible moment. Islam is seething with unrest."

He speaks reasonably enough. Still, I catch a note of fear in his voice, the mahout's fear when the elephant he thinks he has tamed suddenly shows signs of madness. Sparkle and dance as you may, Samiel, I've heard your fear.

"Exactly, your Excellency. We must make Islam an offering: it's now or never."

Show it that even a Christian dog can understand it and love it. But I won't put it like that. Words have lied too much; their credit has run out. I'll say it with stones, with stones and nothing else.

Samiel's face lights up; here's his opening for a witticism.

"As I see it," he says, "you want to prove to them, with walls, that there is no wall." And he ends with a tinkle of crystalline laughter. I go calmly on:

"In reducing my fee, the jury actually did me a service. I'll be losing money. No one will be able to accuse me of being out for gain."

140

"True enough. They'll accuse you of being a fanatic, of trying to encroach on the true religion."

Oh no, I can fend off that charge. I've brought along some documents that support my historical rights to build this mosque. And I enlarge on the subject, ignoring my interlocutor's looks of disapproval.

I speak of the first sanctuaries built by Islam in conquered lands, with columns taken from churches or from even older temples. I speak of the mihrab, the famous alcove which points toward Mecca. It is modeled on Coptic churches.

I can't even be sure he's listening. He takes bits of paper out of his pockets, glances at them, then reduces them to incredibly small pieces, which he puts in a saucer placed beside him for this purpose. I stop and he looks up.

I speak of churches that have been turned into mosques. The best known of these is the church of the Holy Wisdom (mistakenly called Saint Sophia), but there are other examples: Cordoba, Damascus, Diyarbakir, the great mosque of Beirut, the Halawiyia in Aleppo. I cite the portals of the cathedral built by the crusaders in Acre, which were taken down and put up again in Cairo. In those days, Islam took its material where it found it. Why not today?

The cigar is burning away in the ashtray. His Excellency observes me, the lids half down over his darting little eyes. "Put your notes in order and send them to me," he says.

The usual politician's ruse to play for time. My dear fellow, make me a report.

After that, of course, I put away my second document: Le Corbusier, the Huguenot, building a Catholic church at Ronchamp; Bach, the Lutheran, taking the liberty of writing a *Magnificat* and a *Mass in B minor;* Fauré, the unbeliever, begging God to welcome the dead; Montherlant, the pagan, who couldn't help speaking the language of Christianity on stage. One night in Cincinnati I had spoken of these things with a group of friends from different nations, and come

141

home with my head on fire as though foreseeing that a mosque was soon to fall to my lot. But let's avoid these Western references that might damage my cause.

As for mentioning that Ruwan is my brother-in-law . . . His Excellency undoubtedly knows. He must also know that Ruwan won't lift his little finger for my project.

"Put the different maquettes on show," I say in a blank voice. "Let the public choose."

"Yours would be destroyed before the day is out."

"Well then, ask the Prince Regent to settle the dispute."

I looked at the great gloomy portrait hanging on one of the walls of the room. Samiel smiles. The Prince Regent, as everyone knows, is only interested in falconry.

"I'll tell you this much, Jibril. One of the things I regret about my years as a Minister is that I've never had anything of beauty built. Everything that has been built has been commonplace and vulgar. Charity forbids me to mention the Nasr Tower that you've had a hand in. And now, for the first time, I've been shown something I like."

He gets up and paces the floor. He seems to be talking to himself.

"I loved this country. I loved these different colored wools that get entangled, but whose colors never run. I sometimes had the impression that I was weaving them together. Their contrasts highlighted their beauty. Then, one day, the Muslim thread came out of the weft. The fabric has gradually been coming undone. Pull it, and it will all fall apart."

I can't help looking for the offending thread in his office carpet. Samiel sits down again, giving me a last chance to admire his wonderful tactile ears. He's moving in for the kill:

"Jibril, your candidacy is causing discord. Tomorrow, it will cause trouble. I'm afraid I'm asking you to withdraw it."

"I will not withdraw it, your Excellency."

The floor tilts beneath my feet, hurling me into the pit where the bones of the presumptuous are whitening. My skull bangs against a stone wall. I see stars. No, not at all, I'm sitting in the Napoleon III chair facing Samiel, who's looking at me with commiseration.

"I want the jury to turn me down publicly," I stammer. "I want it to take the responsibility, in front of everyone, of choosing the rival scheme."

Samiel shrugs. The jury is divided, it won't decide anything. The project will rot, the sponsors will get tired of waiting. The Government cannot risk such a fiasco. What a mule this little Christian is!

"The next church to be built will be reserved for a Muslim architect. I give you my word."

But that's not for me to say. And there may not be a next church. The duty soldier comes in with a note announcing the next visitor. Samiel seizes it scornfully and rolls it up:

"My dear fellow, I've already been too good to you."

He's right; giving so much of his time to a young puppy. I should have thanked him profusely.

"Furthermore, I could put pressure on you and your family. I've broken stronger backs than yours."

That's also true. With the arsenal of rusty laws and tortuous decrees that are the pride of Marsania, it's easy to stop an architect from building the smallest hut.

"But I'm going to give you a chance. Find yourself a good partner."

"I've had one for ages."

For a moment I had forgotten that El Souss had backed out of the project.

"You haven't caught my meaning. Find yourself a partner just for this project. You may be able to sail under his flag."

Nonchalantly, he's put a tiny visiting card on the table. I can take it or leave it.

I bend down. *Yunis, son of Yunis, architect.* It could have been worse.

Motionless, Samiel waits for my answer.

"I'll take it, your Excellency."

Let's hope he did not notice my violent trembling as I left.

Greenish drizzle veils the waters of the harbor. I want to hate this scheming dwarf who has imposed his will on me, but I surprise something like gratitude in my heart.

This week, the birds of the South have been flying up toward Europe. Each morning I've stood on our balcony looking at their squadrons through my binoculars. Their exodus seemed unending. The world was showing me one of its secret veins.

The two traitors returned from Damascus, having failed utterly. The reply they brought with them was not published.

Black Sunday came and went; the Government didn't budge. The pessimists had had visions of army, police, mobs of fanatics. Nothing happened. Christian workers and Christian civil servants went to work as usual—since the official day of rest in Marsania is Friday. The Christian shopkeepers closed their shutters a little earlier than usual. Then a few prayers were said behind closed doors.

> *Oh God, calm the tempest*
> *And bring us to the haven.*

On Easter Monday, Mark was brought home in an ambulance. He'd been on his way to a Scout meeting with two of his pals. On their way through a tough suburb, they were spotted because of their blue scarves, attacked and pulled off their bicycles. It was bound to happen one day. Mark had a dislocated shoulder. My triumph was modest:

"You see what happens when you go to Scout meetings."

Our mother said nothing. Next day, Mark was running around our neighborhood parading his arm in a sling.

On the Thursday of Easter week, we heard that Monsignor Elias had been deposed. A serious step, but not without precedent. Under the Ottoman Empire, an exarch had been removed from office for failing to collect an emergency tax. More fortunate than his predecessor, our pastor was only exiled to a mountain parish a dozen or so miles away.

Oddly enough, the Forty Brothers and other firebrands didn't fan this particular flame. Their newssheets merely reported the official communication, as if to say, "Let us keep out of these sordid quarrels."

Everybody was talking about the succession. Maybe the Palace would appoint the Metropolitan Matti, who had shown himself to be more diplomatic. Or perhaps . . . "You can't really think . . ." "Oh yes, the Prince Regent wants to appoint Monsignor Carmel."

He was the Latin archbishop who had prudently celebrated Easter. He would wear the two miters, the Latin and the Mozarab, thus ending a thousand years of discord. There could be no juridical objection: we held the same beliefs as the Latins; only the rites and sensibilities differed. Actually, this forced merger was the best way to revive old antipathies. Divide and rule.

I don't know what put a stop to this admirable plan. Possibly Carmel himself had scruples. In Marsania, reforms were rarely carried through. With the help of messengers, Monsignor Elias went on running his little church. A deposed archbishop who was still in post. We enjoyed that kind of situation.

145

Yunis's waiting room. Piled on a tray are back numbers of *Domus,* the Italian architectural magazine. Why do people call our friend a yokel? He's thoroughly in the swim. But the magazines are covered with scribblings, obviously the work of little hands.

"My fourth," says Yunis proudly. "He's interested in architecture."

*"Mabruk!"**

When we're summoned together, the jury will like Yunis because of the callous on his forehead. I too see it as a token of the man's excellence. When I have to choose between several workers, or shopkeepers, I always pick the one who bears the mark of piety.

"I'm sure you know the reason for my visit."

"Won't you explain it all the same?" he replies cautiously.

I unroll the copies of my plans on his rug. He examines the sections and elevations, sheet by sheet. We're unceremoniously down on all fours.

"I've already told you, I like your project," he says. "But you don't need any help."

"There you're wrong. It'll take at least two to put all that into shape."

As though this had been his cue, he points out one or two minute weaknesses. We'll correct them together. Samiel has definitely made the right choice.

On his wall hangs the lithograph of the Kaaba that you find in every humble home. His boy sucks his thumb and stares at me. Yunis shakes his head. He too longs for this white ship that will fill its sails with the wind of God.

"One more question, Gabriel. You could build any number of things. Why, exactly, did you choose a mosque?"

* Congratulations.

The word Christian has not been uttered, any more than it was by the jury. But he constantly hovers around it. That's really what's bothering Yunis. He suspects me of some devilry.

"I saw this mosque in a dream," I said. "I won't rest until it's built."

Only God sends such dreams. And He speaks to whom He will. This time He has deigned to speak to a Christian.

"Give me a day to think about it," Yunis begs.

While taking my leave, I think about the formalities: I'll have to add his name to the plans and to the letter of application, pretending it's a new project and deceiving no one. But the jurors won't say a word; they'll be only too happy to be offered an acceptable product. If they'd liked the vermicelli mosque, they'd have taken it long ago.

Yunis hasn't even mentioned his fee.

That evening, at the Saruns', I explain the situation. The master of the house is away on a business trip.

"I'd rather you won by yourself," says Eudoxia. "For the glory of it. But it's more sensible this way."

Her latest spell of night duty has left dark rings under those enormous eyes. Eudoxia, my friend, I'll end up loving you.

"Last night," she goes on without a break, "a road casualty was brought in, a workman."

"Young and handsome," puts in Safia with a twinkle. She's like that. Whenever she finds a man to her taste, she comes right out with it. She doesn't do it to shock, but out of a certain artistic impartiality.

Eudoxia blushes.

"Shut up, Safia. There's nothing funny about the end of the story. When the young man saw the little cross on my wrist, he wouldn't let me treat him. 'I'd sooner die,' he said."

147

"So why not just let him die in the corner?" That had slipped out of me.

Eudoxia exploded, "You talk without thinking!"

Luckily. If we had to think all the time, we'd end up with an awful headache.

The next day, Yunis calls up. His rustic accent is more striking than usual. Is it the telephone or his emotion? Whatever it is, he's very embarrassed. He beats about the bush until I come to his rescue.

"Well, Yunis, has someone warned you off our project?"

Yunis admits as much. Whoever can have done him this bad turn within twenty-four hours? I don't know why, but I seem to see the sharp face and thin lips of Sheik Talaat.

"Do you want a bit longer to think it over?"

"I'm sorry, it's no use. I've got a wife and kids."

He's really suffering. I almost feel sorry for him.

"It's been nice knowing you, Yunis. May God guide your pencil."

Calm and desperate, I'm about to hang up. But I can hear him breathing.

"I'm ashamed for our country," he finally blurts out.

At long last, we put the finishing touches to the En Nasr Tower: its robe of pale blue glass was complete. As was the custom, the promoters organized a *meshui*.

This wasn't a mere celebration; it was a sacrifice to the powers of darkness, for in our country, all new buildings must be consecrated with an offering. In the old days, the mortar had to be mixed with the blood of a prisoner of war. In the case of our tower, we couldn't get away with fewer than twelve sheep.

My friend Pierrot and the learned hajji Ayub had promised to come and bless the building, each according to his rite. But Ayub wasn't on time, the Secretary of State for Public Works grew impatient and I had to resign myself: Ayub wasn't going to come. In the end, he'd been afraid to give his blessing to this prayer-deflecting skyscraper.

The signal was given, the rejoicings began. The weather was superb. The workers grabbed handfuls of meat off the spits and covered their faces with juice.

"Well, my boy," said the great Sarun, "you're free at last."

"There's still the plumbing and wiring."

"That's practically nothing. Now you can take on something else."

A joke in bad taste. He knew all about my setbacks.

"You'll see," he said with an air of mystery. Then he left me.

A number of society ladies asked to go up to the top floor. I handed out hard hats. The elevator, which had given us some trouble, was in a good humor. The view made the expedition worthwhile: on one side the successive tiers of the city dominated by the commanding presence of the Jeblasan; on the other, a graceful chain of lagoons swollen by the rains of the past weeks.

When I came down, I ran into Red Truck, the contractor, wearing a dinner jacket at four in the afternoon. He slapped me heartily on the back. The penalty clause seemed forgotten.

"I hear you're going to build a mosque," he said eagerly.

"Sure. The whole town knows."

Sarcasm. It took sarcasm to keep me going. Puzzled, Red Truck began scratching a wart on his head.

"If you want to get ahead, Red Truck, do like me: sign up with Muhammad the Prophet."

I don't know what prescience prompted me to say that. Red Truck looked at me with stupefaction. He was prepared for any villainy but that.

149

As a result of this social function, I got my picture in the country's biggest newspaper, between the Japanese architect and Ibrahim El Souss.

"There's glory for you," said my partner kindly.

But it left a strange taste in my mouth.

"Help me, Ruwan."

He took my hand, as cordial as ever. I told him about my latest setbacks. He listened gravely. But I'd swear he already knew about them.

"Of course I'll help you," he says.

I'd been lucky finding him. I couldn't get hold of him on the telephone. So I went to his house after dinner.

"This undertaking of yours is rather insane," he observes.

"But you approved of it!"

"I neither approved nor disapproved. It was your business. To tell the truth, your audacity appealed to me. Today, I'm more aware of the obstacles."

This cautious tone was unlike him. We've gone out on the terrace of the corsairs' house. A servant has brought a small brazier. The two of us are sitting on the ground, I in my Western overcoat, he in the brown wool jellaba that he's been affecting lately.

"This mosque," I say, "will set the seal on our unity. The Muslims will know that a Christian has worked for their faith."

"I hope you're right," Ruwan replies. "But I fear there may be adverse reactions. Some people are already saying that the Christians are too pushy."

The spring night is clear, amazingly clear. The sea is a cloth of silver, beyond the roofs. One by one, the sounds of the city die away.

"And some," he adds, "will say that your part in it would offend God."

"Nonsense! Don't we believe in the same God?"

"That's been a moot point for a long time. For my part, I'm willing to agree with you. But I can't speak for others."

He's put his hands in his sleeves, and the darkness makes his face invisible inside the pointed hood.

"You know, Gabriel, there's only one solution. You must come over to our side."

"You mean join your party?"

"We have no party. You must join Islam."

At last he's come out with it. From now on those words would weigh on us both.

"Islam is our country's future," Ruwan goes on, his voice a semi-tone higher. "Nobody will be forced to join, but those who don't will not be able to make their full contribution. You are a case in point."

He gets up to stir the coals in the *qanun,* his face glows in the firelight. I stretch my legs.

"It's impossible, Ruwan. You know that."

"Why is it impossible? Basically, there's only one difference: for us, Jesus is a man. He was a just and good man who spoke forcefully and revered God. He'd be more surprised than anyone to see himself on your altars."

The neighbors' light has just gone out. I try to figure out where, in this jumble of squat houses, our home on Salt Street is.

"Come, Gabriel, be honest for a moment. Are you so sure about the divinity of Jesus? Are you ready to die for it?"

"I thought Christians wouldn't be harassed in your Islamic republic."

"I've said that and I'll say it again. But think it over. You Christians keep saying that Christ died for your sins. If he was really God, that wasn't much of a sacrifice. He knew he

151

had nothing to fear. Your story only makes sense if Jesus was a man."

A pointless discussion in any case, since according to the Koran this death never took place. At the last moment, the crucified Christ was gathered up to heaven. He was spared the final ordeal because he had been a good servant. That's Islam in a nutshell: being a good servant.

"I bet you never even went to church in America," Ruwan goes on. "Your religion is nothing but loyalty to your clan."

Thirteen hundred years of loyalty, despite persecutions and occasional pogroms.

"What's more, Gabriel, if you'd been born in a Muslim family, you'd be a Muslim. You'd say what I've been saying."

"That argument can work both ways. You could have been born as diehard a Christian as I am."

I've scored a point there. A light breeze springs up and sends a shudder through us.

"If I'd been born a Christian," he says after a pause, "I hope I'd have enough sense to realize that Marsania is a Muslim country."

No, old fellow, don't oversimplify.

"Listen, Ruwan, I have a proposal to make: an alliance— the House of the Prophets will be its pledge—against all forms of mediocrity, dullness and stupidity."

He's absently nibbling salted melon pips. "It's too late, Gabriel," he says at last. "For generations we had to put up with the arrogance of the Christians. Those of the West, and their allies here. They took our religion for mummery. If this alliance you're talking about had been suggested at that time, I'm not saying . . . But don't come proposing it at a time when you are retreating on all fronts."

He's holding the colonialism of the White Fathers against me. For two pins he'd hold the Crusades against me.

152

"Christianity has had its day," he adds. "Look, the world is turning away from it."

Out to sea, the Taffarines lighthouse flashes on and off—Islamic green. And farther away, much farther, another lighthouse, a Christian lighthouse, answers with a long, pale gleam.

"What do you see out there? Countries that call themselves Christian. Selfishness, materialism, injustice. In short, failure. Don't throw in your lot with them."

I stand up. "Ruwan, I'm leaving, before we quarrel."

"As you please. I don't expect you to make up your mind this evening. I ask you only to remember my words."

"There's no danger I'll forget them, my friend."

"One day, I'm certain, you will come over to our side. You'll be welcomed with open arms. And if the Christians want to punish you, we'll protect you against them."

I leave, my mouth full of bitterness and stifled screams. I return home along the narrow, bleached streets, while somewhere a madman is shooting at the moon.

We're finishing our meal. It's Mark's turn to say grace, which he does with a disarming mischievousness. I'm sure his high spirits are more pleasing to the Almighty than sighs.

Going over my head, our mother has let him go back to the Scouts. She regards this as a little revenge on the Muslims for stealing her beloved Ilena.

No sooner has he closed the door than she turns on me: "So, your friend Ruwan has let you down!"

How has she found out about my last visit? Can some slight smell of Islam have clung to my clothes?

"Ruwan has a debt to us," she goes on.

"Perhaps."

153

"A very precise debt. Have you forgotten the Law of Muharram?"

She's been waiting for the right moment to thrust home. In the past, when a Mozarab girl married a Muslim, it was the brother's duty to kill the guilty man. Then, to staunch the flow of blood, a law was promulgated in the month of Muharram. It stated that the Muslim boy's family had to pay financial compensation to the family of the Christian girl, over and above the usual marriage gifts. The sum is fixed out of court, or by a mixed tribunal.

The Law of Muharram was a considerable step forward, but it has largely fallen into disuse nowadays. Except in rural districts, the injured parties are afraid to invoke it.

"We don't need money so badly, now that I'm El Souss's partner."

"That's no reason for forgoing our rights," she replies.

She can be conciliatory as long as no one but herself is involved, but where the family's honor or interests are at stake, she's intransigent. In my father's day, she had to fight for two; he didn't give a fig for our interests. Now it's become an obsession with her.

"Ilena and Ruwan are happy together," I say.

"Yes, happy at our expense."

"By the way, they're expecting . . . she's expecting a child."

She shuts the sideboard quickly. You can see that she's torn. In the East, as elsewhere—more perhaps than elsewhere—we rejoice at the news of offspring. But this little Muslim, who will grow up on the other side of a wall . . . Born of an invalid marriage. This little bastard!

"It will be a boy, of course," she says derisively. A boy, an oppressor, who in his turn will carry off a Christian girl. And this will go on till there are no Christians left.

The ubiquitous Mark has come back into the room and is

154

hanging around like a pet animal, listening to things unsuitable for one of his age.

"I want us to be respected," she declares, "as we were in your father's day."

"We'll be respected when . . ."

I was about to say when I marry Eudoxia. She would accept that sort of argument.

"When I've turned what's in my head into buildings."

"I'll be dead long before that," our mother replies.

She slowly takes off her apron, sprinkles a little water from a ewer on the floor tiles, looks around to make sure I haven't moved and starts in anew: "It's obvious that you're not really the eldest of the family."

She's referring to a son whom her other children never knew. This child, endowed with the greatest gifts, was carried off by measles at the age of two. Our mother has worn mourning ever since. She went to parties in black, gave birth to us in black. Every one of our shortcomings, every one of our bad marks is greeted with, "Oh no, Zacharius wouldn't have done that."

I can't stand any more. I decide to walk around town till I drop with exhaustion. To hell with the subcontractor who's waiting for me at the office.

It's not really with our mother that I'm angry. I'm angry with Ruwan, who calls himself my friend and who's exploiting my unhappiness.

I'm angry with Ruwan, who went to the Lazarist Fathers' school with me and who is now biting the hands that fed him.

I'm protesting Ruwan's living with my sister in contempt of our rights.

The sun is going down, red, weak and sick-looking. My wanderings have taken me into a suburb where there's nothing but huts and rubble. Garbage is being burned along the street, and a pall of disgusting smoke hangs over the whole area. Tell-el-Mahruq, the burned hill.

It was once the garden of the dead. Well-to-do city families had built a pretty village of square tombs, topped with round calottes. They came visiting in their barouches. They prayed, sat about on the grass and picnicked. But in the end the caretakers of the tombs betrayed them. For a few coins, they rented these funerary habitations to the living, and the place became a slum.

My father's burial at Babeluq . . . We bury our dead no later than the second day. But the coffin stays open till the absolution so that the mourners may kiss the hand of the departed. Ruwan came, the only Muslim, or just about. Cordial, dashing in his cadet's uniform. He didn't kiss the corpse's hand, but gave me a friendly slap on the back. He knew how to play it just right. And instead of weeping with our mother, Ilena couldn't take her eyes off him.

"In Arabia," he'd say, "no stone, no stele marks the place of the dead. The camel driver passes over the king's sepulcher without knowing it."

In Marsania, on the other hand, as in all Mediterranean countries, young Islam found an ancient cult of the dead and had to come to terms with it. But one day, maybe it will be strong enough to cast off these borrowings and become purely itself.

Night descends on the necropolis and with it a sense of danger. I head for the road. Taxi? You must be joking. There are no taxis in Tell-el-Mahruq.

All the same, a little while later, as I'm stumbling among the stones on the soft shoulder, a big car comes cruising along the road. I flag it down on the off chance. It stops. As in a dream, Eudoxia's voice, "We've been looking all over for you, Gabriel. If you could see yourself!"

Yes, I know: disheveled, tie to one side, shoes covered with dust. I sink back on the upholstery with relief.

156

"I got the hospital to change my shift," Eudoxia goes on.

The aviator has also taken his car and is looking on the other side of the town with Mark.

"Why this commotion?"

"They were worried at the office when you didn't show up. They gave the alarm. I was scared."

"Scared of what, for heaven's sake?"

She's afraid to put it into words. The Muslim chauffeur drives slowly on the winding road. Two symbols dangle side by side from the rearview mirror: his Koranic amulet and the little cross he was asked to add for good measure.

"What made you think of going to Tell-el-Mahruq?"

"I asked the shoeshine boys. One of them had seen you go by. He said you were talking to yourself. We were terribly worried."

I can't help it, I'm annoyed with her for coming to my rescue, as if I wasn't old enough to take care of myself. And for involving Mark and his bigmouth Scoutmaster in a strictly private matter.

"Walk up! Walk up!" cries the barker on the esplanade. "Come and see the most tattooed man in the world."

While I was busy quarreling with everybody and with myself, the city brought me Timsit.

I was hardly doing anything just then. The En Nasr Tower was finishing itself, and I was still waiting, sadly, for my hopes to be finally dashed.

I'd taken to leaving the office in the middle of the afternoon. El Souss was afraid to say anything. I'd wander aimlessly through the familiar little streets, through porticoes and along passageways. At that season, the fountains were still playing, and I could recognize them all with my eyes closed, for each sang its own song in the balmy air of our short spring.

When you came from the modern quarters, the first was Drink-and-Pray, a thin column of water pouring from a battered bronze disk on which the people of the neighborhood claimed to recognize the effigy of a long-dead saint. A little farther on, the capricious gurgling of Drink-Twice, and the loud waterfall of Drink-Without-Thirst. Then, if you climbed up a stairway, you'd see the mossy lips of Drink-and-Rue, so called because, for a long time, the building across the way had been a prison. This part of the city was full of springs, which gushed up from the depths of the mountain. Fountains for good times and bad, as talkative as washerwomen, till the dog days came and silenced them. Fountains of memory and of forgetfulness, each with its earthenware motto.

One evening, a native clarinet joined in this concert. In these parts, the rich, warm sound of the *raïta* is as common as the braying of an ass, or the cry of the almond sellers. Why should this one have attracted me? Something artless, or only too artful, which, like a sudden breath of wind in our too-quiet streets—a barbaric, spice-laden wind, full of promise, full of menace—aroused a longing to travel.

I'd come upon one of those little squares, which open like wells in the jumble of houses. A few people had gathered and were sitting around on steps. Squatting on his heels, a boy was blowing into his instrument, cheeks puffed out, eyes popping with effort. He wore the wool bonnet of the Nussaris. A colored shape was spinning under a streetlight, which had just come on—one of those swan-necked lampposts that you find at certain crossroads, relics of the munificence of some minister of colonial times. The audience was clapping rhythmically. I drew near.

It was a girl, hardly more than a child, to judge by her looks, clad in an old-rose-colored dress. Her hair was tinted with henna and the bangles around her ankles clinked as she moved. She was twirling in ever-diminishing circles, paying attention to no one, as though dancing for herself alone. It was a warm evening. The birds were falling asleep in the branches. You could make out the faces of women behind lattice windows. I held my breath.

She stopped, made an imperceptible bow, just lowering her eyes, then stared insolently at the spectators. She had the overripe apricot complexion that you see in our mountain children. A little wisp of a thing, a Nussari ragamuffin.

An old man suddenly lashed out at her. "You ought to be ashamed, showing yourself bareheaded in front of men. The Nussaris claim to be Muslims! Pagans, that's what they are. Infidels, and you're a bitch."

The other spectators held back, torn between annoyance and the respect still shown to elderly men here. I was the first to speak up. Others followed suit, and scolded the old man. "Hey there, grandpa, go back to grandma." He sat down on a little flight of steps, choking with rage. But he did not leave the scene.

The little dancer let the storm abate, then opened a wire-mesh purse and nonchalantly began taking a collection. Suddenly, at point-blank range, the black fire of her eyes. Maybe she'd noticed me without showing it. Damn it, I'd been the first to stick up for her.

Brazenly, she went to beg a coin from the old grumbler who'd sworn at her. Clapping broke out again, as she danced round the old man, like a devil dancing round a hermit. He pretended not to notice. Finally, he spat at her and missed. She replied in kind and hit her target.

Timsit spitting on a respectable old man clad in white: my last vision of her that evening. The kids wanted more. But she'd already slipped away down the twisting streets, dragging a sleepy-faced little brother. The night was getting chilly. I made my way home, laughing to myself.

I hadn't seen my fiancée for several days. She was getting ready a little party, her birthday being the pretext. Eudoxia's twentieth birthday!

"We'll marry as soon as I've passed my nursing exam," she was telling anyone who would listen.

The diploma wouldn't be of any use to her, but she wanted it for the glory; it was understood that she'd devote herself to running her home and would give up this absurd hospital work, a childish whim that had taxed her parents' forbearance.

Two days after coming across the little dancer, I longed to see her again. But there was no one on the square with the plane trees but a blind storyteller who punctuated his outpourings with strange bursts of laughter. I went up and down every stairway in the old city. Maybe she had taken her bit of loot and gone back to the mountains. A ragged urchin was following me at a distance, hoping for a coin. I looked over my shoulder. His eyes burned like a rat's.

"Do you know the little dancer in the pink dress? She works with her brother."

"Aïsha?"

"I don't know her name. Where is she this evening?"

He led me to a sinister-looking café from which came the sound of a tambourine. An enormous black, sitting in the doorway, smiled, baring toothless gums. With an almost imperceptible movement, he tripped my young guide up. The boy swore copiously as he picked himself up. "Son of a swine, may those people eat and sing in your fat belly!"

"Those people" were evil spirits, which abound in Marsania.

I went in. The customers shot furtive glances at me. The back room smelled of tobacco and hashish. A huge woman was jigging rhythmically up and down, undulating her arms like bajaj serpents. This was Aïsha. She may have been beautiful, fifteen years ago. That stupid kid.

Time passed, still no sign of the girl. I'm sure I wouldn't have cared so much if I'd known she was always to be found at specified hours, like a reliable purveyor of the picturesque. But she turned up only when she felt like it, or when she was out of money.

At last, one evening down at the harbor . . . I recognized her a long way off by the sound of the big clarinet (one of my friends says the proper translation would be oboe). It was a faux-naif melody, harsh and tremulous, which carried you off to a kind of fairyland. Later, on many occasions, I tried to get that very special timbre from a *raïta* I'd bought. In vain, the only sound I could get was lugubrious.

The little dancer had stationed herself near a shallop that was unloading red mullet. Beyond it lay a world of sleeping boats, ropes, pickling brine and tar. She was still wearing her wine-colored dress, but a white head-scarf made her look more respectable. She was humming, her eyes were closed as if she were dead and her song was drowned out by the clarinet. The whole effect was so singular that some European tourists had stopped and were photographing her with much popping of flashbulbs. Frightful people! I'd have liked to push them into the harbor.

I had sat down on an iron drum. The white Masmuda Mosque stood out above the heap of houses. A breeze stirred the fishing nets.

All of a sudden, the sensation of claws on my knee made me jump. Something was clinging to me. I leaped up, knocking over the drum. The thing was still on me. I dashed it to the ground. A furious chattering started up in the shadow.

The singer broke off and began to laugh: "Kassli, naughty boy!"

I felt sure that she recognized me. Without coming closer,

161

she gave Kassli a tremendous dressing down in an impenetrable idiom. The animal went on protesting.

"He only understands Nussari," she explained. Actually, it didn't understand anything at all. The people roared with laughter, and craned their necks to see the cause of the excitement. The little clarinetist had stopped playing and sat there with his instrument on his knees, looking foolish. The dancer came up to me, undid a leash that was attached to a big bundle and went back into the circle of light, carrying on her shoulder a gray-blue monkey.

"This is Captain Khaïr-ed-Din," she announced in her bad Arabic. "Well now, old fellow, have you had a good day? How many enemies have you slain? How are your wives and children?"

The kids were jumping for joy. The animal rubbed its eyes like a little old lady. It was a Taffarit macaque, Taffarit being one of the valleys where they are still found. The boy broke into a different tune, syncopated, with ornaments and trills, which I imagine had been especially composed for monkeys.

"Well, Captain," she went on, "like it up there?" It had perched on her head and was clinging to her red hair. It looked like a monstrous hat. She smiled, showing her perfect teeth. She began to dance, slowly at first, then faster and faster.

"Hang on tight, General," she kept shouting. The monkey had taken off her white head-scarf and was brandishing it like a banner. I admired the girl's posture and the sculptured curve of her bare feet.

"And now, Captain, you're going to dance alone."

With a little push she sent it rolling on the ground. It started licking its fingers with its blue tongue. She crouched down and clapped her hands. The monkey stood up on its hind legs and began to do a kind of belly dance. It was as repellent as she had been regal. It kept sitting itself down but went on swaying its torso with grotesque movements. The crowd was howling with laughter.

I was both disappointed and fascinated by the ease with which my little savage demeaned herself to become a vulgar entertainer. In the end, the monkey had a fit of sulks, rolled up in a ball and refused to respond. She put it on its leash, which didn't go around its neck, but around the base of its tail. People were throwing coins onto the cloth, which had served as a stage; the takings were meager. She packed up her things in a twinkling and was off without a word of thanks.

They were as proud as princes but they hugged the walls. The girl led the way. The boy trotted behind, with his tambourine like a hump on his back. The monkey jumped in all directions, came back when its leash was tugged and went off again, as agile and wicked as a little devil. I couldn't resist the urge; I decided to follow them.

They climbed steep paths, slipped into alleys which smelled of frying fish. Providence Street, Bu-Denif Street, Riches Street. I was now outside my usual stamping grounds. I hardly knew this neighborhood.

For a moment they vanished and I thought I'd lost them. I started to run. She heard my footfall, looked back and quickened her pace. They went under an arch, and up a stairway, which looked to me like the Zarwatin Steps. She kept glancing back to see how far behind them I was. I was afraid I'd see them disappear through a hole in the wall. I should have shouted something reassuring, but I didn't know what.

The street the fugitives took was almost totally dark, with overhanging houses which leaned across and touched one another. A wretched little lamp swung creaking in the breeze, casting huge shadows. As she emerged from this narrow thoroughfare, the girl turned and confronted me:

"What do you want?"

163

The sky was bright. A fig tree waved its branches above the wall. The monkey started whining.

"I want to know where you live. I loved your dancing."

"We don't live anywhere. A night here, a night there."

"Are you Nussaris?"

"Haven't you got eyes?"

She was ready to bite and scratch.

"You're a Nussari; that means you live with a cousin. There's a lot of them around here."

"Please go away. Leave us alone."

She kept her voice down so as not to arouse the neighborhood. And, without realizing it, I lowered mine too. We may have been enemies, but we were also accomplices.

"I'll go away if you tell me your name."

"My name? If you like. It's Timsit."

She threw me that as a sop and was off again at a brisk pace, dragging her crew along with her. Her dress, for a moment, shone red in the flickering light of the lamp.

Night in the old quarters. Long lines of arches, through which you might glimpse a lantern swinging in the wind. Unidentified things that made you slip. A cat suddenly leaping between your legs. Without knowing how, I come out into the garishly lit El-Watan Boulevard.

Timsit: that means barley in their blasted language. The Nussaris give wretched nicknames to their children—Rag, Flour, Chick-pea—to make the demons think they're not worth stealing. This girl still has hers. Too young to be entitled to her grown-up name.

A late bus comes pitching along, hugging the sidewalk. I rub my eyes, as though I've spent a night carousing.

I've found something that America and the Nasr Tower nearly made me miss: a whole world of tradition and secrets, to which Timsit holds the keys.

Ilena, my sister . . .

She was coming out of the basilica, hoping no one had seen her. Her first instinct is to run away from me, but she pulls herself together.

"Do you still go to church? Does he let you go to Mass?"

"Come off it, Gabriel."

The classical beauty of her face is unimpaired, despite her pregnancy. But there's something submissive in her expression, which is new to her. I take her wrist. I look at the little blue cross that was tattooed there when she was very young. Someone has added branches. It's no longer a cross, but a star.

"Who did that? Ruwan?"

"Everyone used to stare. I couldn't bear it."

The usual ploy of Christians who go over to the other side: they disguise their cross, turn it into a sun or a flower. The bravest cauterize it with red-hot iron.

"The star isn't a repudiation," she goes on gently. "It belongs to both faiths."

Ilena is wearing a loose-fitting green dress, with none of the ornaments the women of Marsania are so fond of. She leans her shoulder against the old wall, and puts her head on one side. Her waistline has become enormous.

"He's growing nicely," she says, referring to the little creature she's carrying.

"He," of course. Why do they all want boys when the Prophet had no sons? Every time she comes into this church, she lights a candle for her child—to be sure he'll be the handsomest, the strongest. She prays for this scion of two races, who will automatically be a Muslim.

"Ruwan's as proud as a peacock," she adds.

"No need to tell me that."

So there was Ilena again, but now a stranger, in the sweetness of a spring morning on Ben-Othman Street.

"And you, Gabriel? What about your mosque?"

165

"No news is good news. I live in hopes."

"Think about Ruwan's suggestion."

"Did Ruwan suggest something?"

"You know he did."

"That I join the other camp?"

"They're not camps. But if you use that word, they'll get to be camps."

She stares at me with an almost mad intensity. The blood has risen to her cheeks.

"Ilena, you haven't been converted, as far as I know."

"Me! What a woman believes isn't important."

She laughs good-naturedly. But I could feel her hurt.

"What an artist thinks," I say, imitating her tone, "isn't important either."

Children come running out of the Morqossiya. One of them hops around us, though we look like any ordinary passers-by. Could we have spoken too loudly?

"Think it over," she goes on in French, with the rather guttural accent she has never quite lost.

"You say that because you're afraid of being isolated."

"I say that because I'm worried about your future."

Ilena my sister. I stand, watching her bulky shape, as she walks away in the mild April sunshine.

We called those big seaside cafés that Marsanians flocked to in the season casinos. The Ras Tarf Casino was one of the most popular. Safia had arrived before me and was eating a lemon sherbet.

"Well, Gabriel, what have you been up to?"

"I'm still waiting for the jury's verdict."

"Waiting is a Jewish notion. Hope is a Jewish notion. Christians abstain."

I loved those crazy ideas of hers; they always held a grain

of truth. She herself wasn't the waiting kind; she went through life without looking back at those who'd let her down, or at projects which hadn't come to fruition.

"Let's get down to brass tacks. What would my lunatic friend say to building a big tourist hotel?"

"Where?"

"On the Taffarines."

Those whale-islands, those sea monsters, that had peopled our childhood dreams!

No one had ever dared touch the Taffarines. Their reputation wasn't of the best. The Knights Hospitalers only managed to stay there three years. A Turkish garrison died of thirst. The lighthouse, which was built too quickly, trembled on its foundations in every storm, with the result that no keeper could be found for it.

Which of these rocks would it be? Zerah and Manarf had permanent populations that might cause trouble; Ras-el-Tourd was too rugged, and the Camel was even worse; little Kelliani had no water at all.

"You can stop guessing," said our friend. "It's going to be Korben."

"But that's your island!"

"We've come to an agreement."

The island of the wild anise. No, I wouldn't be a party to that.

"Come off it, Safia. You buy this rock, then six months later . . ."

"Nine."

"Very well, nine months later plans for a hotel spring up on the very same place. Odd, you will agree."

She looked at me calmly.

"Haven't you ever heard of a straw man?"

So she'd acquired that heap of stones to do someone a favor. I could easily imagine who. Not only had Samiel paid for her studies, he had come to her rescue when she returned to Marsania without money or husband. How could she refuse to do him a service?

"You know I've always longed to reign over an island."

With hindsight, the story seems a little less obscure. First of all, the Saruns commission a market study, which finds that the hotel would be profitable. So they buy the island, with the help of their friend Samiel. But they don't want to show their hand too soon. Samiel suggests his niece.

"I'd just as soon you had no part in this, Safia."

She turned to me with a bitter smile: "Dear boy, I have no scruples left. This is a country where the tombs of my ancestors are desecrated, and I could easily be thrown out tomorrow."

"You're not alone in that predicament."

"If you mean the Christians, believe me, they won't quit. They've clung like barnacles to Marsania from time immemorial."

She rather despised us. The great nomads always despise sedentary peoples.

The waiter appeared in a green jacket. His only job was to place glasses of ice water on the tables. A second waiter took the orders. A third filled them.

"The other paradox," I went on, coming back to the subject of the hotel, "is that the country is seething with unrest and the Saruns decide to build."

"Exactly," she replied, delighted to give me a little economics lesson. "It's the moment to build. The Palace has asked them to do this. When people realize that the Saruns aren't afraid, money will stop bolting to Switzerland."

In fact, to take a rather lofty view, the whole thing was an act of piety.

At this point, the great Sarun made his entrance, as in a well-choreographed ballet. After greeting various acquaintances at nearby tables, he wended his way over to us. He never gave you his hand, he lent it.

168

"The Korben promoters consulted me about an architect," he said, after a few perfunctory remarks about the weather. "I took the liberty of recommending you. I hope you'll do me this honor."

He had his back to the light. His bony face was cratered with dark shadows.

"You understand, Gabriel, I'm merely oiling the wheels in all this. I've got no stake in the affair."

From which I inferred that he must be very deeply involved. But already he was giving me a list of shareholders, from the Bank for Small Businesses to the brother of the Emir of Qatar.

For some years now Sarun had been getting bored with his enterprises, which more or less ran themselves, and had set himself a second task: to attract petro-dollars to Marsania. He had made repeated trips around the Gulf. They were just beginning to pay off.

I set out my objections:

"It's always expensive to build on an island."

"We're aiming at a wealthy clientele. We'll build them a little paradise. They're willing to pay."

I detected a note of scorn in his voice.

"What about drinking water? From May till October it'll have to be brought over from the mainland."

"There are such things as tankers."

"And how will tourists get there when there's a sea running?"

"We'll arrange to use the Chamber of Commerce helicopter. We'll make a deal with them."

"Always supposing there's not too much wind."

Sarun smiled his curious faraway smile. "My dear boy, you're an architect. You build us a hotel. We'll do the rest."

He'd ordered fig coffee as it was easier on his heart. The somber-faced waiter leaned over as he poured it.

"Well, I'm surprised to hear that investors are still interested in Marsania at a time like this." I was beginning to get on his nerves.

"We've lived alongside the Muslims for thirteen centuries," he replied. "We'll manage, we always have. Believe me."

To convince me, he opened his briefcase and took out a little map of the offshore archipelago, strange sea-horselike shapes drifting in the slack water.

"And if things go badly on the mainland," he said, "the Taffarines will weigh anchor."

He bantered on like a lord. Local society accused him of copying his aristocratic manners from Badis Pasha. But they were all his own. And of late, just to show he'd really arrived, he had been speaking Arabic with a slight Oxford accent.

The sound of applause reminded us where we were. The show was beginning. A fat singer in a spangled dress, an exact replica of Oom Kalthum, came onstage. She began to sing: very simple things, about life, its joys and sorrows, with the words repeated over and over again. Sarun disappeared to make a phone call.

"Trust me," murmured Safia. "No one will dare spoil the islands while I'm alive to protect them. I'll put my mosaics on your walls. Right now, Korben is nothing but a block of granite that's tumbled into the sea. We must give it meaning."

The lights had been lowered. *Ya habibi,* sang the voice on the stage, *my beloved, night is falling.* On and on it sang, in great intertwining arabesques. And nobody in the audience got up to tell this woman she was too stout and no longer attractive. This mountainous creature was entitled to be loved; it was scandalous.

But in a corner of the room, a liveried waiter, oblivious of the music, had unrolled his little mat, turned toward Mecca and begun to recite his prayers. Islam, Islam!

"What would you think if I went over to the Prophet's side?" I asked suddenly.

Safia played with her pendant: "I'd be disappointed in you, Gabriel. Marsania is a work of art. The Christians have their role to play here."

As Dr. Samiel put it, the tapestry would cease to exist if the Christian thread changed color.

"You can't help respecting, even admiring, Islam," she said, in a barely audible voice. "But it's not a religion for intelligent women."

Patches of light were floating on the dark sea; fishermen with searchlights were hunting octopus in the shallow waters.

The singer was taking a break. Safia started to sketch my portrait, or rather my caricature, on the paper tablecloth.

Across the aisle from us, a solitary foreign tourist was knocking back her third Martini. A regular, to judge by the way the waiters were hovering around her. One of those crazy, unrepentant lady tourists you read about in novels, whom our city held in its web like a fly. "My father was an ambassador," she kept saying in English, with an accent I couldn't place.

And I was thinking about our island, which was still no more than a splinter in the sea. A white village would bring it to life. Already I could see it, clinging to the slope like a wasps' nest. I had disfigured the coast with the En Nasr Tower. I'd failed to build for the Faithful. It was time I made good.

A fishing boat went by, all lit up, as unreal as a jinni. Sarun signaled that we were leaving. He was going to the hospital to pick up Eudoxia, who came off duty at midnight.

"Guess what," I said, when we were in the car. "I've been invited to embrace Islam."

I'd consulted Safia. I might as well consult Sarun.

171

"Have you? Well, give the matter serious thought," he said, to my amazement.

It's not something he himself would have done. A question of honor and more, perhaps. But an up-and-coming Muslim son-in-law—why not?

Poor me! Even Sarun was pushing me down the slope.

"Eudoxia would never agree," I said, glad enough to have her to cling on to.

"Eudoxia is young," replied the head of the family.

I was walking one evening, at dusk. I was being followed by a man clad in brown wool. He was barefoot. Suddenly he caught up with me, effortlessly, and said:

"Greetings, Jibril. Don't you know me?"

"I can hardly see you."

He threw back his hood. "Now, do you know me?"

An emaciated face, burning, sunken eyes. And such a wonderful smile that you wouldn't have dreamed of pitying him.

"Yes, brother," I answered. "I have met you before. But where? Be so good as to remind me."

He shook his head, smiling. "Guess," he said. And side by side we strode along dark paths through the landscape of the night.

At that time, I was still immersed in schemes. I had to plan, design, keep after the contractors and lay concrete foundations.

Then I'd meet Timsit, who lived from day to day with a touching trust in life. And I'd feel somehow ashamed of myself.

In the end, she'd consented to talk to me. She came from the region Marsanians call The Land of Clouds, although the clouds stay there barely three months of the year. The peasants had planted their fig trees on slopes that were so steep they had to hang on to the branches to gather the fruit. Her father had been sick for years. No one knew what was the matter with him. Six brothers and sisters, plus two, maybe three, who died in infancy. Her mother, she told me, was only thirty-five and her hair was gray under the henna. But Nussari women never know their age.

I was still wondering in which hole in the wall she had made her nest. When I walked her home in the evening, she'd let me come with her as far as Drink-and-Be-Quiet, the loneliest of the city's ancient fountains. Then she'd bar my way and make me go back.

Once, in the shadow of a doorway, I'd tried to kiss her. She sank her sharp teeth into my cheek and I bore the scar for a long time afterward. Yes, I was well and truly bitten, as they say in French. Bitten in both senses of the word.

Eudoxia was reviewing for her nursing exam with a rather comical earnestness. At first, she asked me to test her on her lecture notes. But I made a poor job of it, and in the end she decided to work on her own. We stopped seeing each other.

One evening, however, she called to tell me that, when walking home from the hospital, she had noticed, on one of the squares, a marvelous little dancer with a monkey. I must drop everything and go and see her.

Had I been found out? Not at all. The guileless creature had simply wanted to share her enthusiasm.

The next day, I went once more to pick her up at Berthome Bey. I was gradually getting used to this haunt of sickness and death, where the horrors were masked by a facade of bougainvilleas. The management had finally got around to poisoning the stray dogs that fought over the contents of the garbage cans; but others would come in their place.

All we had to do was find Timsit. I hoped she had

173

changed squares, as was her wont, and eluded us. But no, there she was, the conscientious artiste, under the catalpa trees with her two assistants.

Eudoxia slipped unsuspectingly into the front row. I was just behind her. The dancer seemed not to have noticed. She was spinning slowly, singing a mountain air. I still knew only part of her repertoire. A harmless-looking policeman was watching over the heads of the crowd.

"Have you dined well today, Captain?" Timsit asked.

The monkey grimaced, showing its blue gums.

"The Captain says music doesn't fill the belly," said Timsit.

"He can come and do the dishes in my restaurant," a man in the audience called out, and got a laugh.

"And now," Timsit went on, "Captain Khaïr-ed-Din will show us the richest person here tonight. Off you go, Captain!"

The monkey jumped off its perch, made a beeline for Eudoxia and held out its little paw to her. It was astounding. I tried to figure it out. Eudoxia earned a miserable wage at the hospital and her parents rationed her pocket money. Khaïr-ed-Din had got it wrong. But one day, she would certainly have far more money than all these spectators put together.

Eudoxia fumbled nervously in her purse. She had no loose change. Without giving me time to offer mine, she put a banknote in the monkey's paw.

"Thank you, bloated capitalist," said Timsit. Where on earth had she picked up that expression? The audience roared with laughter and looked respectfully at Eudoxia, despite her simple dress.

"A dance of thanks to the bloated capitalists," announced the theater manageress. She began marching around, in a parody of a procession, with her brother in front and the macaque behind. Strutting, waddling and puffing out her dress, a caricature of self-importance. The clarinet blared like a bugle.

A few drops of rain fell. Timsit rushed to take the collection before the crowd dispersed. She smiled at each person who gave her a coin. Then she stood in front of my fiancée, shaking her iron begging-bowl. She had no right to do that. Eudoxia had already given generously; I held back her arm.

The dancer let out a torrent of abuse in her own language.

"The little bitch," said Eudoxia, on the verge of tears, as I led her away. And that was the end of the show for the evening.

The following day, I found Timsit under the catalpas. It was unusual for her to be in the same place three days running. Could she have gone there deliberately, in order to see me?

There was no show that evening. She was sitting on the ground sulking. Her little brother was asleep with his hood over his head. The monkey, attached to a stout thong, was struggling frantically to get free.

"Hey, you," she cried. "You never told me you had a wife!"

She hadn't let me take the slightest liberty with her. But that did not stop her from making a jealous scene.

"I've never seen a street dancer behave as badly as you did," I said.

"No wonder!" she snapped. "I'm the worst little bitch in our village." She was fiddling with her bracelet.

"Your wife was really cross. What's more, she's not even beautiful, with those eyes like five-pataka coins."

"No one would agree with you there."

She was sitting on her heels. There was always a heady, rather pleasant fragrance clinging to her. I suppose it was a perfume she rubbed into her skin to keep from smelling bad. Maybe she washed herself as well.

"And how do I know you haven't got a second wife?" she spat out. "And a third? Rich men are all the same."

Money was an obsession with this little beggar girl.

"In the first place, I'm not rich." Seeing her disappointment, I added gently, "Maybe I will be, one day, when I've built lots of houses. But I'm just a beginner."

"Do you build houses?"

"You know the big tower, down by the lagoon? Well, I'm one of the people building it."

Timsit shook her head: "It's too high. It'll fall down."

If I'd wanted to impress her, I hadn't succeeded.

"Secondly," I went on, "I'm not allowed two wives. I'm a Christian."

"A Christian?"

I thought she'd guessed. But she hadn't been living in Marsana long enough to appreciate its subtleties. All city dwellers were alike to her.

"Christian son of a dog!" she cried, rather half-heartedly.

Her kid brother had woken up. He was looking at me with his little bright eyes, half hidden behind his high cheekbones.

"Be polite to the gentleman," he said.

It was the first time I'd heard his voice. The macaque was clinging to my leg and rubbing its damp cheek affectionately against my trousers.

"Thirdly," I said, refusing to be sidetracked, "the girl you saw is not my wife. She's my fiancée."

"So what's that?" she asked, pointing at my ring.

"It's an engagement ring. On our wedding day, I'll transfer it to my left hand."

The prospect seemed to overwhelm her and she leaned back against the tree trunk and fell silent.

"Aren't you performing this evening?"

"No. My soul is sad tonight."

She must have got that expression from one of her songs.

"Anyway," she added, "I'm only a stranger here." *Taber-ranit.*

"Listen to me. I'm going to do something for you. Tell your father he can come to Marsana for treatment. It won't cost him a penny. I'll fix it up with the hospital."

"Do you know the manager?"

"No, but my fiancée works there."

I expected her to brush aside a suggestion involving her hated rival. But no, she sat there, thinking it over.

"It really won't cost anything?"

"I've told you it won't. Your father just has to get here."

"He can do that. Our cousin has a taxi."

One of those incredible boneshakers that can occasionally be seen hurtling down the mountain roads.

"Okay," she said at last. "But I can't write. You write to my father. When he sees a nice letter, he'll believe you."

With great difficulty she spelled out the address, and I took it down in my notebook between two architectural sketches. The boy had started to play softly on his clarinet. The monkey was hunting for fleas in its thick coat. I rose, with a little gesture of farewell. She got up too.

"Your fiancée . . ."

"What about her?"

"You'll never marry her. She's too pretty and too rich for you," she said, shamelessly contradicting her previous declaration.

One morning, Eudoxia asked me to go with her to the church of Saint-John-Underground before she went on duty at the hospital. This church was even more modest, more tucked away than our basilica. Some said it was founded by Saint John the Evangelist when a storm drove him off course on his way to Patmos. And that the city itself bore his name:

Mars Hanna, John's Port. But the legend is a little too good to be true. In Arabic, an "h" is not lost as easily as a hat in a high wind.

The two of us were alone in the gloom, lit only by the soft sheen of the gilding.

Her lips pressed against the iconostasis, Eudoxia was murmuring an inaudible prayer.

I felt too torn to pray. I kept hearing Ruwan say, "Christianity, religion of women."

I thought I'd recognized his voice, coming out of the loudspeakers, that for some time now had been inundating the city with lines from the Koran, or with ambiguous prophecies. In the past, this kind of amusement had been confined to Ramadan and family celebrations. But now, anyone could rent one of these machines and treat the neighbors to an earful. The police didn't do a thing.

Islam, religion of men.

A campaign was launched against a brand name that Sarun used for one of his products: Hamdullah (God be praised). It was certainly a sacrilegious name for a cigarette. With his customary astuteness, he dropped it at once, and the offending product became *El Hamd* (Praise). The colors on the pack didn't change; neither—I imagine—did the clientele.

A night watchman shot down a terrorist who was planting a bomb in a bank. The funeral served as a pretext for a great volley of rifle fire. I can see us now, standing on our balcony at around one in the morning, waiting to be able to get some sleep. A gang of youths passed chanting, "Christians, no good! Christians, get lost!" I'd firmly gagged Mark. After all, the demonstration was almost good-natured.

The police didn't lift a finger. They couldn't very well arrest all the people who had gone to a funeral.

Soon the violence escalated. A shot fired from a window put paid to General Fitussi, the Town Commandant. This

178

honest man had made the mistake of coming out publicly against the new militants. Inquiries led nowhere.

At the Saruns', sensible people commented on the event, "It's just an internal matter for Islam."

I threw a stone into the fish pond of their wisdom: "Their tactics are obvious, gentlemen. When they've eliminated their liberals, it'll be our turn."

Timidly, Eudoxia backed me up, like a dutiful fiancée. The master of the house showed an impressive calm. That's how I was at the time: one moment bitter and vengeful toward the people of the Crescent, the next moment ready to defend them against all those summary judgments.

Despite warnings, I decided to attend Fitussi's funeral at the Haj Sadoq Jemma, also called the Mosque of the Sabers. It was the officers' favorite mosque, and the recent order banning infidels was momentarily forgotten. I recognized a number of Christians who held public office, and foreign military attachés. But neither the Prince Regent, nor the Prime Minister troubled to come. They were keeping their distance from this all-too-loyal soldier.

The imam read the sura for the dead in a solemn voice, very slowly, very beautifully. However, I had a feeling that he did not condemn the murderers. Gray beard and secret passions.

The cortege then went to the Bab-el-Jenub Cemetery, where the dead man's family tomb was: a miniature temple like any number of others, hastily rewhitewashed. A few Muslim friends made discreet signs to me. The sun beat down mercilessly. A second prayer was said by a friend. Before it was over, a handful of leaflets had mysteriously been scattered in the crowd. I picked up one of them:

Ahmed Fitussi, we fought against you. But now you're down, we shall not haunt your tomb with our hatred.

The Navy launch picks us up at the Harbor Command. One more of the privileges Safia accepts without hesitation. Dear boy, you know the Prince's fleet has to go on missions. I'm taking along two surveyors to correct the faulty Ordnance Survey and plot the contours because everything depends on that.

Eudoxia dashes up at the last minute, breathless, carrying over her shoulder a pretty purse that will be spoiled by the spray. She had overslept. Her exam was yesterday. She looks completely washed out. Safia kisses her and pours her some coffee from a thermos bottle. Then she suddenly turns to me and says, "Remember last time? The sea was like a millpond."

She said it quite deliberately to show her power over me.

"What do you mean, last time?" asks Eudoxia, who is not supposed to know about last summer's escapade when she was down with flu.

There are three women in my life at the moment. But I can't feel too guilty. Each sings her own song, and each is listened to.

Far ahead of us, in the heat haze, a freighter is heading for Europe. An unidentified fighter plane cuts a long paraph in the sky.

On the island, the two girls help the surveyors. They have wisely brought along big straw hats. I've only got my little pocket calculator which converts angles into distances and heights.

At lunch, the Muslim surveyors take a little of the Saruns' sweetish, yellow wine, made on the country estate. Every year Eudoxia's father gives the exarch a small cask of it to use at Mass.

"It's just a foretaste of what you'll drink on the other side," I joke.

The two men laugh. Islam has not outlawed wine; it has

simply reserved it for use in Paradise. In fact, Islam holds wine in higher esteem than we do.

While we are getting on with the surveying in the afternoon, I reveal my plans. Here, I'll put honeycomblike cells, each with its own balcony. Farther on, the restaurant overlooking the sea.

"My turn," Safia breaks in. She will put in as many mosaics to trap the unwary as the estimates will allow. And these mosaics will be trompe-l'oeil views of the village itself: the arches, the fractures, the clusters of houses clinging to the hillside—a whole mock labyrinth to delude the visitor.

The two girls leave me to my work and go off to bathe. Safia floats like seaweed, while Eudoxia splashes about as if she were drowning. And, needless to say, as she's coming out of the water she gets stung on the foot.

"It's a pity," she says, inspecting the damage, "that my revered father never built a swimming pool in the garden."

Her revered father has a horror of water.

At the end of the day, rather than go straight home, Safia suggests a detour to Zerah. The launch threads its way slowly through the channel, between the cliffs of Ghorr and Manarf, which stand like two castles frowning at each other across the black water. We pass close by the hull of a Greek steamer, wrecked on a shoal. Storms are still breaking her up, but her name is quite legible: *Selene,* planet of dreams. She was a cruise ship and was passing through the straits on a fine June night. Our captain gives her a friendly blast on his hooter.

"She answered," says Eudoxia.

We land at a little pier. There's a row of rotting huts on a beach. Women are cooking out of doors. An old man is scraping the scales off a fish, showering the gray sand with silvery dust.

Arabic is little used here; Faranghi reigns supreme. Between two bloated Berber faces, I glimpse quattrocento features; the races are even more mixed here than in Marsana. Some of the people are worried about our proposed hotel.

We'd better watch out, the natives of Zerah are tough. Not so long ago, they used to flash their lanterns to lure ships onto the rocks. Last summer, they got into a fight with some young people from the city who were diving for amphoras: you're scaring off our fish, the islanders told them. We must win these people over, or they'll sabotage our site. Yes, my friends, the hotel will buy your bream. Yes, I promise you, we'll hire your sons and daughters.

"Let's go and see the opera singer," says Safia. "She's the only tourist attraction here."

The two surveyors have stayed on the launch. They're none too keen on these savages, who eat unclean food. Some kids have gathered around us, or rather around Eudoxia. Why is it that whenever we go out, children flock to her?

We cross the island's one stream. The singer lives in a hovel nearby. She's German or Dutch, no one knows which, and was on the cruise ship the night it went down. She swam ashore here and has never left. Her reason went to the bottom with the boat.

"Madame Isolda!" Safia calls.

And out she comes into the rays of the setting sun. Her corpulent figure is clad in rags, her bare feet are covered with bruises, and long blond hair falls over her shoulders. The islanders feed her, out of charity or superstition.

Safia addresses her in French, "Madame, you have nothing to fear. We are admirers."

She stares at us with her pale, haggard eyes. And suddenly, in the deceptive light of the dying day, breaks into an operatic aria, which I do not recognize.

"Abuna Pierrot, you who are wise, what do you think of Christians who let themselves be converted? What would you say if I, for example, went over to the Fridolins?"

He does not throw up his hands in horror, he collects his thoughts for a moment:

"If you ask me, Islam is the religion of sensible people. One performs one's duties and one is in the clear with God. A Christian, on the other hand, is never in the clear, never at peace. So, one fine day, he gives up the struggle."

The pink, chubby face under the graying hair. The eyes that will always shine with the light of childhood.

"The Islamic virtue is faith," he continues, "the Judaic virtue is hope, the Christian virtue is charity."

He looks down at the workscarred hands spread out on his knees. He offers no further arguments.

"Go where you have to go," is all he says.

Projecting houses, propped up with shores. Street vendors selling lupine seeds marinated in brine. A labyrinth of bluish-white walls. The old city is a big peppermint stick melting in the sun.

Some English nobleman wrote, "You land at Marsana, thinking it is just another port of call, and the trap closes round you."

People will still show you the evil-looking café where he went every evening to smoke dreams, and the porch where he was found dead, a little mummy curled up in a grubby burnous.

A young man, who knows nothing of all this, strikes a match on a doorpost.

"From here to the first fountain is seventy-seven paces," said the old negro of my childhood. "Then from the foun-

183

tain to the Mosque of the Plum Tree: another seventy-seven paces."

Counted city. Coded city. Enigma city.

The pair of storks still keep their vigil on the ramparts above the square, and another seems to have joined them, making a *ménage à trois*. Little boys continue to spin wool all along the city walls, using the nails that have been driven into the stone. At Charbit's lemonade stall, fat men in yellow slippers sit reading newspapers. *The sign of the magic needle*, the tailor's board announces to the world. *"Arro!"* cries the donkey driver, vainly trying to get his beast to move.

Yet something has changed in the city. The spring is heavy with signs and omens. "Yesterday," Eudoxia tells us with a shudder, "we had a baby born without a brain." "We" being the hospital, which takes up more and more of her time.

I have some small purchases to make in the *qissariya,* a covered market—the name harks back to a long-vanished Caesarea. The mosque cuts off the view. Grass is growing on its dome, like the down on an old man's head. I'm just on my way when a procession marches by to the droll sound of a native trumpet. Tunics of pistachio-green, banners, shouts, long live the local saint.

The binding force in all this is called Islam. And without it, we Christians of the East would be but a shadow of ourselves.

But fidelity is my motto.

Old Katrin fumigates the house against evil spells. She trained us from our infancy to recognize different odors: benzoin, frankincense, sandarac. "Forget it, Katrin," people would say, "that's Muslim stuff."

Our mother spends her afternoons in secret conclave with her elder sister on the blue plush sofa. The humming of the fan drowns out their deliberations. No matter, I already know the outcome: "Marsania is no longer a place for Christians."

Mark is becoming more insufferable than ever, interfering in everything, always putting in his two cents' worth. He doesn't even bring home good report cards!

"That'll do, Mark."

"That'll do, that'll do," he parrots. "Tell your friend Ruwan that'll do."

"I don't see where Ruwan comes into it."

"Don't you?"

He stands up, eyes flashing. His voice comes out as a strangled squeak; it's breaking rather belatedly.

"Ruwan is the leader of the Demons of the South. Everyone knows that except you. And you know it too, only you pretend not to, because it suits you better."

I spring to my feet and slap him in the face. He sits down again, choking back his tears. The insolence of the kid! He could at least have cried.

The following day, by strange coincidence, we find the words *Family without honor* painted on our door. This time it's not the Forty Brothers, nor the Brothers of the Chain, but our Christian neighbors. They're reminding us that the daughter of the house was carried off by an infidel, and that the compensation still has not been paid.

The family on the ground floor are very huffy. They don't want people thinking they are implicated. And they start scraping off the damn paint since Mark wouldn't and I was afraid to.

"Family without honor," croaks young Mark, to no one in particular.

Our mother has said nothing; but she's gone to lie down.

Once more I draw up a list of possible remedies. The head of Ruwan's family is still—at least in name—the crippled old colonel. A reasonable man who's fond of me. I'll call on him and he'll see that justice is done.

That won't do. I must tackle Ruwan. He's humiliated me. It's his turn to suffer.

I'm shown into the old reception room. The thick walls have kept it cool. Ruwan comes in and greets me. He doesn't realize why I've come.

"Sorry, old boy, I've spoken to two members of the jury about your mosque. I think they'd be willing to back you now, but the Saudis won't have anything to do with it. And without their money, the project can't get off the ground."

He sounds so sympathetic. He'll make a wonderful cabinet minister.

"Everyone blames the Saudis," I say icily.

"No, I assure you . . ."

"I'll take the next plane to Riyadh. We'll soon see who wants what."

I detect some embarrassment beneath the easy manner. I savor it for a moment, then launch in:

"As a matter of fact, I didn't come to talk about my work, I came about the Law of Muharram."

"The what?"

"You've not forgotten, have you? You're the husband of a Christian."

"A Christian woman has indeed consented to join with me in holy matrimony."

Let him banter on. I'll be patient, very patient.

"Yes, Ruwan. When such a thing happened in the past, there'd be war between the two families. Luckily we now live under a more humane law."

"I gather you've come to ask for money. And it's taken you a year to get around to it. Bravo."

Hands in pockets, he stares at me.

"The Law of Muharram has saved a lot of lives," I say.

Can I be threatening him? No, of course not. Ruwan and I have been friends for too long. I continue my plea:

"The courts nowadays fix very modest payments. We can

go by the most recent judgment. It's simply for the principle of the thing."

Ruwan has bent down to tighten his sandal.

"How much?" he asks, after a pause.

"I haven't even tried to find out. Maybe five hundred piasters. That wouldn't ruin you."

"Do you mean that? Is Ilena only worth five hundred piasters? She will be flattered."

I hate his guts! I tried to hold out a compromise, and now he's turned my concession against me. What does he think he is, with that striped tunic and that short beard?

"You don't understand, Ruwan. The money itself isn't important. My mother wants a gesture. That's all. You know what people of her age are like."

He looks conciliatory but says nothing.

"My mother has had to put up with unpleasant comments in the neighborhood."

"In other words, you're asking me to please your neighbors."

His laugh is hurtful; it may even hurt him.

"Let's get this clear," he goes on. "Ilena came here of her own free will. I chose her, she chose me. I will not pay a fine for that, symbolic or otherwise."

I avoid his eye. He shakes his head and says, "We love each other."

That's easily said. But is there really love in Islam? On the woman's side, yes, undoubtedly. Witness the fat singer in the spangled dress at the Ras Tarf Casino the other evening. But what is there on the man's side? Possessiveness, a certain respect for the mother of his children. A kind of friendship too. More than that? I don't know.

"I hear you're going to build a hotel with Sarun."

"That's the idea."

"The country has other needs."

"You're telling me! I've applied to build workers' houses."

"I might be able to help you there," he suggests, with unexpected diffidence.

He's trying to redeem himself. He wasn't willing to back me up on the mosque. But an apartment house is different. It's less compromising.

"No, thanks. I don't want to be beholden to you."

I see him flinch. At last, I've hurt Ruwan.

"As you like, dear boy," he says. "I meant what I said."

He snaps on the lights. The sickly glow from the lamps reveals the ribs of the pointed arches, the peeling distemper. This must be the conspirators' room, where they hatch terrible plots against the Prince, Dr. Samiel, the Christians, the Jews and God knows who else.

Ruwan walks part of the way with me. On Saraïtin Street, a woman is selling hot snails, which people are eating in the open. A horse is drinking at the fountain and you can see each swallow of water go down its long throat. On Bu-Hanesh Street, the seller of reed pipes has laid out his wares. My friend picks up one of the pipes and draws a few notes from it to the amazement of the kids in the suk.

> *I remember, says the flute, the marsh where I was cut,*
> *And I weep my lost youth.*
>
> ABDUL HASSAN EL WESTI

Snow is falling on the foreign city: wet deceptive snow, which melts as soon as it touches the ground. I hurry along the sidewalks, holding up the collar of my old raincoat around my sore throat. I go as far as the kiosk on the boulevard and buy Eth Thawra, *the Revolution.*

Eth Thawra *used to be a clandestine extremist weekly. It's now become Marsania's main daily newspaper, the only one you can find outside the country. Naturally, it's expensive, since it has crossed the sea by plane. It's my one luxury, and I won't be able to afford it much longer.*

Before unfolding it, as always, I run my fingers over the Arabic letters of the banner; tracing the curve of the Wa or the blade of the R.

The boulevard is brightly lit. Through a gap between the houses the Two Churches loom up in the darkness. It looks as if one is perched on the other. The one at the bottom braces itself against the load it is carrying. The one on top effortlessly displays its illuminated dome to the night sky. And sometimes, I get the feeling that in the course of a more brilliant existence I've contributed to this architecture.

"A package for you, Mr. Gabriel," says the landlady. I'm a discreet lodger, without many visitors. She'll give me a good reference if need be.

I take the parcel with a sigh. That's how they got my friend Muwaffaq: an explosion, and three lines in the newspaper. I press my ear to the wrapping. I untie the string, take off the paper. Surprised to be still alive.

Come off it, you idiot, they're only propaganda leaflets against the regime in power in Marsana, and you said you'd distribute them.

"Well," asks our mother, "what about the compensation? Ruwan owes us compensation."

"He refuses to pay." I simplify. "He says we're no longer living in the Middle Ages."

"I like that! The way we Christians are being treated, you'd think it was the Middle Ages."

I've never known her so ruthless. Usually, she's the first to slip a coin to a beggar, or help an old servant. She gets up, taking the combs out of her hair, tearing the sleeve of her dress.

"I'm just a poor, weak woman. We have no one to defend us."

All her life, she's avoided dramatics and high-flown language. It's unbearable.

"I'm just a feeble old woman," she repeats. "This would never have happened in your father's day."

There's a sudden gleam in Mark's eye!

Our city was just settling into the summer heat when Timsit's father decided to come down from his mountain. The Berthome Bey Welfare Bureau had agreed to pay for the treatment. Eudoxia was delighted to have been able to arrange this. She thought he was the father of one of the workmen on the En Nasr site.

I dreaded one thing: Eudoxia's running into Timsit in the hospital corridors. But the man on the gate would never admit Timsit in her cheap finery—and she didn't seem to have any other clothes.

I came upon her, a few days later, as she was washing her feet in the Drink-and-Sing fountain.

"Can the Captain swim?" I asked, looking at the animal.

"The Captain can do all sorts of things," she replied solemnly. "He can even run in the snow, up in the mountains where we live. But he can't swim."

"You must teach him."

"My father's better. He wanted to thank you. He's at the Café of the Peaks, if you'll come and see him."

A low dive, kept by a Nussari up in the Esh-Shaffa quarter. I went there right away with Timsit and her theatrical troupe.

I liked the fellow on sight. Like many Nussaris, he had

rather prominent cheekbones and the same bright eyes, under jutting eyebrows, as his children. He answered to the ceremonial name of Abd-el-Hayy—Slave of the Living One.

"Show your hospital papers."

Case history: complications following pleurisy treated by a village apothecary. Of course, he hadn't been cured in that short time, but the condition had been arrested.

He started off with a few remarks about hard times—in the manner of our tenant farmer, Micallef, though less foul-mouthed—then went on to speak of his family. Of his wife, whom he called "the mother of my children," and who had no equal when it came to baking. Of his eldest daughter, Tilenlit (lentil), who had just married a rich man in his forties. Of young Timsit, the prettiest of the lot, who made such a useful contribution to the family income.

"Her real name is Zohra," he told me. "Flower."

She'd refused to tell me for fear of arousing the envy of the demons. But I preferred Timsit.

I'd given the old man a cigarette, and he was rolling it endlessly between his fingers. He was wearing a brown burnous with white stripes, the uniform of his tribe. The little dancer was sitting beside him, even though, in our country, women were not allowed in cafés. Everyone seemed to know her. People called out to her in Nussari and she gave as good as she got.

"Your daughter has a sharp tongue," I said.

He took this as a criticism, and was quick to answer it, "Marriage sweetens a girl as the sun sweetens an apple."

Obviously, he was expecting me to ask for her hand. My religion, of which he must certainly have been informed, presented no obstacle. In those remote mountains, the Koran had never stopped anyone from striking a good bargain.

I stayed a while longer, then rose to take my leave. His face bore no trace of disappointment. He could wait.

191

"God bless you! Come and see us at Tinferwin. We'll kill our best chicken."

Cats sneaked in and out of holes in the walls of the narrow alleyways, like a band of starveling ghosts attracted to the places where they may once have known happiness.

The Pope, secret commander of a crusade in the service of Western imperialism.

MEHMET ALI AGCA
author of the attempted assassination,
13 May 1981

For pity's sake a little peace. A little detachment. On my way through Qasrum on business, I decided to revisit Olive Tree Pass.

A little goatherd asks me the time. Saïf, a Christian village, a white nest peopled by women in black. Wasps are dancing around a brass water tap that has been left running. I solemnly turn it off. Hey, old Hanna's house is shut up. He must be dead, and now nobody sits on the bench where he carved a motto.

At the edge of the vineyards, the path peters out. Sloe trees clutch at the passer-by and show him all that remains of their flowers, as if to say, "We'd prepared a welcome for you. But you've come too late."

Noon, the sun beats down, and I've taken off my shirt. The birds are silent. All that can be heard is the persistent chafing of the insects—a great motionless whirring.

Greetings, old tree. It stands alone. No one knows who planted it; probably a passing peasant. For centuries, the sea wind has been sweeping into the pass. For centuries it has been buffeting the olive tree. At each gust, the tree clings a

192

little tighter, grows ever more gnarled. Its trunk is now huge, swollen all over, as if imprisoned beasts were trying to break out of the bark.

Far below me, the sea, creased only by the V-shaped wake of a little cutter creeping over its surface like a water spider.

I climb higher. The inland slope comes into view, drier, almost colorless. A wadi meanders along the bottom of the valley, with wide sandbanks and shimmering mirages. Man's only mark on this landscape: the twin arches of the Issawen Bridge. But the cunning river decided to flow beside, not under them.

This is where the land of the Nussaris begins—the old province of disorder and insubordination. We Mozarabs have always paid our taxes promptly to our masters. Don't mention that sort of thing to the Nussaris. Only yesterday, they'd pillage their neighbors when they were short of bread, or when a wind of adventure blew. For years, we felt that the threat was in the South.

What does the South betoken today? All I can see are the peaks of the Four Bridegrooms, the dark fleece of the Timaritin forest, watered by melting snow till the very heart of summer. And in resplendence, crowning all, the startling white barrier of the Amoragal Mountains.

Land of monkeys, genii and legends. A Nussari pedlar told us some of these legends, as we sat around our fire, and his mimicry made us think we could understand him. These folk speak a very ancient language whose alphabet is lost. Apparently we all spoke Nussari before the birth of the Prophet, before the coming of Christ.

"What will you do in the city, Gabriel?" asks the mountain. "The city is a hive of intrigue, a fountain of bitterness."

If I went over to Islam, my plan for the mosque would be accepted at once. The Lord would bear me no grudge: He is above such things. And to appease the Christians, I'd leave a testament proving my fidelity.

Tilit, tilit, sing the mocking mountain cicadas. The sky has clouded over and the sea is now prussian blue. I roll my clothes into a ball to offer less resistance to the storm.

And in the evening light, as the first drops were falling, just for pleasure, I rang the bell on Olive Tree Pass.

"Where are you going, Gabriel?"

Now, we're walking along the shore, and the shells are lacerating our bare feet.

"And where are you going?" I asked.

"You'll soon find out."

I'm carrying a sack full of stones and I stumble. The man with the wonderful smile turns toward me.

"Courage, brother. We're on a pilgrimage to Mecca."

I'm sitting on the edge of my bed, bathed in sweat. Light from the streetlamp filters through the blind, throwing strange patterns on the tiles. El hajji Jesus! That was all I needed.

I put a foot to the ground to convince myself that I really am awake, and go into the kitchen for a glass of water. Half past midnight; this is no time to wake up. Mark has left his bedroom door open. The room is empty. The bed hasn't even been slept in. Another Scout meeting, I bet. He's the limit. But this time he's in for a surprise. I'll be waiting for him.

I must have fallen asleep again. I'm roused by a furtive sound. The boy is coming in with unnecessary stealth.

"So here you are at last!"

That unabashed boyish face.

"They've blown up the Transfiguration."

"What did you say?"

"The chapel. Didn't you hear the explosion?"

That little white presence, which tamed the brooding mountain.

"I'm going out again," Mark announces. "I just came in to get my sweater and a flashlight."

"You're going out now?"

"The Scouts are holding a torchlight procession on the mountain as a protest."

Mark grabs me by the shoulders.

"Come with us, brother."

This chapel is a symbol. We built it about a hundred years ago, without asking permission from the Ministry of Religious Cults, on a stony patch of hillside bought from some shepherds. Our first act of defiance after years of submission. And the best part of it was that we were given official blessing once the deed was done.

A covered pickup truck goes along Bu Hanifa Street collecting volunteers.

"Great news!" Mark announces. "Gabriel is coming with us."

"Only till sunrise," I say. But no one understands my reservation. The truck puts us down in front of the Aïn-el-Bey mausoleum. The noise wakes a sleeper in a burnous and he lets out the traditional oath:

"Cursed be the religion of your father."

We take the path that Mark and I climbed on my return from the New World, when I still believed in happiness. The flashlights reveal dense, thorny scrub. Now and again, someone bumps into a branch and stifles a cry.

"No one will see your torches at this hour."

"Oh yes they will. Word has been passed from house to house. All the Christians are awake. They're looking at the mountain."

At our feet, the streets of Marsana weave an intricate,

luminous pattern that is extended by the lights of the ships in the harbor.

Our chapel has been reduced to a heap of rubble. Only the icon was found intact. We can comfort ourselves with this little miracle.

The Scouts have taken up their places along the top of the mountain, and the torches are lit one from another. I keep in the background, as it behooves a chance visitor. But that doesn't stop the aviator from spotting me and acknowledging my presence with a little smile.

The cry goes up, "We shall rebuild you!" Faces glow in the firelight. For a moment the darkness is dispelled. A better generation taking over from one that is mediocre, timorous, bankrupt.

We were beautiful. We were strong.

The following day, *El Umma,* the official newspaper, deplored the explosion, but reminded its readers that the chapel had been built in defiance of the authorities, under a weak government. The journalist had the effrontery to go on: "We had suspected for some time that the mountain of Marsana would not be able to wear a baptismal cross for much longer."

Needless to say, the perpetrators of the deed remained unknown. When the whole town was saying their names!

That same night, unfortunately, an inscription insulting the Faithful was painted on the Bey's tomb. A few undisciplined Scouts going down the mountain. In one hour, beauty had degenerated into stupidity.

I made a detour by the Esplanade, from where you could see the top of the Jeblasan. The little white presence had indeed disappeared.

And I returned to my office with that emptiness of heart one feels when one has stopped loving.

The blue-eyed emir is watching the fire from his balcony. Houses are burning in Bab Tuma, the Nazarene quarter of Damascus, making the summer evening yet more suffocating. All day long, the mob has been killing and looting. The emir sent his guard to save what could be saved. He opened his residence and the fugitives crowded in. The chaos was indescribable. Seated at his gate, on the edge of the town with its narrow creeper-shaded streets, he gave the thugs a silver coin for each Christian prisoner they brought him.

The emir can remember the day when he himself went to the giaours. The general, son of the king, had promised to let him leave for the East. Instead, he languished five years in damp dungeons in the land of the giaours. But that ordeal is now forgiven.

From his balcony, the Emir Abd-el-Kader contemplated the nearby Umayyad Mosque, with its three towers: the minaret of Qaït Bey, the minaret of the Bride and the minaret of Jesus, the highest, for it is there, according to Islamic tradition, that on the last day the Son of Mary will return to live among men.

I had one more tricky matter to deal with. I found Yunis at home bouncing his youngest son on his knee.

"How are things going with your scheme for the mosque?" he asked.

"Our scheme, you mean. I've left it in your waiting room."

Two large cartons containing the plans, sections and drawings, with the notes copied out more legibly.

He raised his eyes, pretending not to understand. I looked around at his petty-bourgeois comfort, the fringed sofa, the frilly curtains. All the cheap trash I wanted to throw out of the window. Actually, Yunis is wise, he doesn't draw attention to himself.

"As long as this scheme bears my signature," I say, "even

with yours alongside it, it will get nowhere. It will have to take its chances with your name alone."

Now he's really embarrassed.

"I thought I'd explained, Gabriel. I've been advised against any kind of collaboration with you."

"I'm not talking about collaboration. Gabriel's plans no longer exist. They are Yunis's plans."

The child has buried its face against its father's chest, as if I were a madman.

"Really, my friend, I can't," Yunis stammers, overcome by emotion. "I'd be accused of copying from you."

"Nobody will say a thing. They'll be delighted to have a good scheme presented by a good Muslim."

But I already know he's agreed. He's liked the scheme all along, and he knows that without him, there's no chance of bringing it to fruition. He's humble enough to father another man's child.

He's been thinking about the House of the Prophets quietly, on his own, as if he sensed that in the end it would fall to his lot. He has redrawn the ablutions court. He has also noted that the antiseismic precautions were not stringent enough. I plead guilty, with extenuating circumstances: the antiseismic specifications run to 150 pages of small print. The matter is in good hands.

"I'll turn the fee over to you," he promises.

"For God's sake don't. If that were found out, the whole thing would come to grief."

With tears in his eyes, he watches me go down the steps.

"The Koran is all-embracing," Ruwan once said.

Meanwhile, Sarun was having a dock built on Korben. There had never been such a rush. The government was

198

trying to quell all the rumors about the political crisis, and the imminent fall of the Regency.

And, needless to say, Red Truck has been given the main contract without my having been consulted. He crowed about it every time we met.

I was asked, somewhat astonishingly, if work could possibly begin on the foundations before the plans were finished. I launched into an embarrassed explanation, from which Sarun concluded that he could go ahead. A gentleman from Qatar arrived with a briefcase, and left again seemingly satisfied.

Soon the place where Safia had dwelt alone with her art was shaken by blasting. Boulders were blown up to make foundations for the houses. Our island had shrugged off the naval bombardment, but this was too much.

I put plugs in my ears and gritted my teeth.

We had all sorts and conditions of people working for us; most were Muslims, but there were Christians from both Churches and even a Jewish topographer. To avoid running a daily shuttle, tents had been erected wherever the terrain permitted.

"When the hotel's finished, will you let me spend a night there with my wife?" a foreman asked. "Just one night." I promised I would, though I had no authority to do so. It was as if commitments suddenly carried less weight. As if one's debts could be settled in counterfeit money.

The grass was trampled. The gulls deserted their clifftop nests. Safia cried out in horror and decided she'd make the mosaics at home. Only one thing mattered: to get ahead with the work. After a few days, I told myself my misgivings had been groundless and that Sarun, the able helmsman, was going to chalk up one more success.

It couldn't last.

One fine morning, the workers announced that they were

going on strike. Life on Korben was too hard. The pay was too low.

"The weather will be good from now till October. What are you complaining about?"

"We don't see our families anymore."

I stepped in. I got the men a bonus. The Christians were prepared to go back to work, so was the Jewish topographer. Not so the Muslims. They said they were sorry, begged me not to be angry, but went on with their mutiny.

So it was more than a simple little strike. It was political. Hadn't Ruwan said, "The country has other needs than this hotel"?

Red Truck was fuming. He'd never been defied in this way before. Luckily—unlike dreamers of my sort—he knew his workforce. He knew how to deal with these men, and, if need be, bring them to heel.

"We'll maroon them," he roared.

"We'll maroon them," Sarun agreed after some hesitation. The Palace raised no objection. This was the first time it had risked a clash with the Forty Brothers and other Demons of the South.

Our barges weighed anchor, leaving the strikers on the island with the tents and the remains of the provisions. I no longer had any say in the matter.

The response came soon enough. "Starvers," "Exploiters": the Brothers' newssheets let loose. Demonstrators marched through the streets.

To add to our troubles, the fishermen of Zerah sided with the mutineers. They brought them food and drinking water. Then they took them all off the island in small groups. The Palace sent a gunboat to keep an eye on the operation. It couldn't very well fire into the crowd.

So the site and all our equipment remained abandoned. We were off the hook but had been made to look ridiculous.

For a whole week Eudoxia refused to speak to her father.

200

I allowed myself the luxury of defending him. He had, after all, tried to create jobs.

Misfortunes never come singly, and a cousin who was passing through told us that Samir, the pelican, had died at his residence in Qasrum. The old philosopher had been savaged by a stray dog. Throughout the country, wisdom was on the wane. The ritual sentences were read, as at the funeral of a man.

Can overwork bring on nosebleeds? Anyway, that's what happened to me one morning. I'd had the unfortunate idea of taking a hot shower, and came out of the bathroom with blood streaming down my face. Our mother screamed, and spread her fingers as if to ward off a spell. She had seen Gabriel's corpse go by.

But young Mark went around the house brandishing a dishcloth and shouting, *mawut liz zubab* (death to flies).

Ruwan on the phone. He wanted to announce the happy event himself. Of course it's a boy.

"Congratulations on Ruwan II," I say, with as good grace as I can muster.

"Abdullah," he tells me. "A name Christians use too. I chose it out of consideration for his mother."

No one is better than he at making such little gestures, and they tie an adversary's hands. Rumor has it, incidentally, that he's dropping his own first name. Ruwan doesn't sound Islamic enough. From now on he'll be known as Abd-el-Wahid, servant of the One God.

He insists I come to the small seventh-day celebration to be held in the baby's honor. I'll be the only representative of Ilena's family.

Ruwan and I cannot quite manage to burn all our bridges. Something of our friendship always remains.

"I'll come on one condition. That you publicly disown the bombing of the chapel."

"The bombing of what?"

Hell, does he take me for a complete idiot?

"Forgive me, Gabriel, I haven't been out of the house in the last few days. It was a very difficult birth."

"That doesn't stop your followers from taking orders from you. The bombing was their work."

"I neither ordered, nor do I condone any bombing."

All of a sudden, he starts breathing heavily.

"But to be quite objective," he goes on, "I do have to say that the position of the chapel, on top of the Jeblasan, might have seemed provocative."

Now he sounds like a foreign minister. A moment's silence on the line.

"Well then, I'll see you at our little ceremony."

"What about my condition?"

"I disown the bombing of the chapel," Ruwan says at last.

Hardly an official denial. However, I am sufficiently easygoing—or rather cowardly, let's face it—to leave it at that.

Of course I don't say a word to our mother about this insulting birth. She'd been praying it would be a girl!

Most of Ruwan's guests are bearded young men in white robes. They are perfectly amiable; he must have given them a talking-to. For a moment I forget the storm clouds that are piling up over Marsania.

"Whatever you do, don't imagine we have anything against Christians," says one of those nice young men. "We merely want to clarify our relations."

"Obscured by this decadent monarchy," adds another.

"Which has always tried to set the communities against one another," puts in a third.

That's largely untrue, but what does it matter, since we are being shown goodwill?

202

Beat, beat o tambourine. Beat and leap and rattle your disks. Make this child's good fortune resound. And you, little ragged girl, who are allowed in because this is a celebration, wiggle your tongue in your mouth and let out one of your most piercing cries.

A few feet above me, Ilena, surrounded by women, her cheeks flushed, apparently satisfied with her lot. Unapproachable.

And the baby? Insignificant, podgy and yellowish. Nothing like the little king that I'd been expecting—that I'd been dreading.

"He already weighs nine pounds," a matron informs me.

I'm the first to leave. Ruwan sees me to the door.

"You were just right, Gabriel."

Actually, I'd hardly said a word.

"So you see," he adds, "everything is still possible in Marsania when everyone does his bit."

The din coming from Ruwan's house can be heard at the end of the street. Yet nobody complains. Blessed is he to whom Allah has given a son.

The next day, our mother turns on me with fury in her eyes.

"You were at Ruwan's last night! And it's a boy!"

You'd think she hired spies. But the town does the job for her free of charge.

"You'll just have to hurry up and get married, and produce boys. Lots of boys."

The old priest in the black turban goes by, mumbling into his beard.

"Be careful, children," Katrin warns us, "never speak to him. He's possessed by a demon."

Some Muslims imagine that our priests, as heirs to an older

*tradition, know all sorts of magic formulas. They come and see
them on the sly to ask for talismans. And this priest, swallowing his
pride, agreed to sell some.*

*He lives alone in the back of a tumbledown church. His wife is
dead.*

We run after him with the local boys, shouting, "Boo! Satan!"
*He turns around and casts some spell on us and we take to our
heels, scared to death.*

Conference of Islamic heads of State in Mecca. To avoid
attending, our Prince Regent comes down with a diplomatic
illness. But the weeklies publish a photograph of the other
presidents and sovereigns entering the sanctuary barefoot.
Who, these days, apart from Islam, can attain such communion?

Meanwhile, I receive a visit from the emissaries of the
Swiss company that checks on very tall buildings. It is com-
pulsory to have a certificate for buildings over thirty meters
high. The gentlemen graciously say they are satisfied.

One evening, as I'm leaving the office, I am accosted by a
young man. White tunic, jawline beard; he can't be one of
our friends.

"El hajji Abd-el-Wahid begs you to come to his house."

It takes me a few seconds to realize that he means Ruwan.

"Right away? Are you arresting me?"

The young man is profusely polite. He's showing me into
a cab.

Fine opening gambit! What's it all leading up to? For a
moment I have visions of grand negotiations, a plan for
everlasting peace. We Christians, for example, would recognize the preeminence of Islam, and in return would be allowed to go about our business. But if Ruwan had any such
ideas, he'd talk to someone more powerful than I am.

Evening crowds. It's been another very hot day. The red garden flowers have replaced the purple ones—and they will be the last. Street vendors are selling the first prickly pears. Sometimes these are peeled, like potatoes, and left floating in bowls.

Ruwan, with one of his lieutenants, is in a room I've never seen that opens onto the patio. He's a little thinner, his green eyes are burning feverishly. Some passion is consuming him.

I pick up the family tabby, which stiffens under my caress. We have a proverb which says cats are Muslim.

"He's like you, Ruwan."

"Go on! What an idea!" He laughs. And I get a glimpse of my old buddy.

"Bring in our thug," he commands.

Enter the thug, swaggering and smiling round at the assembled company. He's one of those cocky, idle-looking young males that you find in all Mediterranean countries. In the corner of his mouth, there's a small but deep scar.

"You may talk freely," says Ruwan, rocking gently in his wicker chair. "You're among friends."

"What do you mean?"

"Tell us about your adventure with the red sports car."

I shudder. I can see what they're getting at.

"The red sports car? I dunno . . . Well, I was with my pals one night in Bir Falastin. That's where I live."

The wells of Palestine. The wretchedest neighborhood in the city.

"We were hanging around, when all of a sudden this red jaloppy turns up."

Mercilessly, Ruwan cuts in, "Had you seen it before?"

"Yeah, sure. In Bir Falastin, they say it's a gift from God when a well-built guy comes across the red automobile."

Arms folded, deadpan, Ruwan's lieutenant is guarding the door.

"There was a chick at the wheel, all by herself," the thug went on. "That's the honest truth, I swear."

In Marsana, it's not done for a woman to drive alone in certain neighborhoods.

"She comes along, hugging the sidewalk. Damned if she doesn't give me the glad eye. I'm thinking, this is my lucky night. The other guys are all egging me on."

Who drives a red sports car through the city streets—all alone? I know only too well.

"Go on," says Ruwan. "You're in my house. You'll come to no harm."

"We went to the upper part of the city. We stopped outside a white villa."

"Where?" I'd asked the question, and was surprised to hear my own voice.

"Hard to tell," answered the little tough. "She took all sorts of detours so I wouldn't see which way we were going."

And to avoid being tracked down again at home. The white box, bordered with hibiscus, where Safia lives under the eye of a fat, illiterate duenna.

"We'll spare you the rest," says Ruwan ironically.

"As you like," the guy answers.

Handsome? Not even. Coarse skin, hair growing low on the back of the neck. Sexy-looking, that's all you can say. No, let's be fair, there is a certain beauty in his look. I keep at him, I'm rubbing salt into my own wound.

"When did you get back home?"

"She woke me in the morning. It was still pretty dark. She drove me back, taking all sorts of detours again. But I'd know that house if I saw it."

"Sure, you'd know it," I say between clenched teeth.

"I'd know the inside too," he goes on, jeeringly. "There's a black glass table shaped like a crescent."

206

The sophisticated furniture Safia ordered from Italy. He must have washed her windows one day. I stand up.

"This is an odious trick. You are trying to compromise a friend in order to compromise me."

The guy looks at me so insolently that I can't stand it any longer. I slap his face. A drop of blood oozes out of the corner of his mouth. He's hardly moved.

Sometimes, when I look back on that scene, it's as if we were rehearsing a bad play at the El-Tor Street theater. I see the young face with the hooked nose, the sallow skin. The grubby shirt. How old can this thug be? Eighteen? The room begins to spin.

"Gently," says Ruwan. "This young man is my guest."

"Excuse me." I sit down, completely drained.

"Christian women can kiss my ass," says the thug. "Jewish women can kiss my ass."

I shrug. He pulls a ring out of his pocket and triumphantly slips it on his little finger.

"How about this?"

It's the ring Safia always wears. A little silver rose, antique and beautifully crafted.

"You stole it."

"I don't steal from a woman who's a good lay. She gave it to me."

Obviously.

"That'll do," Ruwan cuts in. "Leave the room."

Throughout the proceedings he's been drinking tea in tiny sips. What payment has this witness received for his services? Money? The satisfaction of helping a political cause?

"We wanted to open your eyes," says Ruwan calmly. "You associate with scum."

"How can you be so unfair! Safia is an artist. She's admired abroad, and even in this lousy country. You can't expect her to behave like other women."

"I wouldn't know. At that price, art doesn't interest me."

The way he says that sends shivers down my spine.

"You're not going to do anything to her, I hope."

"We don't kill women," he says superciliously. "At the very most, we flog them in public, now and then."

For some time, I've been hearing conversation inside the house. I try to distinguish the voices.

"Don't worry, nothing will happen to your friend," Ruwan goes on. "This is a special favor to you. The last, no doubt."

I reply in a humorous vein, "Thanks, your lordship."

"You can even keep the ring, if you like."

It's valuable. I take it awkwardly and stuff it into my pocket. So now I'm beholden to Ruwan, five minutes after being his victim.

"It's time to choose, Gabriel."

"There's no choice to make. This is a multifarious city with a multifarious population."

"A pluralistic society," says Ruwan, aping the language of the intellectuals.

"You know perfectly well Marsania is a medley of colors, and the different elements highlight one another. You exist because I exist. You exist because Safia exists."

The municipal water carts are going silently down the long curves of Princess Fawzia Street, as they do every evening, imbuing the air, as they pass by, with a long-forgotten coolness.

"Here you are at last," shouts Mark. "You were seen with a Demon of the South. We thought you were in danger."

For two pins, he'd have raised the alarm.

"I was with friends at Ruwan's house," I say calmly.

"Back home," said Timsit, "the men count in Arabic and the women count in Nussari. The men call a mule by one name, the women call it by another. I think I have a right to talk like a man, as I've been to the city. What do you think?

"Back home," she goes on, "the father takes his meals alone, waited on by one of his children. You aren't allowed to smoke in his presence.

"Back home, last year, my second sister was made pregnant by a jinni. My father drove her out of the house. She died of cold in the snow, and was found with her face all black. My father is a just man."

Safia in her garden. What will she say this time? I toss the little rose into her lap.

"Massud says 'Hi.' "

"Massud? Who's he?"

"You know, the little thug from Bir Falastin. The handsome, curly-headed guy."

She looks up, realizing it's no use pretending.

"How did you come to meet him?"

"We were introduced by a mutual friend."

I jeer at her. Bully her. She heaves a sigh and gets on with her work.

"Are you going to bawl me out?"

"Maybe you were expecting me to congratulate you."

She rises to her feet.

"Shut up, Gabriel. I'm not your wife, as far as I know. Nor your fiancée. And talking of fiancées, may I remind you that yours would like to see you?"

Poor Eudoxia, so deserving, so neglected.

"I'm a woman on my own," she says. "My husband left me childless. I'm still entitled to live."

She is getting mightily on my nerves.

"You're a fine one to reproach me with Massud or any-one else. You with your little street dancer. Maybe you thought I didn't know about her."

I must have been a laughingstock.

"You've got it all wrong," I say. "My friendship with Timsit is something very pure and chaste."

She looks skeptical. Sweat is pouring down my neck and chest. I'm at my most unattractive. I'm about to make myself still more odious.

"Well, how was it with Massud? Did you get your money's worth?"

"No complaints on that score."

She bursts into shrill laughter that goes on and on. Insane laughter. I throw her to the ground and beat her till blood trickles from her mouth.

No, we must banish that vision. Safia is still sitting there quietly. She has put down her watercolor and is examining the little silver rose.

"Oh, how did you find it?"

There's not a trace of mockery in her smooth, full face.

"It was stolen from me in the street," she explains. "You know how they do it. Someone jostles you and slips it off your finger. Like in Chicago."

I purse my lips. That went out in Chicago years ago. A donkey cart is skirting the fence. The sun is drowning in the bay and no one is going to the rescue.

"Why didn't you tell me?"

"I keep my troubles to myself."

I look at the sketch on her easel: a curved landscape. Safia believes the horizon is curved.

"Do you expect me to swallow that?"

"I don't see why not."

"Well what about Massud?"

"Who's that?"

"Come off it! Massud, the seducer from Bir Falastin."

210

She looks genuinely surprised. Has she been rehearsing this scene? Has she been practicing in front of the mirror?

Forget it, I haven't said a thing. I don't flog women.

And I walk off into the dusk, clutching the little silver rose that I didn't even show her.

Toward the end of this strange spring I had the feeling I was being followed on the street. Sometimes by a big bruiser dressed like a fishmonger, sometimes by a kid with a limp that didn't stop him keeping up with me. They were quite open about it, and stared at me brazenly when I turned around. It was almost as if the object of the exercise was to let me know I was being tailed.

Work on the Korben site had started up again after a fashion, with Christian labor, and strikebreakers recruited on the quiet. But the heart had gone out of it.

"We'll see what happens after Ramadan," said Sarun.

Whenever he set eyes on me, old El Souss would look pained, and I guessed what was going on inside his gray head: "Poor Gabriel, he's dogged by bad luck. The only thing he's managed to finish is the Nasr Tower, and that was for someone else. And the wiring and plumbing aren't done yet."

But I saw Timsit every evening, and was almost happy.

Eudoxia wrote me a dignified note: "Gabriel, isn't your fiancée worth visiting anymore? There must be stiff competition. Don't worry, I'm not the clinging kind."

I thought about her more often than she imagined. Once or twice, unbeknown to her, I'd stationed myself outside the hospital and watched her come out in her little light-colored dress, so serious, so touchingly convinced of her power to alleviate the suffering of the world. I observed her from across the street. Anyone at all perceptive would have sensed, seeing this blue, rather frail, figure that she belonged to the great family of the exploited.

And a few yards away, my personal spy was watching me watching Eudoxia. This time, he'd be able to report some good of me.

One evening, my patience ran out; I turned sharply on my heel and walked toward him. It was the kid with the limp. He was shaking, but stood his ground. His face was convulsed, horrible. But lit up by magnificent eyes.

Hit him! Thrash an explanation out of him.

He asked me for a light. Mechanically, I apologized and walked off down the boulevard under the fluffy pink trees.

"I've got men following me too," Timsit told me.

"That's because you're attractive."

"No it isn't. They offer me money to go back home."

"You should jump at it." I was teasing her.

"One day, I will go back to my village," she answered gravely. "But the time hasn't come."

She always gave you the unadorned truth. You had to take her as she was. I asked her what these mysterious characters were like. She was no good at description. But there was no mistaking the lame kid.

So someone was watching me, and wanted to get me away from Timsit. Ruwan, obviously. After all, we were still brothers-in-law. No doubt he hoped to fit me into his scheme of things one day. Having cleared the first stumbling block from my path, in the person of Safia, it was logical that he should attack the second, in the person of the little dancer.

I called him up. To my surprise, he himself answered.

"Well, old brother?"

His usual manner, half-affectionate, half-annoyed.

"Ruwan, tell your heavies that I've seen enough of them."

212

"What are you talking about? In the first place, I have no heavies."

"They follow me on the street."

"You think you're so interesting? You think you're dangerous?"

The next day, Timsit told me she'd been threatened. As I've said, she wasn't one to embroider the facts. She'd never bother to lie; it was beneath her.

"Still the kid with the limp?"

"Yes."

"What did he say?"

"That something would happen to me if I stayed in Marsana."

"Are you scared?"

"Oh no. I can take care of myself."

Clearly, these threats were in response to my phone call. I'd challenged Ruwan and his response was to double the stakes.

"Go and live somewhere else, Timsit."

"No, I like it where I am."

I went home, clenching my fists. That same evening, Ruwan called back.

"I've seen the heavies," he said. "A kid with a limp and a big fat butcher."

"I'd call him a fishmonger."

"They're certainly not my friends. They're Sarun's men."

I came down to earth with a bump. Was Eudoxia, that gentle creature, having me tailed by her father's henchmen? No, the idea could only have come from him. She didn't even know about it.

Quite honestly, Sarun had reason to be annoyed with me. I'd been a rotten fiancé. And he was generally regarded as a ruthless and somewhat devious man. There were rumors about the way he had discredited a rival. He wanted Timsit out of the way. So he threatened her and offered her money. It made sense.

But a frank talk can clear up any misunderstanding. In these troubled times, Monsieur Sarun, we cannot afford a private quarrel. What, within reason, do you expect of me?

I'd made up my mind to visit him in his tobacco warehouse. And as I was rehearsing my plea, he suddenly seemed to be standing before me: his long cadaverous face, with the bow tie under it, like a kind of signature. He listened to me without a word, then bending forward, broke into one of his curious smiles.

One evening, Timsit stood me up. I went from archway to archway, fountain to fountain in search of her. I was about to give up when a slip of a kid came to my rescue:

"Are you looking for the girl with the monkey?"

So our idyl was the talk of the town.

Timsit was weeping silently in the doorway of a bakery. Maybe for the first time in her life. Her little brother was weeping too. Cockroaches were running along the wall, maddened by the specks of flour.

"Where is Khaïr-ed-Din?"

I'd noticed at once that the monkey was missing. She pretended not to know me. I shook her.

"The Captain is dead," she said at last. "Some men came. They put him in a sack and banged the sack against a wall."

She raised her red-rimmed eyes; suddenly they were full of hope, as if I could bring the Captain back to life. I wondered naively if she would be so grief-stricken when the killers did me in.

But I was just a rich gentleman, an incomprehensible being washed up by the tide, which could carry me off again. Whereas little Khaïr-ed-Din had shared her joys and sorrows.

"How many men were there?"

"Two, and the lame kid. At least they got a good scratching."

Her laughter cut me to the quick.

"Where have they put the monkey's body?"

"They took it with them."

To prove to their master that they had carried out their mission. I leaned against the wall, my heart heavy. I too had grown fond of the little devil.

Timsit began keening like a wailing woman at a wake. She had lost her child, and her livelihood.

"I'll buy you another."

"You won't find one. The Nussaris never sell their monkeys."

"Don't worry, I will."

She was excited for a moment, then her grief took over again.

"Anyway, it wouldn't be Khaïr-ed-Din."

Some passers-by had gathered around. I tried to distract her attention.

"It's all your fault!" She spat the words in my face.

She was quite right. If it hadn't been for me, Khaïr-ed-Din would still be peacefully pursuing his theatrical career.

The following day, she told me she'd decided to return home. The enemy had tried to buy her departure, now he was getting it for nothing. Playing for time, I said, "You can't go home to your parents empty-handed, especially without your monkey. Wait a day or two and I'll get you some presents."

Then, all I had to do was go shamefaced and contrite to Eudoxia and beg her forgiveness.

But Eudoxia made the first move. She appeared in my office, smiling bravely.

"I've come to release you from your vows, Gabriel. We weren't made for each other."

She took off the engagement ring that was to have become a wedding ring and set it down on my blotter. A little round, empty, ironic thing.

The only reply I can think of is a question about her father.

"Have you at least told Sarun? He'll hit the ceiling."

It is a very serious thing to break off a Mozarabic engagement. And the girl who has the nerve to do so does not easily find another taker, even when she's as rich as Eudoxia.

"My father can think what he likes," she answered gently.

I labor the point: "Your father has been having me tailed."

"I'm sorry, Gabriel. If I'd known, I'd have stopped him. But that still makes no difference."

She's sitting there, broken up, on the verge of tears. Mechanically, I leaf through the plans for the Taffarines hotel.

"There was Safia too," I say. "I imagine you'd guessed."

"I didn't mind too much," she says with a shrug. "She's four or five years older than you. And anyway, no one can make a life with Safia." Is this an olive branch?

"Eudoxia, I'm a swine."

"Not at all. I'm the one who made the mistake."

The two of us on the avenue swarming with people. The city is carrying on its nightlife with an air of insouciance. But next week is the dreaded Ramadan. Friends call out from the terrace of a café. An engaged couple enjoying a stroll, they think. The lemonade seller turns his swan-neck taps. Leaning against a pillar, a Demon of the South, in white robe and leather belt, observes the comings and goings.

"If you like," I suggest, "I'll write you a letter, acknowledging the wrongs I've done you. You can show it to your next fiancé."

"I don't need a letter, Gabriel."

We're passing the Prince Regent's Palace. The years have lent charm to its nineteenth-century facade. It's guarded on alternate days by the *Whites* and the *Blacks.* Today the *Blacks* are on duty, with their countrified faces and their bayonets like huge steel nibs. I have a fleeting vision of them dipping their weapons in ink to write a petition to their colonel.

"There'll be no 'next fiancé,' " she says firmly.

We're standing together under the trees, which summer has strewn with blood-red flowers. I'm already late for my meeting with Timsit. Will she wait for me?

"None of this would have happened if I'd been able to work properly and build the House of the Prophets."

"I know," she says, understandingly.

In a moment she'll hail a cab. In a moment part of my life will disappear.

The next day, to everyone's surprise, the Government falls. We'd come to believe that Samiel was indestructible. But he'd shilly-shallied too long and his credit had run out. The Prince Regent, that insubstantial being, had finally got the message that all was not well. Wearing a black frock coat, Samiel climbs the Palace steps to tender his Government's resignation. An enormous crowd gathers on the square. What savior will emerge? Perhaps the *Master of the Hour* announced by the prophets of Islam.

Timsit and I, turning our backs on all the excitement, visit the tomb of El Hanachi, the saint with the serpent. In front of it, humble candles are burning. In our country we've always venerated the reptiles that ward off rodents. But the monument is only a large, slightly lopsided cube, topped with a fluted dome. I glue my eye to the slit in the door. Timsit scolds me: the old fellow doesn't like being disturbed.

217

"What I like best about Islam," I'd said to Ruwan not so long ago, "are the saints."

"The saints of Islam thank you for the compliment," he'd answered imperturbably.

He himself was not too much in favor of these old, vaguely heretical, cults. I thought I'd pull his leg: "When you die, in sixty years or so, all your faults will be forgotten and they'll build you a pretty white mausoleum. The good folk will come and pray to you to cure them of their toothache."

And since everything happens at once, the forces of evil chose that very night to get even with the En Nasr Tower. At three in the morning, I was undeservedly enjoying the sleep of the just, when Red Truck pulls me out of bed.

"For Christ's sake!" he grumbles. The explosion has blown out the glass from top to bottom. There'll be pieces in every garden for a mile around. It has melted the elevator shaft, ripped out the plumbing. Just the carcass, the great concrete skeleton, remains. No one will have the patience to pull it down and it will stand as a monument to our folly for a long time to come.

The representative of the Swiss insurance company is also on the scene. He has already notified us that the policy does not cover acts of terrorism. In front of all those dismayed men, I suddenly burst out laughing. This Victory Tower, this eyesore, had at last got its comeuppance! Since returning from America, I'd managed to complete one single job, and this was it. And here it was in ruins, mortally wounded. If a calamity is bad enough, it becomes hilarious.

"Poor boy," says Red Truck, loud enough for me to hear, "grief has sent him off his head."

Dawn spreads out over the city. The first furtive calls can be heard from the gardens. The order never changes: first the birds wake, then the donkeys, then the flies, and last of all, men.

True to form, no one claims responsibility for the explosion. The Forty Brothers merely point out that the tower was of foreign design. They've begun sending out press releases like a government department.

White sky over Marsana. Summer settles in, the terrible Middle Eastern summer. I make my way through the narrow streets to the Café of the Peaks, where Timsit, seated between two sleepers, is playing cards with her little brother.

"You wouldn't listen to me. That tower was too high. It was bound to fall down one day."

I wander aimlessly back to the modern quarters, my mind a blank. For some time I've been getting a curious pang of unease whenever a car slows down behind me. I'd been thoughtless and untrustworthy. Now I was going to pay for it.

The composition of the new government is announced. Prime Minister: Amor Pasha, the man with the fine snowy head of hair. He must have been chosen for his looks. The Mozarabs are represented by our friend Sarun. At last this former commercial traveler has made it.

"Now that Sarun's a minister, I can't very well make it up with his daughter," I tell Safia on the telephone. "I'd be accused of opportunism."

The street is quiet, apart from a few groups gathered around transistors.

A little later, the Forty Brothers make it known that they put no faith in the new team, headed by an old hack.

"And how's Eudoxia?" asks our mother, who doesn't miss a trick. "You don't mention her anymore."

"Eudoxia's fine, thank you," I say, throwing down the newspaper on the table.

Those were days when God seemed to have rejected Jesus and us with Him. How had we failed? Hadn't we served Him better than the so-called Christians of the West? But our sighs and prayers left Him unmoved. God had gone over to the other side. Cold and inscrutable, He held himself aloof from us. This was the God of Islam. And this, perhaps, was Islam's main shortcoming, a lack of tenderness.

My throat was a little dry as I got out of the bus. Some newly shorn sheep were waiting on the sunbaked square. They had been herded together, head-to-tail, as is done in these parts, with the rows fitting into one another; arranged in this way, they never dreamed of moving.

A sentry was sauntering up and down in front of the house. A neighbor had brought some peaches. Such was Monsignor Elias's exile. Tragedy? Comic opera?

The prisoner occupied the only room in the house that opened onto the courtyard. He was reading, moving his lips; he didn't seem to know who I was.

"I'm the son of your friend Hilarion."

"Dear Hilarion! How is he?"

"He died six years ago. You saw him to his last resting place, Monsignor."

"May the hand of the Almighty be light upon him," he replied, unruffled. Then he asked me to sit facing the light. His sight had deteriorated considerably.

"Yes, it's really you, Gabriel. Forgive me. One can't be too careful these days."

He ordered the customary coffee from a young curate, who had dropped in to see how he was getting along. All the familiar objects had been left behind at his official residence. "Except Lazarus," he said.

Lazarus was parading in the courtyard, trailing his magnificent tail and pecking the ground every three paces, like a punctilious gentleman. His name was a reminder that the peacock had personified eternal life in early Christian art.

"He should sing for visitors."

"He's stopped singing," replied the young curate with a knowing air. "The courting season is over."

Aware, maybe, that we were talking about him, the bird came boldly in and stood in front of us, darting his absurd little head from side to side. These creatures' necks must be too frail to hold their heads up. The old man took some grain from a saucer and scattered it. "I never go to sleep unless Lazarus is in my room with me. The country may seem peaceful, but it would only take one fox . . ."

Clearly, he was not about to be released. The new government couldn't risk antagonizing the *Demons*.

"And now," he went on, "let's hear about you. You've caused a bit of a scandal." His memory was coming back inexorably.

"I have nothing to say," I answered. "What's broken is broken."

Elias, in the midst of his own worries, had taken the trouble to arrange a match between a student from a good, but poor family, and Sarun's daughter. And instead of making myself worthy of the honor . . .

"Eudoxia was too good for me. She is a generous, unselfish girl. She was the first to understand my scheme for the mosque."

"Ah, that mosque," Mar Elias cuts in. "It was bound to fail. If you had done me the favor of consulting me."

I look at his hands, speckled with liver spots. I look at his soft gray eyes, under those beetling brows. I look at his book, which he can no longer read.

"This House of the Prophets should have been built ten years ago," he adds unexpectedly. "Everything was still possible then."

In those days, there was little talk of oil. It was before the Muslims realized they were the most blessed of men. The

221

Demons of the South were dozing in the bottles where King Solomon had shut them up.

"I've become a nobody," Monsignor Elias goes on. "The exarch's residence has been closed; the police have put it under seal. There's not even the telephone here. I have the papers read to me. How do you glean a little truth from a newspaper?"

"Between the lines, maybe?"

"I've become a nobody. All the same, one of the Prince Regent's aides came to see me yesterday. Just imagine, he wanted me to put people's minds at rest with a statement."

He shrugs and his gray eyes shine with pride.

"Still, we can hope that Sarun's influence . . ." I've pronounced his name in spite of myself.

"Sarun accepted that post against my advice," says the old man. "He's now a willing hostage, whereas I'm an unwilling one. There's not much difference."

The curate is sitting there on a stool, trying to look as if he's not listening. How are we to know he doesn't work for the Minister of the Interior?

Monsignor Elias opens his book at random and pretends to read a passage:

And it shall come to pass in that day, that the Lord shall hiss for the fly that is in the uttermost part of the rivers of Egypt and for the bee that is in the land of Assyria . . .

The folio volume has fallen from his trembling hands. I stoop to retrieve it. As I do so, he whispers a few words in my ear, "When the Palace announces that I have resigned of my own free will, you'll all know it's a lie."

The curate has withdrawn, offended perhaps. The afternoons are much pleasanter at this altitude than at sea level. The old man leans on my arm, and we go out to a seat on the porch. Above our heads hang the unripe grapes of a headstrong vine.

As though talking to himself, he reviews some old memories of his life as a monk. The ravine which snakes down to the Dead Sea, across the plateau of Judaea, the Monastery of Saint Saba, with its silvery domes, clinging to the sheer rock face. If they hadn't begged him to come back, he'd still be there listening to the falcons chasing one another through the gorges.

"I came to announce . . ."

"No, my son, you're not going to announce your departure. We've already lost Fahim Bey, Iskandar Pasha, Alfred Sebbagh, Edward Sebbagh. What will become of us if everyone leaves?"

It's not that. They've just gone on vacation a little earlier than usual, taking some extra luggage.

"Things will be better after Ramadan," I say, faithfully repeating Sarun's words.

"Those who leave are traitors," replies Elias. "They are sapping our community's strength. That's the word I want put out."

Things have come to a pretty pass if one can't go to Cannes or Saint Moritz anymore!

"Don't worry," I say, "I'll be the last to desert."

And I explain my plan. As soon as Mar Elias understands that it involves the Nussaris, he grows wary. For all the centuries we've known these people, no good has come of them. But they will become our ally.

Because once the Jews have been thrown out, and the Christians crushed, who will be next on the list? The Nussaris, of course. The liberties they take with Islam, the shameless behavior of their women, what they eat, what they are, everything will be held against them. After the infidels have been dealt with, it'll be the heretics' turn. I'll go and warn them and get their support.

"You mean to negotiate with the Nussaris?" Monsignor Elias asks incredulously.

"I have a close friend among the Nussaris." Better not specify the sex.

I gloss over the difficulty of finding a qualified spokesman among these savages. The identity of their headman, the Grand Muqran, is their best-kept secret. Yesterday, though, Timsit swore she knew him.

"I shall need a letter of credence, signed by your hand," I go on.

The old man's cheeks flush at the idea of still being useful, of becoming drawn into a plot. He asks me to bring his writing materials and gets rid of the curate by ordering another coffee.

From Elias VIII, Exarch of the Christians, to the Grand Muqran of the Nussaris, health and prosperity.

May the just and good Lord guide thy feet and heap His blessings on thy head.

The sky is heavy with threats; but these can still be averted if men of goodwill unite.

The bearer of this letter comes in my name.

Back in the office, I'll correct one or two of the downstrokes, and erase some of the superfluous diacritical marks.

"Perfect," I say, "except the Nussaris won't believe me. They'll say I've stolen some of your stationery."

Elias smiles, fumbles in the folds of his robes and produces a small object wrapped in a handkerchief. One more treasure preserved from the oppressors: the seal of the exarchate. Having no ink pad, he breathes on its surface and makes a pale print.

When I leave, the new sentry lets me pass without a word. But it will be known that I came here, and that I was given a letter. So I won't sleep at home tonight. I'll ask Nahas, our engineer, to put me up. The police won't come looking for me at the house of a Muslim.

224

*To consider minorities as politically and economically inferior
smacks of dictatorship and injustice.*

Colonel QADDAFI
Green Book

As we crossed the Tin Tazart viaduct, I saw it was being
guarded by troops. Obviously the government was afraid
the bombers would strike again.

Timsit had never taken the train before. She preferred
the warm, intimate atmosphere of the bus, with its vegeta-
bles and chickens. She was curled up on the seat.

"Where's this Eudoxia?" she asked for the tenth time.

"She's gone. Gone for good."

"Good riddance."

"May the demons feast on her bones," added the little
boy.

Their antipathies were as violent as their affections. I tried
in vain to explain that Eudoxia had all the good qualities
and I all the bad.

The train made its way through interminable gorges full
of giant oleanders. Poisonous to mules, if the young musi-
cian was to be believed. His sister was absently singing a
love song to herself:

> *I planted almond trees*
> *Because of your big, black eyes.*

Did she really know the famous Muqran? "No one's allowed to know his name," she said. "But my father has told
me which village he lives in."

Every six years, a new Muqran was chosen by the village
chiefs. The election was held in secret. Those taking part
were forbidden to reveal the result—ever since the fateful

225

day† when the Prince Regent's troops seized the Muqran Mohand-wa-Mohand, and impaled him alive.

"When I've seen this man, maybe he'll want to hold me as a prisoner."

"As long as you're with me, you won't come to any harm," said Timsit. "I swear by the Prophet."

It then occurred to me that she may have got it into her little head that we were going to see the Grand Muqran in order for him to marry us. I'd have to clear up that misunderstanding.

"I've been sent to sign a pact with him against the Forty Brothers."

"Against the Brothers? No one can do anything against them."

"You're wrong. They're only pharaohs."

This old name, transmitted by the Koran, had become synonymous with despot. It appealed to her and she spent some time rolling it around her tongue.

"God will hurl the pharaohs into the sea," said the little boy, half remembering the story of Moses. He may have looked a sleepyhead, but he had a bellicose imagination.

The Jebel Express puffed slowly into its terminus. A crowd had gathered on the platforms. It was the first time I'd seen so many Nussaris together, and despite some intermarrying, the local type stood out clearly: deep-set eyes, prominent cheekbones, straight hair. The passengers jumped down from the train: more or less seasonal workers hurrying to get out of the big city before Ramadan. We too had only a couple of days in which to complete our business. After that deadline, despite the Nussaris' lack of piety, the obligation to fast could provide an excuse for not seeing us.

There were police at the station to see who had got off

† The year 1134 of the Hegira

226

the train. What on earth were they afraid of? I'd put on a burnous and was too hot.

"Wait till tonight," said Timsit. "You won't be sorry to have it."

Apparently, no one had noticed us. Mules for hire were standing under big trees from which fluff fell like snow.

"Where are you from?" asked the man in charge of them, boring through me with gimlet eyes.

"The gentleman's come to buy monkeys up-country," Timsit explained.

"Then change mounts at Aït Faraït," the man advised. That was the next leg of the journey. He charged us a little extra for the return of the beast.

We then had to choose an animal. Timsit rejected three for reasons best known to herself, and picked out a big gray mule.

"You must never take the first one offered," she told me.

And we set out over the mountains, taking the hazardous shortcuts she knew so well. She made me get on the pack saddle. I insist we change off.

"You won't make it on foot," she answers scornfully.

Wherever there's the slightest shelf of land, there's a field of barley squeezed onto it—some are still an acid green, others a gold that seems to sing on the dark red of the earth. Below us, clouds of dust rise up from threshing floors, where donkeys, mules and cows walk around in circles until they're ready to drop. Every peak is crowned with a tiled village.

The land of the Nussaris is teeming with people. The folk of the plains took refuge here in time of invasion, and escaped starvation by eating acorns. Nowadays, the men go to the coastal towns or to Europe, leaving their wives and children. But they nearly always return to live out their days at home.

On the outskirts of one of these hilltop villages, we meet

a group of girls carrying enormous fagots, which look strangely out of place in this country without woods or forests. They line up to let us pass, hiding their faces, then all together turn their nice red cheeks toward us, laughing merrily.

Timsit finds us a room. Her little brother plays a solo on his clarinet, and the men of the village dance, three steps forward, three steps back, grasping one another by the elbows.

The evening has brought a surprising chill to the air.

The next day dawns white and stifling, with wispy cottonwool clouds: leftover rain that hasn't fallen. The boy catches a chameleon on the path, and only with great difficulty can I get him to release it, as this creature is an ingredient in the Nussari pharmacopoeia. The stones hurt my feet through my thin rope soles. I try to get news of the city, but my transistor batteries have gone flat.

Halfway to our destination, we see our first black swine. The Nussaris let these creatures roam free all year and they become so wild that they have to be shot before they can be eaten. A highly controversial matter! For centuries, village theologians, flying in the face of the evidence, have been doing their utmost to prove that these are not pigs, but a distinct species unknown to the Prophet.

Here at last is Ouresker, clinging vertiginously to a mountain peak.

"This is only the lower village," Timsit tells me, "Ouresker-el-Tahtani."

The upper village is still hidden from view. We make our way past thorny hedges, past orchards where bird-scarers are click-clacking. This nest of houses looks dead, but dozens of pairs of eyes are watching our approach.

I show my letter of credence. The village headman holds it upside down.

"How do we know this really is Mar Elias's signature?"

"This girl can vouch for it."

And Timsit obligingly swears. It's fortunate that a woman's oath is accepted in this Godforsaken land.

"Get back in the saddle," the headman orders. "You'll be taken to the Grand Muqran."

"But I thought he lived here."

"No, he lives in the sky. Hang on tight."

I'm blindfolded and someone takes the mule's halter. Timsit is furious at being told to wait for my return. My guide makes all sorts of detours to confuse me. I'm aching all over when I arrive.

The blindfold is removed, the ceremonial starts once more. A new dignitary has my missive translated. Then, with the blindfold back on again, I'm led through the village on foot. Up and down we go, at every step. I swear they're making a fool of me.

A little old man sitting on his heels, leaning against a wall in the gloom of a low-beamed room. I go toward him. He has a little pointed beard, and his eyes sparkle with shrewdness. "You are in the presence of the Grand Muqran of the Nussaris," my keeper informs me.

As is customary, we begin by talking of the harvests, the flocks, the health of this one and that one. The old fellow speaks fluent colloquial Arabic. He must have been a peddler for ten or twenty years in the lowlands.

"Mar Elias is a just man," he volunteers.

We're alone together. True, they'd frisked me earlier to make sure I wasn't armed. And a light step in the adjoining room reminds me that even here there are bodyguards.

I have prepared my speech carefully. Marsania is in turmoil, O Grand Muqran. If the Nussaris think they can stay out of trouble, they're wrong. Everything points to their being the next victims. The fact that their married women go unveiled, even in the city. The way they turn around and stare after men. The black pigs they make into smoked bacon. And it's not just pigs; there are rumors of snake stews.

My host makes a gesture of denial. I'm willing to grant that it's a legend. But the fact is that the Nussaris have the art of cooking up everything that swims, runs, flies or crawls. It was their favorite pastime long before the coming of Islam. And in all innocence, they have carried on with it. They've dried their magic herbs between the pages of the Koran.

A servant puts down one of those carbide lamps used in outdoor markets; the harsh white light casts enormous shadows. While I'm speaking, the Muqran mutters intermittently to himself. Is he reciting ancient prayers that are now forbidden?

I've brought with me some of the leaflets that have been handed out in the city in the last few weeks: "Children of Marsania, your language is Arabic, your faith Islam." He looks at them without surprise. After all, his intelligence network is a thousand times better than mine. There are all those knife grinders, itinerant workmen, scrap-iron merchants.

"You'll share my meal," he says.

An earthenware pot with a conical lid. Am I about to taste their fricassee of bat? Not a bit of it, it's a perfectly normal half chicken. My host takes the best piece with his fingers and serves me. He eats practically nothing.

A boy fans us with a little branch. On his account I've stopped talking.

"Go on," commands the Grand Muqran.

The same threat hangs over both our peoples; is it not therefore the moment to conclude an alliance? That means if the Christians are attacked in Marsana, the Nussaris will rise up and help them. And vice versa.

I've been left alone. I wrap myself in my burnous and lie down on my mat, but I can't sleep. Through the single loophole in the room comes a breath of warm air from outside. At this distance, Marsana has lost its power to do harm. But tomorrow, it will be in the grip of Ramadan.

Damn it, I too am a Nussari, despite the veneer of a few centuries. So is my sister Ilena. And what of my friend Ruwan, who claims to be an Andalusian Arab? Haven't we all drawn our lifeblood from this mountain?

I get up to look for some water and step over the body of my guard. A few huddled sheep are dreaming in the little courtyard. A donkey twitches its ears as I go by; it's still on the alert. A little unsleeping figure passes in front of me, and stops a moment. His Excellency the Grand Muqran is meditating. He has not seen me, or pretends not to have.

What shall I say about the next day's talks? They were the same, except that the Muqran called in his advisers. As I await the outcome in my cell, I repeat the maxims of Es Sitifi, the Machiavelli of the Maghreb:

If the need is urgent, ally yourself with the devil. But the devil has duped cleverer people than you.

If you are consumed by ambition, ally yourself even with the Christians. But they are bad friends. Turn against them as soon as you can.

Not content with writing, Es Sitifi put his principles into practice. He was said to have received money from the Norman kings of Sicily. But history does not tell us how he betrayed them.

"Alliance concluded," the Muqran announces with a big smile. He's used no more words than he had to for so simple a thing. Naturally, nothing will be written down; that would be too dangerous, and contrary to local custom. In case the people in Marsana doubt my story, I'm presented with one of those black stones, veined with yellow, which are only found up here, and which the Nussaris hardly ever part with.

Timsit is waiting for me in the lower village with a new

mule she has managed to borrow free of charge. She's already heard, heaven knows how, that the treaty has been concluded.

"Let's be on our way," I say at once. The heat is abating. Looking back, we see Ouresker-el-Tahtani hanging over us like a huge decayed tooth. When all's said and done, how can I be sure I've seen the real Muqran? The Nussaris are quite capable of producing a false one to mislead possible assassins.

"What was he like?" Timsit asks.

"Little pointed beard, sharp nose, no bigger than an eleven-year-old child."

"That's him all right," she says with impressive calm.

And we take to the treacherous paths which plunge down to the sea.

From the top of the keep, brother Charles scans the horizon. But nothing has changed: the blue-black cone of the mountain, and the long rocky ridge with the cleft like a wound. Baleful old fortresses. A breeze from the south warms the winter morning.

He is the only European in those parts—and the only Christian, except for a slave whose freedom he has bought. The civilized world is at war, and strange passions are seething within the borders of Tripolitania.

What does this new wind hold in store for him? He already knows. He knows he will be put to death in the name of Islam—of a certain Islam. He has been resigned to this for a long time.

For it is through Islam that he found his way back to God. Accordingly, he decided to live out his days in its shadow.

In the distance, the wind has raised a little dust. The wind, or someone who is coming. And all is well.

Turning our backs on the roller-coaster villages, we traveled for three days, Timsit, the mule and I. No one raised any objection to my setting out alone with this girl. Her ability to defend herself must have been well known. She was as tough as the mule.

A little water still flowed in the wadis, but the mountain was beginning to smell of burnt broom. Our route wound from valley to valley. When harvesters called out greetings, Timsit replied in her own language.

"They all think I'm your wife," she said, without batting an eyelash.

And to pull her leg I said, "The Grand Muqran promised me that all the Nussaris would become Christian."

She didn't even seem shocked. If that was what the Muqran wanted, it must be a good thing.

In the early evening, when the heat had let up, the mountain took on blue tints, and when I looked back toward this wall of shadows, this rampart we had not crossed, I thought I'd been wrong not to push on into this unknown kingdom, far from our pettiness and our quarrels.

One night, as we were sleeping, wrapped in our burnouses, on the grass-grown roof of a shepherd's hut, the call of the jackal rent the silence. "Don't worry," said Timsit, "that's Si Yakub. He's a sly old thing and he doesn't go for men."

Our path was marked with little cairns, known as *rejems*. The bigger ones, so they say, contain the bones of holy men. But when I asked Timsit their names, she invariably answered, "It's the lord of the path."

It was arranged that she would leave me at the Olive Tree Pass. On the morning of the fourth day, as we were toiling up a bare slope, she pointed toward a slight dip in the mountain ridge ahead of us: "We're nearly there."

I was so used to approaching this pass from the other side

that I hadn't recognized it. She began to laugh. What a booby; he can't even find his way home!

Midday surrounded by flies, midday soaked in sweat, on the Olive Tree Pass. The heat haze shimmering on the watery plain.

The mule shied. There was a shape under the lone tree. Was it a boulder? No, a man was getting to his feet, coming out to meet us. Good Lord, Micallef. Our tenant.

"I spent the night here," he says. "I knew you'd be coming by."

"How did you know?"

"The shepherds saw signals on the mountain."

The same flashing torches, which in days gone by warned that the regent's soldiers were coming.

"I talked to the shepherds and came up to meet you," says Micallef.

"That was good of you."

He brushes aside my thanks and goes on, "The police are waiting for you in town. They've searched the house. They're sure you're hiding hereabouts."

"My conscience is clear."

Someone in the city must have reported my departure for the land of the Nussaris. But they'd have trouble pinning anything on me.

"Don't the mountain folk know what's happening?" asked Micallef.

"What is happening?"

He points in the direction of the capital: "Rioting."

"Have you any news of my mother? And my younger sister?"

"None at all. But nothing's happened to them, or I'd have heard."

Timsit is patting the mule's flanks, unmoved by these rapid exchanges in Faranghi. I pull myself together.

234

"What have the police got against me? I'm not responsible for what happens in Marsana in my absence."

"The leader of the Demons of the South has been shot. He may even have been killed."

"Ruwan ibn Maher?"

"Yes, I think that was the name."

"Who shot him?"

"A Christian. I didn't get who it was. People are saying that you supplied the gun because of your sister Ilena. There's been rioting ever since."

What perfect Marsanian logic. Ruwan seduced my sister, therefore I hired an assassin.

And there on the hilltop I start to laugh insanely.

For a long time, I leaned against the olive tree, gazing down at the sun-parched countryside. The vineyards, the orchards, and the cemeteries surrounded with cypresses. I alone had changed. I now had a price on my head.

Micallef was sitting on his heels, fanning himself with his straw hat. Wily, a bit of a thief, but faithful. Nascent shadows were making long seams on the face of the landscape. And out here, the goings-on in the city no longer seemed real.

"I must be getting back," said Micallef at last, shading his eyes with his hand. "They'll be worrying about me. They worry about everything nowadays."

"As you like, Micallef."

"Don't follow me down, I beg you."

"Where on earth am I to go?"

"To the Plain of the Fevers. No one will look for you there."

He showed me the way. He left me bread, cheese and some plums. Then he disappeared along the dry bed of a little wadi. Between two humps in the ground, a white spire pointed upward like a finger.

Then Timsit got to her feet. There was nothing more to

say; it was all settled. She loaded her little bundle onto the mule and bade me good-bye just as if we were to meet again the next day. And away she went. After a while, I looked and saw her receding into the distance, leading an animal that limped slightly. She didn't look back. She'd become no more than a tiny silhouette wending her way back to the wildness of her origins, swallowed up by the landscape, forever incomprehensible.

Exile. To save money, four of us cram ourselves into one damp hotel room. The women are in the neighboring attic. We share the sour autumn and the rickety washbasin. As long as we can bear one another's company.

As head of the family, a position I could well have done without, I sent Ruwan our apologies. For he did recover from the attack. He'll be crippled for life, that's all. I said he could publish my letter.

"You're crazy, Gabriel. You might as well write to the devil."

In any case, he did not reply. And one day, one of my friends put an end to the discussion in these terms:

"Spare us your remorse, old fellow. What you did was well done."

What did I do? I merely arranged an alliance, too late to be of any use. By the time the Nussaris got moving, the Christians had already lost out.

For God was out of reach, and France too far away.

But this evening, things are very different. Everyone believes that Ruwan was shot on my orders.

Shafik has found a little temporary job. My poor mother works as a cleaning woman. Leila is looking in vain for piano pupils. Every morning we rush for the overseas newspaper, hoping to read that Ruwan and his gang have fallen.

236

Alas, the Forty Brothers' tentacular hold on Marsania gets stronger all the time, like fig trees that have taken over an old house and are slowly bursting it open.

Gray night, bitter night over our destinies. But each of us, as he left, was bequeathed a little bit of sunshine that will burn forever in his breast.

Am I awake? Surely; a sleeper turns over and his iron bed creaks. The curtain moves, letting in a wan light. Someone is coming toward me, as in a dream. It is Mark, the terrorist. How ashen his face is! Smiling, he takes my hand: "Remember your promise, Gabriel. Tonight, I'm sixteen."

The promise I'd made on my return from America: to light a bonfire on the mountain of the Transfiguration the night of his sixteenth birthday.

O Morqos, you are nothing but a pile of bones beneath a white stele. And we dared not carve your name on it for fear of reprisals against your remains.

The Chapel of the Transfiguration is nothing but a pile of rubble on the mountaintop.

And my heart is nothing but an old rag that is getting drier and drier.

Long are the days of Ramadan. This one has been longer than ever. While there is light enough to distinguish a black thread from a white, my brothers, you shall live with your thirst.

Never had Ramadan been so strictly observed. Brigades of volunteers have seen to that under the compliant eye of the police. They are young, they are fanatical, and they wield sticks. They have even stopped Christian restaurants from serving lunch. In their immaculate tunics, they are the kings of the city.

The cannon has thundered, the long wait is over. At last one can make peace with one's body. The streetlamps come on and it's possible, once more, to distinguish the black thread from the white. But this man-made light does not count. It cannot shift the frontiers of sin. From every house come laughter, shouts and the babble of children's voices.

A group of people go along the street toward a house where the table has been laid for them. They are young militants. They have done their duty. Now they are joking and enjoying themselves.

The eldest walks in the middle of the group—striped tunic and neat beard. He's only a few years older than the others, but takes a more lofty view of things, which stops him from joining in their fun. He's already sizing up the responsibilities of power. What will he do with the Pashas? What will he do with the Christians?

Hidden under the archway, the boy is waiting for him to come by. He's made a study of his movements. He knows that every evening Ruwan crosses this square in the old city with his little band of followers.

I grab his shoulders and shake him: "Get out Mark! You've got no business here." But I am far away in the mountains of the Nussaris on an illusory diplomatic mission. No one has noticed the lone boy on the street corner. Everyone is too busy eating and drinking.

Two shots ring out. Two shots, the newspapers said, though the second cartridge was never found.

The attacker has fled. He runs down the narrow streets and passages. But he doesn't really know this part of the city. His pursuers gradually catch up with him. People interrupt their meal, lean out of the window. Shouts of "Death!" come from all directions.

The pack has cornered him in a blind alley. He hammers on the door of the last house—one of those blue doors with huge studs on it. Seek, and ye shall find; knock, and it shall be opened unto you. . . .

I didn't see it happen, I didn't know about it. I was in the mountains and suspected nothing. I had, in fact, opted out, and another performed for me what he believed to be my duty.

238

For two days, the body of my little cousin Mark was exhibited on the square. Then the women of the family were allowed to claim it.

And Micallef, on the Olive Tree Pass, pretended not to know in order to allow me a few more hours' peace of mind!

Messages . . . Messages in Arabic on the walls of the foreign city. Messages in the subterranean tunnels where trains run. Undesirable messages on the seats of Metro cars.

The real inhabitants—those whose papers are in order, who enjoy civil rights and who have learned from the cradle that they are the most intelligent people on earth—the real inhabitants pass by these messages without understanding them. They don't want to see them.

They are the work of other inhabitants who are seldom seen, but who are there nonetheless, in their tens of thousands, in the interstices of the city, in the garrets, the slums. At nightfall, they come furtively out of their lairs and take possession of the city by means of their magic writing.

Look, here's an alluring shopfront: *Lobster tails à la crème de vin jaune.* I lower my eyes and see another statement: *Aïsha, you'll be mine forever.* It's barely decipherable; scrawled in clumsy, tortured letters with a piece of coal. But it *has been written.*

I walk blindly along the boulevard. The Church of the Madeleine. Emir Abd-el-Kader is said to have gone there to say a prayer after he was freed. I climb the steps. But the stones of the Madeleine have nothing to tell me.

The streets, the squares, the cities that I carried within me and that were never born.

I go underground again to read once more what the walls have to say: *M'Barek, I'll be at Brahim's Café on Saturday. God loves us. Islam will conquer. O my children across the sea, God bless you. Unite against the police.* The great formless poem that runs like blood through the veins of the city.

New Year's Day in the foreign city. At midnight, all they could think of doing in celebration was to blow their horns. Is this what two thousand years of civilization amount to? Where are the flutes and tambourines of Marsania?

On the square stand some Christmas trees provided by the municipality. One of them has fallen over, but its fairy lights go winking on.

Cold countries!

Listen to me, I've got a question for you. Answer off the top of your head: What does Marsania mean to you?

"To me," says the first exile, "it's ground raw meat, with onions, mint and a big piece of pita bread."

"To me," says the second, "it's the old city at night, with its long vaulted alleyways, lit only at the crossings, here and there a hooded shadow, fleeting and elusive."

"And I see cats scavenging in garbage cans," says the third.

Naturally, living abroad has divided us into tiny clans: a microcosm of what we used to be across the water. I even accepted an invitation from Gregory, our erstwhile aviator. He lost an arm in a futile battle. Then he married a girl from Verrières-le-Buisson. Now he works in one of those French banks that try to ensnare Arab capital. He won't listen to talk about the past:

"Exile lends enchantment to the view," he says firmly. "The East that you keep on about never existed. Think of what it was really like. Think of the details!"

Hell, I'm still being followed. A little dark fellow with tinted glasses that are certainly a sham. I stop outside a bookshop, he stops outside a lingerie shop. I go on, he goes on.

That's how they got Daud. They tailed him. One day, in a

quiet street, they gunned him down. But Daud went in for arms trafficking. I merely serve as a mailbox.

I swing round, I walk toward the guy. When I draw level with him, it will be easy. He'll just have to push his weapon into my stomach.

"Hi there, Arab, another Arab's watching you. Hi there, jackal, another jackal's passing you."

He pretends not to see me, averts his eyes and looks into a travel agent's window. Next time.

One day I too will put on tinted glasses and grow a mustache. I already have a false passport. All I have to do is look like the photograph. I'll go to the harbor taverns and eat grilled octopus with sour wine—even though there is no more wine in Marsania. I'll have my shoes polished by the shoeshine boys—even though they've all been sent to re-education camps. I'll walk in front of the Palace, where new masters have replaced the princes. And I'll melt into dark quarters where plots for revenge are being hatched.

"One day," says the old negro, "a Jewish woman prisoner poisoned the Prophet's food. He found out and sent for her.

" 'Woman, why did you wish me dead?'

" 'I said to myself, if he's a false prophet, the earth will be well rid of him; if he's a true prophet, he'll spit the poison out.'

Whereupon Muhammad forgave this creature so full of faith."

I've been put in charge of liaison with Rome. For we have men in Rome too. I deliver packages, get the latest news and, before catching the train back, I revisit some familiar place to draw strength from its beauty.

Do you know the *Cimitero dei Forestieri?* You take the subway to the *Porta San Paolo.* You walk around the pyramid that an Augustan profiteer had erected over himself—so white you'd think it was made of sugar. You follow the old reddish wall adorned with umbrella pines. A little gate opens onto a cool enclosure.

No one was there that morning, except a tiny woman in a black shawl who was kneeling by a grave, digging the earth with a trowel. I'd just read a few inscriptions when she rose to her feet and walked toward the custodian's house. Something about that elegant step seemed familiar. I quickened my pace, making the gravel crunch beneath my feet. She turned around. Safia!

I knew I'd see her again—on the day of her choosing.

"Hello, Gabriel," she said, as if we'd parted only yesterday.

Her full, lively face, those magnificent yellow eyes unchanged. She takes off her scarf, and out tumble gray locks that she has had the coquetry not to dye.

"I've come to pay my respects to the dead," she tells me. Two dates on a slab, one name: Avram Samiel. All that remains of a prime minister.

This incurable passion the Jews have for tombs.

"I know you didn't really care for Samiel. But he too was an artist. Master of weights and counterweights. Master of curves and countercurves."

And his masterpiece was Marsania.

We took the streetcar back to Safia's apartment. She lives on the most peaceful of the Seven Hills, the one you never hear about. Her windows look out on a garden.

"This is my boudoir," she says.

"Do you still paint?"

"More than ever. But you wouldn't recognize my style."

She opens her door with a mischievous air. I'm stupefied. The whole apartment has been painted in trompe l'oeil to enlarge its modest dimensions. And there, running around the walls, are the arcades, columns and terraces of the village of Korben, with glimpses of the blue-green water that lapped the shores of the Taffarines.

That's how I'd imagined those Islands of the Hesperides, but it was Safia who had brought them into being.

"I daren't sit down," I say, "I'd feel I was plunging into the water."

How wonderfully at ease she seems. This daughter of a wandering race has managed better than any of us to find a niche for herself beneath new skies.

"Do you own the place?"

Despite the confiscation laws, she'd been able to sell her little villa on the heights of Marsana for a not too disastrous price. She'd also sold the turquoises and aquamarines that we loved. She lives on modest commissions. Here, of course, everyone loves art. It's not like back home where the purchase of paintings was just a social obligation. I say "was," for in Marsania today, it seems, they don't even know what painting is.

"You're as beautiful as ever, Safia."

"Shameless flatterer."

I refuse the proffered cigarette.

"You're not so bad yourself, Gabriel. The forty-year-old ravaged look suits you very well. When you were younger, you were too . . ."

"Too . . . ?"

"A bit too full of missionary zeal."

We go on bandying trifles, although my train ticket is in my pocket and life is about to separate us once more. We recall, one by one, figures from those happy times.

"I've seen Ruwan on Marsanian television," I say. We pick up the signal occasionally. Ruwan is not a cabinet minister; merely a secretary-general of something or other. But still powerful, apparently. He was getting about in his little invalid carriage, his face distorted with the effort. I've heard that the slightest movement is torture.

His wife, my sister Ilena, has smuggled a letter to us.
She's had another child, a daughter, and is bringing her up
secretly in our faith. Not the boy. He belongs to Ruwan.
But the daughter, God willing, will be a Christian at heart.
This is the revenge of Mozarab women who marry into
Islam.

"Will you never have done with Jesus?" Safia jokes.

I thought of the imam who led the prayers in an Andalusian mosque until the day he informed his dumbfounded
congregation of his conversion to the Gospel; perhaps he
too was a Christian woman's son.

The bells of a nearby church strike the hour. They ring
out louder and more confidently than the bells in our country, whose tinkling always sounded apologetic.

"At first," Safia says, "they'd wake me up at night. Now
I'm used to them. Time flows over me without hurt."

Her face lights up with a touching smile. We have exhausted our list of dear ones, but for a single name. I ask the
question I hadn't dared ask anyone:

"And what happened to Eudoxia?"

"Eudoxia is a nun at the Convent of Sidnaya, near Damascus."

The one the Crusaders called Our Lady of Sardenaya.

"That's my fault," I say.

"You have nothing to feel guilty about. That girl was not
for you. She belonged to God."

"To God? But Safia, you don't believe in God."

"Maybe I don't," she answers with a little laugh.

The village of Korben looks out at us from its lattice
windows. We are the only millionaires who will ever put up
there.

"Safia, it was you I loved. You know that, don't you?"

"Actually, you were in love with a number of people.
Not to mention a hotel and a mosque."

At that I lash out at her:

"And are the thugs on the *Piazza di Spania* as handsome as those from Bir Falastin?"

"Why wouldn't they be?" she answers imperturbably.

But her calm, settled air belies her words. There are no more affairs in Safia's life. Only her art, her imaginary village, her marvelous umbrella pines in that peaceful cemetery. And possibly, through a narrow chink, the God of the Old Testament.

"I'm a free woman," she continues, as though reading my thoughts. "It wasn't an easy status to achieve in Marsania. But I was determined and I managed it. And I continue to live that way here. People can say what they like."

And I'm such an idiot that all I can do is put on my jacket, as my train's leaving shortly.

"Guess what. I'm going back to Marsania soon."

"As an architect?"

"No, as a political agitator."

"You're out of your mind."

We're going down the narrow brick stairway.

"You've got to forget that country," she says. "It has nothing further to offer you. You knew it at its best, just when the fruit was getting overripe."

Why don't I stay with her, now that I've found her again? Instead of going back to my shadowy life.

As I was walking away, I looked back and shouted, "Next year in Marsania!"

And I saw her looking after me, shaking her head.

I went down through the gorge of the One-Eyed Horse, eating the bread Micallef had given me. But the only suggestion of horse was the bones of sheep that had fallen from the plateau one misty day.

On I walked till I saw ahead of me a golden triangle of land with a toy farm to one side of it. It was only the Plain of the Fevers.

245

"Gabriel! Do you know there's a price on your head?"

The farmer and his family: hardworking folk who came to drain these marshes where egrets feed. A big antenna on their roof picked up the news, which got worse from day to day.

"You'll cross the straits with a fisherman," they decided. One or two large dhows haunted the shallows, gathering sponges that Liz Taylor has proclaimed to be the softest in the world.

We made the crossing at night, and the youngest crew member hummed old love songs.

At dawn, we saw that the straits were swarming with small boats. Bigger gray vessels were watching the goings-on: "The Sixth Fleet."

Too late. All the Sixth Fleet could do was look on. I landed in the little foreign port, with its gaily colored houses. Some Marsanians were encamped on the steps of the Latin church, surrounded by mounds of baggage and howling children. Suddenly a man came up and embraced me:

"Bravo Gabriel!"

It was Red Truck, the contractor, unshaven and haggard, but jovial nonetheless.

"Bravo Gabriel!" chorused the others.

Those wretched people were thanking me for having had the leader of the Demons of the South gunned down.

An absurd ovation, earned by another. A senseless homage to a dead boy.

And the stars of heaven fell unto the earth even as a fig tree casteth her untimely figs.

And finally, one winter evening, I saw Sarun again, in the little church on the Rue du Danube. The stove was drawing too strongly, the nave was packed. I was nearly overcome by the heat and the incense. And the choir was singing the old canticle:

246

They shall lift up their voice,
They shall cry aloud from the sea.

There were all sorts of people there. The matrons who used to keep the shop on Spinners' Street. Iskandar Pasha, our only Mozarab general, weighed down by victories he had never won. And the children born in exile who spoke French like Parisian kids.

Higher and higher rose the voices in their inexorable beauty. And I dreamed a dream: behold, a city arose from the sea. Behold, Marsana emerging from the abyss and calling to her children.

Suddenly I caught sight of a tall silhouette barely stooped by age. Sir Bat, clad all in black and leaning on a stick. When the service was over, I went up to him:

"Sarun, you have disappointed me. Forecasting used to be your job. And you were never wrong."

He looks slowly in my direction and wrings out a smile:

"That's not true, Gabriel. I saw it all coming, and I saw it from afar."

We leave the church together, he leaning on me as on a walking stick.

In fact, of course, I said nothing. I did not stir from my pew. His eye, his great staring nocturnal eye lighted on me. And he went away without having recognized me.

"Stop that woman!" shouts the man with the megaphone.

She's already melted into the dense crowd. They'd have had to bar the street, check all the people one by one as carefully as you go through hair looking for lice.

Ah, there she is. They've got her. Bring her back. Show her terror-stricken face. But it's all a mistake. It's only a stout old matron.

"Bolt your doors and bar your dwellings," says the radio.

247

"There must be no hiding place for the enemy of religion. There must be no rest for him who has offended God."

The enemy is Abbas, the last Prince Regent of Marsania. He fled from his palace disguised as a woman—thus revealing the true nature of his heart.

"We will cut out his tongue, we will gouge out his eyes," screams the radio.

The following day his body, still dressed as a woman, is found on an empty lot with thirty-two stab wounds.

The sailor points indifferently into the mist: "The islands." And tosses his cigarette butt into the sea, like a routine offering.

The clouds drift across the horizon. A fit of bad humor has blotted out the last sight of Europe astern. The deck is full of folk returning home because the civilized world no longer needs manual labor. Children crash into our legs. A fat, heavily made-up woman is quietly throwing up, her knees spread wide.

I do my best to blend in with the crowd, but I'm of a different species. I'm a political animal, the only one making the trip, I dare say. The organization is always sending agents to Marsania. But news soon dries up. Last month, Masfud was caught carrying arms, and shot.

The ship gives a friendly blast on its siren, as though to salute a companion. There are two of them, in fact, motionless, slightly fantastic shapes, rising high out of the water. Their names come back to me: to starboard, Ras-el-Tourd; to port, Korben. The island that we were going to build is unchanged. Short grass has grown over the scars we made. Brambles have filled in the holes. In the end, our dynamite did no more harm than the naval shells when the Regent's fleet was playing at sinking the great rock.

With the naked eye, I can see wild goats leaping. Safia had suggested shooting them in order to save the clumps of ornamental shrubs she was going to plant. It was never done, and the damn creatures have eaten everything—our bougainvilleas, our columns, our vistas.

A little farther off, the pervasive smoke of burning seaweed rises from a third island. The fishermen's wives and children, who are sitting on the shore in front of their huts mending their nets, wave to us as we go by.

"An opera singer used to live there," I say to a countrified fellow sitting next to me. "I heard her sing one evening. A foreigner with long blond hair."

He looks at me incredulously. This woman did exist, I swear it.

A murmur wells up from the deck: the great Arab prayer. Praise to the Lord for having brought the boat to its haven. The slow, full words rise and fall indefatigably. Words of hope I do not share, but which I have heard so often that they have become part of the substance of my being. And I repeat them too, softly, on the face of the deep.

The mainland is still invisible, but already we can smell it: the tang of scrubland in the fall, the fragrance of tiny tobacco fields. "Can you smell the island, Farida?" a father asks his little daughter. He's wearing the embroidered skullcap of the Amurian region.

Then, as though in answer, the mist rolls away, revealing a coast bathed in sunlight. The islands were only the first bastions of the white city huddled at the feet of a cliff.

As long as there's a Marsana, the Jeblasan will brood over it.

I count the belfries. None is missing. Then, my heart thumping, I set about counting the minarets, as there ought to be three more than there were before. To one side, the dark shape of the En Nasr Tower still dominates the lagoon, several heads higher than the surrounding buildings.

249

To pull it down would have been too costly, and no one dared complete it.

Just now, I was down in the toilets between two trembling sheet-metal partitions. I examined my face in a rather cloudy mirror. Who's going to know the once-handsome Gabriel with these gray locks and all these lines?

Dragging his leg, the pilgrim arrived at the gates of the city. But no one remembered him after such a long journey. (Ibn Atuf)

We go round the mole and enter the channel. A building I've never seen juts out over the tangle of the port: a prayer in the form of a three-master, a dream in stone, which cleaves the harbor with its bow. What used to be here? Warehouses, customs sheds, I believe. Now there's the madman's mosque, the giaour's mosque. And those who land on this shore lay their doubts about the existence of God at its feet.

Passports. Mine, of course, is forged. My name is Abd-er-Rahim, and no one is more Muslim than I. The policeman in his fine uniform looks at my cheap jacket and badly pressed pants.

"Where were you working?"

"In Paris, in the building industry."

Not a complete lie. Builder I was, builder I still am.

He could easily call my bluff. All he'd have to do is get me to recite the *Fatibah*. Or if he rolled up my shirt cuff, he'd see the cross tattooed on my wrist.

But it never occurs to the fat gendarme to do so. I've slipped a ten-piaster note between two pages of my passport. It's not that I have a bad conscience; I simply want to speed up the formalities. Others in the line have done likewise. A sigh of relief. A rubber stamp. Next.

In the end, I left my suitcase stuffed with subversive literature below decks. The crew can enjoy it. And I threw my black glasses overboard.

Revolution Boulevard—formerly Prince Ismail Boulevard. Little ragamuffins are trying to buy my currency off me. It's amazing what the government will tolerate. It will soon be as lax as the late monarchy.

I turn around, a little fuddled by the sun. The three masts of the stone ship tower over me. It's not exactly as I'd imagined it. But it's my design all right, radiant in its reality.

"That's the Mosque of the Republic," the meringue seller tells me.

"You mean the House of the Prophets."

He grins from ear to ear: "Now, you're a man in the know."

Yes, I know the seven secrets of our city. And the seventh is "seven colors." And I know that these colors are the seven peoples who used to live here on good terms: the Muslims of local stock; the Hanafites or Kuluglis, descendants of the Turks; the Mozarabs, to whom I belong; the Latins, who came by sea; the Sephardic Jews; the Nussaris, who hardly count as men; and the jinn or genii, who live under the earth and inhabit the waters, but who, like the six other peoples, had their own cadi, their own doctors and their own feast days.

Are these lost secrets? History has not said its last word.

And I make my way through the little winding streets without anger and without hatred; I walk under the arches and the corbels, moving slowly toward the heart of things.

SHORT GLOSSARY FOR THE WESTERN READER

ABD-EL-KADER (Emir), 1808–1883. Descendant of the Prophet, an Algerian political and religious leader. Defeated by the French, he was kept prisoner in France for five years. Later he was allowed to retire to a palace in Damascus with a pension from the French government. In 1860, while a Muslim mob was slaughtering the Arab Christians in the city, he rescued several hundred of them, and was granted the Grand Cross of the Legion of Honor by French Emperor Napoleon III.

He wrote several philosophical and mystical books in which he compared religions to children born of the same father to different mothers. His main French foe wrote: "His face is pale and looks like the conventional portrait of Jesus Christ."

AÏD-EL-KEBIR, also called Aïd-el-Adha or Great Bairam: greatest feast in Islam. Pious families are supposed to kill a sheep to commemorate Abraham's sacrifice. The Hajj, or pilgrimage to Mecca, usually takes place at that time.

ALMORAVIDS, also called Al-Murabitun: confederation of Berber tribes, whose religious zeal and military enterprise built an empire in northwestern Africa and Spain in the eleventh and twelfth centuries. Its name means "those who tied themselves" (to God). Some present-day political organizations have chosen the same appellation.

ANDALUS: Muslims of Berber or Spanish stock who lived in southern Spain. Expelled by the Christians between the thirteenth and the fifteenth centuries, they took refuge in Morocco or on the shores of the Mediterranean as far east as Egypt. They built many mosques and fine houses in their new homelands.

The Jews from Andalusia were similarly scattered.

252

CHARLES (Brother), alias Charles de Foucauld, 1858–1916. French explorer and hermit who chose to live in the middle of the Sahara Desert among Tuareg tribes. Murdered by fanatics from Libya.

Now honored as a saint by the Catholic Church, he also was an admirer of Islam.

EMPAIN (Baron): renowned Belgian businessman, developed new suburbs in Cairo at the end of the nineteenth century. His European factories provided streetcars for Egypt.

EXARCH: Eastern Christian bishop or archbishop, or deputy appointed by a patriarch to exercise jurisdiction over certain parishes abroad.

FATIHAH: the first chapter of the Koran, recited on many occasions.

GIAOUR: a derogatory term for a non-Muslim, especially a Christian, used in particular by the Turks. Literally: nonbeliever.

HANAFITE: one of the four schools of religious law in orthodox Islam. Predominant in Turkey and Central Asia.

JEWISH (or half-Jewish) PRIME MINISTER: such a fact may sound strange in an Islamic country. But many Jewish or Christian examples can be found in the not-too-distant past.

JINNI, plural *jinn* or *jnun* (also *genius,* plural *genii):* spirits dwelling in all conceivable objects, also capable of assuming human or animal form. Belief in them is very strong in the Middle East.

LULL or LULLE (Raymond): great Spanish alchemist and philosopher of the thirteenth century. He traveled to North Africa four times in order to convert the inhabitants to Christianity, but was expelled each time.

MARSANA: synthesis of some large cities in the Middle East or North Africa. Capital of Marsania.

MARSANIA: synthesis of Egypt, Lebanon, Syria, Iraq, etc.

MIHRAB: niche in a wall of all mosques showing the direction of Mecca. The Faithful face the *mihrab* during their prayers.

MINBAR: pulpit for the teacher in a mosque. According to the historian Ibn Khaldun, caliph Omar tried to prohibit minbars in the early years of Islam.

MOZARAB: means arabicized. A name for Christians under Muslim rule in Spain, but could also be used for most Christians in the Middle East. In the novel, the Mozarabs are a synthesis of several Arabic-speaking communities:

—the Copts of Egypt (largest Christian group in the East);

—the Maronites, Syriacs, Greek-Orthodox and Greek-Catholics of Lebanon, Syria, Jordan;

—the Assyrians and Chaldeans of Iraq, etc.

The relationship between the Muslim majority and Christian minorities, especially in Egypt, is vividly described and explained by Jean-Pierre Péroncel-Hugoz, *The Raft of Mohammed,* Holmes and Meier, N.Y. 1985.

NUSSARIS: in the novel, synthesis of several proud mountain tribes of the Middle East and North Africa. Some of them are Muslim dissenters.

OOM KALTHUM (1898–1975): an Egyptian woman of the lower classes, who became the most famous singer in the Middle East.

RAMADAN: the ninth month of the Muslim calendar. Muslim ordinance prescribes abstention from food, drink and sexual intercourse between sunrise and sunset. Ramadan trains Muslims in self-discipline and scrupulous obedience to God's commands; it is not related to penance for sins.

SEPHARDIM: originally, Jews who lived in Spain until their mass expulsion in 1492. In liturgy, their descendants still speak Judeo-Spanish. The designation Sephardim frequently signifies all Southern Jews, whether or not they have ties with Spain.

SEVILLA: one of the main cities of Andalusia. See Andalus.